QUEEN OF SERPENTS AND SHADOWS

BLOOD AND SALT BOOK FOUR

ALEXIS CALDER

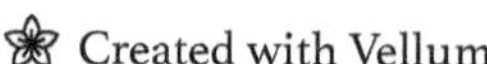 Created with Vellum

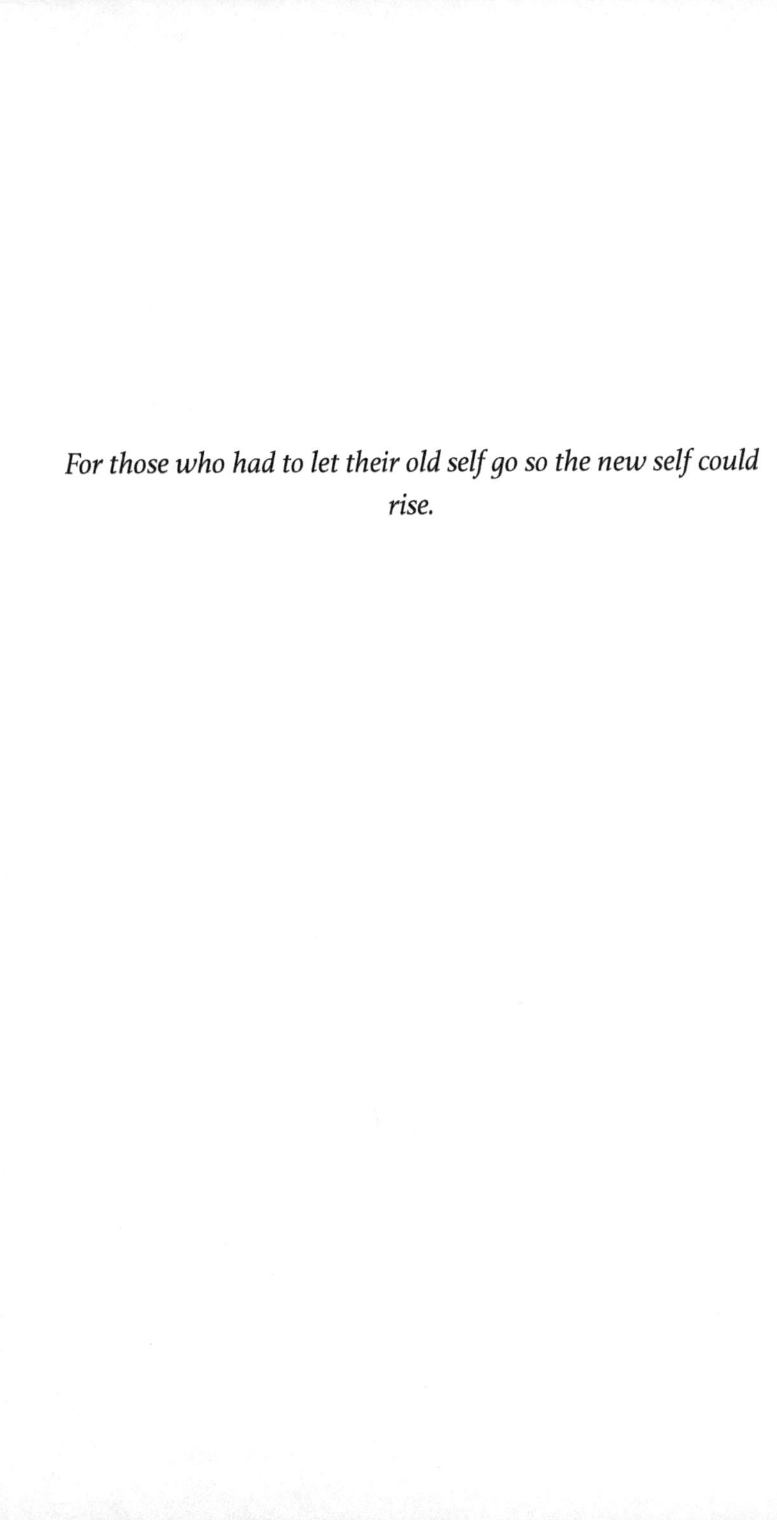

For those who had to let their old self go so the new self could rise.

KINGDOM OF BLOOD AND SALT

1

ARA

THE WATER SHIMMERED like jewels in the early morning light. Bright fractals sparkling and blinking with the push and pull of the waves. The ship cut through, oblivious to the light dancing on the previously dark water. It made my insides twist, the warning impossible to mask.

We were sailing for Drakous, but the weight of expectation around Nyx's promises pulled me down. We couldn't abandon Drakous after the dragons had come to our aid, but Nyx was after humans. We were in an impossible position.

I looked back, squinting toward the place Athos had been. I couldn't see it anymore, but I knew it was there, a city barely clinging to life. Half of our soldiers were making their way through the passes of the Darkspire

Mountains, destined for Drakous and a battle that might be over before we even arrived.

The others were tasked with defending our city, but we all knew what that meant. It was the only reason I'd even agreed to leave. We all knew there was nothing we could do to defend ourselves if Nyx decided to come for Athos. If we stayed behind, there'd just be more bodies when she was finished. In Drakous, against the fae, there was a chance we could win.

Something tickled my insides, wriggling and twisting, calling my attention to the water. I could feel again. A connection to the depths that I thought was lost forever. Somehow, I'd tapped into my magic again and though it felt like an echo, it was still there, that familiar sensation I'd lost. I shoved the feeling away, hoping to tamp it down enough that I wouldn't alert the gods.

Something shimmered just below the surface and, for a moment, I caught sight of a sea serpent peering above the waves. My heart stopped as I made eye contact with the creature, a sense of understanding passing between us before it returned to the depths.

My magic might be returning, and it might put a target on my back, but with allies like the monsters of the sea, it would be worth it. I could actually make a difference in this war. Though I might not see the end, I could help save everyone I loved. The thought made me smile. It was the first time in a long time I felt empowered.

"You look pleased," Laera said as she joined me. She leaned against the railing, her own gaze dropping to the water below. The boat bumped against a large wave and sea spray misted our faces. I wiped my eyes, reveling in the feel of the grittiness of salt against my face. For a brief moment, I recalled my father's favorite saying, the reminder that humans lived by the code of blood and salt. The smile faded. He wasn't even human. And neither was I.

"I forgot how much I hate water," Laera sneered. She used her tunic to dry her face. "This is why I prefer to stay in palaces and send my spies to do the digging for me."

"Did you find something?" I asked, turning to her. Our departure had been rapid, but I knew she was tasked with trying to get any information she could before we charged into the fray.

"Nothing yet. I'm still shut out. I don't know what bargains my father made, but he's got someone I'm not familiar with on his side. It's like he's closed off my power. I didn't even know he was aware of that part of my magic." She squeezed the railing so hard her knuckles turned white.

"I know what it's like to be cut off from your magic. I'm sorry," I offered.

"I'm not cut off from all of it." She released her grip. "I just can't get into the heads of any of my usual charges. I'm starting to think they might all be dead. But that would mean my father killed his entire council."

"He probably did," Ryvin added as he joined us. He gave me a small smile and a nod before returning his attention to his sister. "I want you to try Selena."

Laera's brows shot upward. "The woman who ran away as soon as things in the tunnel got difficult?"

Ryvin nodded. "Yes. We know she wanted nothing to do with our father, but she'll do anything to save her own skin. Plus, if word gets out about her daughter..."

"Our sister?" Laera sneered. "Every time I think of it, I want him dead even more."

"We'll watch his head roll before we see the Underworld," Ryvin vowed.

"I don't see how Selena helps us. Even if I feel oddly obligated to her offspring. She's probably hiding in some forgotten building in Athos waiting for the chaos to settle so she can scurry out and claim her riches in the fallout. Which, honestly, she deserves after what our father did to her. You do realize what she can claim if we're all dead?"

"Just try it, will you?" he pressed.

Laera crossed her arms over her chest. "Fine."

"Thank you," Ryvin said.

Laera's upper lip curled in disgust. "Gross. Don't start being nice to me now. I don't think I can handle that."

Ryvin looked like he was holding back a laugh. He shrugged, then moved closer to me, taking the place against the railing on my other side.

"I'll be in the captain's quarters. Trying to break into the mind of someone who is useless to us," Laera announced dramatically.

Vanth joined us, his brow furrowing as he watched Laera walk away in a huff.

"What was that about?" Vanth asked.

"She's never been one for taking orders," Ryvin said.

"You actually gave her an order?" Vanth asked skeptically.

"I requested nicely," Ryvin clarified.

"I'm sure she'd rather be ordered," Vanth mumbled.

"Do you really think she might find something from her?" I asked.

Ryvin shrugged. "I find it hard to believe that the queen cut off all communication with her best friend. She was playing the long game to get her court back. I'm guessing that's the biggest reason Selena chose Athos."

The ship rocked gently, and I returned my attention to the water. There was so much building, so much that had been hidden. Ryvin set his hand on mine. "We're going to defeat him. It's the only option. I refuse to let him win. And I will not lose you."

We hadn't had time to address the change in our relationship, and I wasn't sure how to move forward with him. If I was being honest with myself, the day he'd offered to give me all of his magic had thawed something in me. He'd demonstrated that taking my magic wasn't about power. It was an attempt to keep me safe, no matter how misguided it was.

"Why do the gods fear my magic when yours is so deadly?" I asked.

"Because I can't use my shadows against a god. You can do what you did to that vampire to any of them."

I returned my attention to the water. "But now you have that power, yet they allow you to live."

"I don't think they'll allow me to live long, Asteri," he confessed.

Fear flared and I spun to face him. "What do you

mean? You said taking my magic would prevent them from killing me."

"It does. Without magic, you're not a threat. But what I did was never about keeping myself alive." He tucked a stray strand of hair behind my ear. "It's always been about protecting you."

"The assassins after you…" The group that had attacked us had survived when they shouldn't have. They weren't typical bounty hunters. "They weren't sent by your father, were they?"

"Don't worry about it." He offered a small smile.

"Don't shut me out. You promised no secrets." I pressed my palm against his chest. "Don't you dare."

He grabbed my wrist, lifting my hand from his chest, then lowered his face, pressing a kiss to my knuckles.

"Don't try to distract me." I tugged my hand away. "Who were they?"

He sighed, then lowered my wrist, weaving his fingers between mine. He held my hand like he was afraid I'd float away if he let go.

"You're right. They weren't sent by my father. They were sent by the gods. Before you say anything—" he held his other hand out and I closed my open mouth, then glared at him. "It means they have upheld their end of the bargain and no longer see you as a threat."

"I am not okay with you taking my place for this. Especially after what I did in Athos. They're going to know I tapped into my magic." As my anger rose, shadows swirled around us, twisting and spinning into a cyclone of darkness.

"You need to take a breath." Ryvin looked nervously at the dark tendrils.

I closed my eyes and tried to slow my racing pulse. I was not going to watch him sacrifice himself for me. There had been far too much of that in our kingdoms' histories. When I opened my eyes, Ryvin had taken a step back, but he was still clinging to my hand. The shadows had dissipated.

"I'm sorry. I'll work on my emotions. But you have to promise me something. Right now."

He lifted an eyebrow in silent question.

"If we survive this war, we figure out how to get rid of my magic for good. I don't want to live the rest of our lives running from the gods."

He moved closer. "I was gifted more magic than most, and now I think I know why. It's enough for both of us. It's enough to help us survive. We'll both use mine and figure out a way to destroy yours."

I stood on my toes and kissed him. His arms moved around my waist, pulling me closer. I nuzzled into the embrace, burying my face into his warm chest. If only I could stay here like this. If only I could ignore reality and live in a place where we could just exist and enjoy each other's company.

But that wasn't our path. He kissed the top of my head and I breathed him in, allowing myself one more moment of safety before I stepped away from his embrace. The expression on his face hardened, taking on a seriousness that told me he was steeling himself the same way. Neither of us asked for this, but we would do all we could.

2

Bahar

Hundreds of ships waited in the distance, all of them poised to attack Drakous. Winged dragons made of magic flapped idly over them, the creatures seemingly tethered to the unmoving ships.

They hadn't struck yet, but I could see the display for what it was. This was a show of power. Meant to intimidate and overwhelm. It wouldn't work. The Fae King's ego was already getting the best of him. He'd waited to attack until I returned. He wanted a battle. He wanted to say he defeated me.

I flapped my wings harder, the fear for my kingdom dissolving as I moved closer to land. The sun glinted off the scales of my army. Let the fae see us. Let them see what five hundred dragons looked like as we blotted out the newly returned sun. Let them feel fear.

Instead of banking toward land, I aimed for the waiting hoards. The wingbeats behind me didn't hesitate as they followed my lead. Words weren't necessary. The second I unleashed my fire, they broke into attack positions and we charged.

The strange magic dragons launched toward us, breathing their unnatural flames, their aim awkward and inconsistent. They were easy enough to avoid, so I rolled to my side, focusing on the ships below us.

Archers filled the sky with a cascade of arrows, some clattering against my tough scales before they fell to the sea. I swooped down, releasing fire at the attacking ships.

Men screamed, leaping from their boats into the sea. More scales glinted in the water, and the survivors screamed as they were pulled under. For the first time, I started to think that maybe it wasn't so bad that Ceto's child was my ally. Having her for a sister-in-law might be beneficial.

The dragons around me attacked the ships with the same fervor, using flames and claws to send the sailors to their watery graves. Some of my dragons went after the magical creatures, exploding them into a burst of dust as their fire engulfed them.

The Fae King had tried once before to take my city, but he couldn't win. This wasn't going to be any different.

I made another pass over a row of boats, launching a blast of fire as I flew over them. The sailors screamed. Some tried to put out the flames while others took their chances in the water. Ceto's monsters were getting a feast. After this battle, I would be sure to burn offerings for her. I might even do like Athos and commission a temple. Having her as an ally rather than a concern in the sea could make Drakous even more powerful.

Flames tore through the air and I twisted, my wings just missing the unnatural fire. Heart pounding, I turned, facing down the abomination that had released the gruesome fire. These dragons were deadly, but they were false creations. An insult to all dragons.

The sun dimmed as hundreds of dragons coming from the city flew toward the battle. More of the magical dragons flooded the sky, quickly outnumbering my own warriors.

The massive creatures had a wingspan twice as large as mine. They moved forward as a unit, creating a shadow over the sea as they charged. Below, I heard the cheers of the sailors, who'd apparently been expecting this.

A wall of fire exploded from the creatures and I watched in horror as dragons fell to the sea. My people. My warriors.

These creatures might be made from magic, but their fire was still as deadly as mine.

A glint of gold caught my eye, and I noticed my brother heading straight toward our new challengers. Fuck.

Kabir was charging with his unit, the dragons dodging the bursts of fire as they got closer to the monsters. These were not the same as the magical dragons we'd fought before. I could feel the heat of their flames, the wind coming from their wingbeats. And there was something else, something that sent a shiver right down my spine. Whatever it was, these new monsters were not going down easy. The first ones we encountered were weak, but they seemed to have improved the magic on these new additions.

I joined the ranks, flying with my warriors, all of us falling into the battle formations we'd practiced so many times. Claws glinting, fire at the ready, we rushed toward the hoard of massive creatures.

One by one, we released our fire, orange flames merging with the fire of our enemy. Dodging and twisting, I flew into the waiting masses, tearing my claws through their flesh, releasing fire where I thought they might be more vulnerable.

My dragons followed, completing attack patterns of their own. We fought with claws and teeth and flame. One of the massive creatures lunged for me, its jaws just missing my neck. I slashed along its face, drawing dark green blood.

It screamed, but didn't hesitate as it snapped at me again. When I avoided it, the creature attacked with claws, tearing through my scales as if it were human flesh.

I growled, then released a fireball into its face. The dragon shook it off. No turning to dust, no sign that I'd injured it at all.

These things weren't going down. Not a single one fell to the water. Not a single one had turned away.

A roar tore through the air, the sound making my whole body tense. I hurtled a burst of flame at my attacker, then launched upward, breaking free of the throng. Below, I saw the masses surrounding the gold dragon. The attacking hoard closing in on my brother. I dove, with a roar of my own, drawing as many of the beasts to me as I could.

Just as I arrived, Kabir fell. My heart felt like it was torn from my chest and I let out a bellow I didn't recognize as I plummeted after him. His dragon form was breaking and twisting as he neared the water, forcing him into shifting. I flapped harder, managing to swing below him, his weak human form landing on my back with a thud.

Two dragons flanked me, moving close, and I knew they were there to catch Kabir if he fell from my back. I didn't feel any movement. He didn't grab onto my scales.

With a roar of grief I bypassed the battle, wincing as arrows pierced my sensitive wings. As soon as I reached the shore, I slid my brother from my back. One of the dragons who'd followed me shifted quickly and raced to the fallen prince. It was Zarthan, our best healer. I didn't even know he'd joined the fight. He shouldn't be here. He was too valuable to risk.

My blood ran ice cold.

If the healers had joined the fight, the city had already fallen.

"I've got him. You go," Zarthan yelled.

I nodded, then shot into the sky. My people were being annihilated. Dragons were dropping from the sky, their human forms hitting the water where, to my surprise, the creatures ignored them. But they weren't splashing, they weren't fighting for air.

We were being destroyed. One at a time, dragon by dragon; the fae were killing us off. Part of me wanted to rush back in and show the fae what dragons were made of. But that was pride, not leadership.

I made a sound I never thought I'd make. The call for retreat.

My warriors hesitated, some of them still fighting for their lives.

I roared again, then rose skyward so they could see me before making the final call.

Three times.

This was real. We were falling back.

The problem was, I knew we couldn't fall back to our city.

I glanced to shore where Zarthan was loading my brother onto the back of the third dragon who'd joined us. Likely another healer, since he had a strap on his back to accommodate fallen warriors. No other dragon would allow anyone to ride them.

Hating myself, I retreated, flying away from my home. We'd regroup. This wasn't over.

WE REACHED the winter training camp just after sunset. It had been years since we'd utilized this space, but there were still buildings and some basic supplies stocked for emergencies.

I didn't have the list of the fallen yet, but I knew we'd lost too many good dragons.

Healers and anyone with basic healing skills quickly worked to clean wounds and tend to the injured.

I walked around the makeshift hospital, offering encouragement where I could and placing coins on the eyes of those who were gone.

"How is he?" I knelt next to my brother, who was still unconscious.

"He'll recover," Nissa said. She stood, and I noticed the blood staining her tunic.

"You're injured. You need to get that taken care of."

She lifted a brow. "I've been healing longer than you've been alive. I'm fine. And your brother is going to be just fine."

"You're too valuable to lose to pride." I couldn't help but stare at the bloody tunic.

She lifted it, revealing a small cut that was stitched neatly. "I told you, it's under control."

With a grunt, I nodded. "Alright."

"I know you're worried," she said. "But as soon as he is healed enough to shift, he'll recover completely."

"What about the others?" I asked as I looked around.

She pressed her lips into a tight line. "We lost a lot. I've never seen anything like those other dragons before. We weren't prepared for that."

"I know." I couldn't say it out loud, but I knew if we didn't figure out how to eliminate whatever magic created those, we'd lose.

"We've faced worse odds," she said, her tone full of false optimism.

"I've known you too long to think you actually believe that," I replied.

She shrugged. "We'll figure something out."

"Sure." I sighed, then walked away, leaving the injured behind.

There was no time for feeling sorry for ourselves. I shoved aside all the fears of failure. We would find a way to defeat the Fae King, even if it meant taking him to the afterlife with me.

"YOUR HIGHNESS," Zane, one of my best scouts bowed, then approached.

"What did you see?"

"They have completely taken the city. None of the dragons are fighting back." He looked like he was struggling to remain in his human form. His whole body was tense and his hands were shaking.

"You're certain?" I asked.

"We saw them patrolling. Nobody is in the streets other than their soldiers."

I shook my head. "They lured our army away to Athos. But they severely underestimate us if they think they'll be able to hold the city. It's only temporary."

Zane smiled and some of his tension eased. "Tell me what you need. I'll get a team ready."

"I need all my generals," I said. "We're going to make him regret everything."

Most of my best fighters had gone with me to Athos. We'd been so certain that the battle would happen there, we'd left behind too few men to guard the city. They gathered around me, surrounded by rocks and dirt, a far cry from the expansive war room in my palace.

An eagle flew past and I watched as it dove toward its prey. The large bird rose with a squirming rodent in its beak. By the way the creature dangled, I could tell it was already dead. Nearby, I caught a rustle and saw another rodent dive into a hole, finding safety in the ground.

My lips curved and I looked over at Patro, an old friend who now fought by my side. "Do you think you could draw up a map of the tunnels?"

He lifted a skeptical brow. "You can't be serious. Those death traps we played in as kids? They have to be collapsed by now."

"Are you talking about the ancient waterways?" Jasmine, one of my newer generals, asked.

I nodded.

"Those haven't been used in generations. There's no way they're usable."

"We don't need them to be usable. We just need at least one route to get us into the city. From there, we can eliminate the Fae King once and for all." I balled my hand into a fist, imagining myself squeezing the life out of my enemy. He took my city, he threatened my mate, there would be no truce.

"Get me a scribe," I called.

A younger dragon who'd been standing just beyond the circle of generals scurried away, then returned quickly, panting. He shoved the scribe forward.

"You summoned, Your highness?" The scribe looked terrified. I'd argued with my father for years about the waste of having a scribe with us when we fought. He'd insisted it was necessary for someone to record our efforts. I suppose now I was grateful we had him with us.

"I need to make a map of the tunnels under Drakous," I explained.

The scribe's shoulders eased and his expression changed from dread to excitement. "Of course! I studied all the ancient maps. I think I have the entire system memorized."

"That's incredibly lucky," Patro murmured.

"Or it's proof that the monsters who stole our city don't belong there," Jasmine said. "The gods are on our side."

"The gods don't take anyone's side but their own," I replied.

"We'll just have to make it work on our own," Jasmine said. "Tell us what you need."

"I'm going in with a small group. The rest of you, be prepared to take the city as soon as I kill the king," I replied.

My generals cheered, and for the first time since I left Drakous, I felt hope. The Fae King might be near immortal, but all I needed was to get close enough to use my fire. Nobody could withstand dragon fire.

"You, what's your name?" I called to the younger man.

"Doren, Your highness," he said.

"Doren, come with me. We've got things to prepare." I led him away, gesturing for the rest of the generals to follow me.

3

Ara

There wasn't much space below deck, but it was enough for some practice space. We'd been down here for a while already and sweat rolled down my temple. Ryvin wasn't even breathing hard.

"You can't go easy on me if you want me to actually learn," I reminded him.

"I'm not," he assured me.

I gave him a skeptical look, knowing he was always thinking about how he could keep me safe. I knew that now. I trusted him. The thought sent a rush of something warm through my chest. I hadn't truly realized how much I'd missed feeling that around him.

"You're not even trying to get to me," I pointed out.

"When you pose a threat, I'll fight back," he said playfully.

I'd been trying everything and all I'd done was kick up the dust on the floor. The boat pitched just enough that I had to brace myself, the rocking sending me a little closer to him. I moved with it, charging with my knife.

Ryvin dodged, spinning away from my attack with a fluid grace that was only possible for fae. With a scowl, I turned, then ducked, aiming lower in the hopes of throwing him off. He jumped back, avoiding my blade again.

Pushing a loose strand of hair from my face, I turned to him, annoyed by how easily he avoided me. Frustration was building. It was a reminder of how much slower I was than the fae I'd be fighting.

I slid the knife back into the sheath on my thigh and balled my hands into fists, studying the cocky expression on Ryvin's smug face. He didn't have to go easy on me when he wasn't even trying to get to me. So far, I'd failed to even get close enough to use the weapon.

Annoyance and a desperation to prove that I could handle myself crept in, making my cheeks heat. I wanted to win. I wanted to best him. He wasn't even fighting back and I couldn't reach him. What was I going to do in a real battle? This was exactly why Vanth had to stay on my heels. All those years of training had been worthless.

Until I found my magic. Anxiety made my insides twist. I'd called on my own magic, summoning water and getting help from a sea serpent. I'd missed the connection from using it, but even if I could access it again, it wouldn't help me here.

But something else could. Something darker.

I couldn't hide the smirk as the idea crept in. I'd been so focused on defeating Ryvin on my own, I'd forgotten that I could use his magic. Pride had won over reason, making me want to prove myself as a fighter. But I wasn't fighting other humans. I couldn't win with human rules.

"What's that look for?" Ryvin asked.

I could feel the darkness swirling, Ryvin's magic coming to me as if it were my own. Shadows billowed around me, and I welcomed them.

"That's what I wanted to see," his voice was a purr, sending a chill down my spine.

He lifted his hands, sending his own shadows my way, but I deflected, creating a barrier of darkness that rose around me like a shield. Giving it all I had, I pushed the shadows forward with a grunt, sending them to him.

The ship rocked and I threw my arms out to catch myself, sending the shadows outward. When I regained my balance, dark clouds floated around my ankles, hovering over the floor like a haze of night.

Ryvin was picking himself up off the ground. "Well done."

"Why didn't you just say you wanted me to use magic? You said we were going to fight," I pointed out.

"I want it to be instinct. Not reaction. I want you to use it with intention. Strategically. As a first option." He wiped dust off his sleeves, then moved closer to me. "You can't win against one of my father's men with the skills you learned in Athos."

I frowned, hating what I was hearing. Not because it wasn't true. And not because the magic wasn't intoxicating.

I felt powerful when I called his shadows. I felt strong. It was addictive. But there was risk in using it.

He brushed his fingertips across my cheek, his brow furrowed as he studied me. "What is it?"

"What if I take too much?" I knew the consequences. "I can't risk taking all your magic."

"You won't," he assured me. "You'll feel it. And the more you use it, the more you'll notice it."

"I almost did, though. When we were fighting in the throne room. I could have killed you. And you'd have let me. You wouldn't stop me if I took too much. I can't risk that."

"What if I promise to tell you if you're going too far?" He set his hand on my waist, the touch scalding. I could hardly concentrate on his words when all I could think about was the feel of his hand on my body.

I gritted my teeth and pushed away the increasing sense of need. "You have to. Or I won't use it."

"I will. I promise."

I nodded, then tilted my chin, looking up into the swirling gray depths of his eyes. Since the moment we met, he'd captured me with those eyes. I should have known I'd be helpless against him.

He leaned down and my breath caught as I anticipated the kiss, but I felt a hand on my thigh a second before he grabbed me and spun me, turning me so my back was against his chest and my blade was at my throat.

"You tricked me," I hissed. "Rude."

"We're still training, Asteri," he whispered, his breath hot against my cheek. Shivers went straight to my core. He had a knife to my throat and all I could think about was getting his clothes off. It was a good thing I didn't have to fight him. I'd never win.

For a moment, I imagined using that knife to cut apart his tunic until the torn fabric was in a puddle on the ground. I gritted my teeth and forced the image away. "You're a distraction, you know that?"

"Teach me a lesson then," he said, his voice husky enough that I knew the closeness was getting to him too.

The blade was near to my throat, but he wasn't letting it touch me. I'd felt the bite of that blade more times than I'd like to admit, and I was sure those memories were what had him recreating the situation now.

My arms were by my side, pinned by his other arm. Like my past opponents, he was so much stronger than me that I couldn't just push my way out.

Magic it was.

I felt for the shadows, then closed my eyes. Taking a deep breath, I visualized the dark tendrils traveling up my body, staying tight enough that they wouldn't be as obvious. I could feel the coolness of them as they stretched forward, pushing their way around Ryvin. Tensing, I ordered the shadows to twist around my captor's arms, then I demanded the shadows pull. I didn't realize I was screaming until I was stumbling forward, free of Ryvin's grip.

The knife clattered to the ground, and he was left with his arms wide open, extended on either side of his body. Tendrils of darkness twisted around them, keeping his arms in place.

Grunting, he struggled against his confinement. I stared, watching in awe at how I'd been able to control the shadows with such precision. It wasn't the big emotional reaction I'd created in the past. This made me dangerous. It made me powerful.

I dropped down and grabbed the fallen knife before slowly approaching him. Blade pointed out, I paused in front of Ryvin. "I think I won."

He winced, finally dropping one arm to his side, then the other. "You definitely won."

I slid the knife back into its sheath, then helped him brush away the last few clinging shadows.

"You're getting better," he said.

"It's not too much, is it? I don't want to leave you with nothing."

He smirked. "Do you remember what I did in Athos?"

I swallowed hard. I didn't let myself recall that battle. No, not battle. Slaughter. He destroyed everyone with precision. He left me and his men standing while those trying to harm him were brutally eliminated. The power he'd used then was beyond anything I could comprehend.

"I could have continued to fight after that." He rubbed his thumb against my wrist comfortingly. "I told you, I have more than enough power for both of us. Unless you're actively draining it from me like you did in the throne room, we're fine."

I nodded, still feeling uneasy. "What about my magic?" We hadn't discussed the fight in Athos yet, but I knew we had to address it.

"Try to use my magic and avoid tapping into yours," he said.

"Do you think that's what I did? Accessed mine through you?" I asked.

"I'm not sure. It could be that, or it could be going back to you. Magic doesn't like to be forced to be somewhere it doesn't want to be," he replied.

"Alright." I think we both knew it was going to be a problem. But all we could do was add it to the ever-growing list of things we needed to address. If we survived the Fae King and Nyx, we'd figure it out then. Right now, I needed a distraction. Anything to get my mind away from how dangerous things were for us.

Ryvin's hand was on my waist again, his fingers under my tunic, brushing against my bare skin. I stepped closer, then slid my own hands under his tunic.

"So naughty," he whispered. "I thought we were training."

"We deserve a break, don't we?" I asked playfully.

A creaking sound made me drop my hands and turn toward the light coming from the now open hatch.

"You two decent down there?" Laera called.

Ryvin let out a low, frustrated growl.

"From that sound, I'm glad I asked. You've got ten seconds till I come down."

I sighed, then smoothed my tunic. "We were training, that's all."

"Right. I'm pretty sure even the shifter could have felt the sexual tension floating up from down here." She climbed down the ladder, then walked to where we were standing in the center of the open cargo hold.

"You likely won't ever hear me admit this again, so pay attention." She crossed her arms over her chest as she turned toward Ryvin. "You were right. Selena's been in touch with my mother this whole time. And I have news of Drakous."

Her nostrils flared, giving away her anger despite her attempt to keep her expression neutral. "Our father has already taken the city. He killed the officials they left behind and he's holding the princess hostage."

I covered my mouth with my hand. "No."

"What about the youngest prince?" Ryvin asked.

She shook her head. "I have no idea. Maybe he ran."

"How did the city fall so quickly?" Ryvin asked. "They've never been breached."

"Remember those strange dragons we saw in Athos?"

My mind filled with the creatures that charged our allies in the sky. They'd seemed easy to defeat, but there weren't that many of them. I could already anticipate where this was going. Athos had been a decoy, which meant there were likely a lot more for the real battle.

"I don't know where they came from, or how he had access to magic like that, but there were thousands of them. They blotted out the sun. The dragons who were left to defend the city were so busy fighting those creatures that they didn't defend their walls." Laera shook her head. "It's over."

I dropped my hand. "It's not over. We can't let him win.

We have to find out what those monsters were and how he's so strong. There has to be an explanation."

"Even if there's an explanation, it doesn't mean there's a way to defeat him. Sometimes you just lose," Laera snapped.

"What happened to killing him yourself?" I demanded. "What happened to the angry woman who demanded justice?"

"She's also realistic," Laera said. "I will risk my life, but I will not commit suicide."

"It's only suicide if we aren't smart about it," Ryvin said. "He'll expect us to charge in. He'll expect a glorious battle. It's why he has those dragons. He's preparing for doing things the way they've always been done."

"Does the Dragon King know this information?" I asked.

"I'm not sure," Laera admitted.

"Is this where the party is?" Vanth called.

We all turned to watch the shifter making his way down the ladder. When he turned to face us, his expression hardened and his posture tensed. He was instantly back on the battlefield. "Who do we need to kill?"

Laera rolled her eyes. "Shifters."

"Drakous fell." I explained what Laera discovered. With each word, I could see Vanth tensing more.

When I was finished, we were all silent for so long I started to contemplate clearing my throat just to hear a sound other than the waves against the ship.

"We have to get to Drakous," Vanth said. "The dragons

will be outside the city. They won't be stupid enough to try to charge in. They'll be planning."

"They're probably already there and our soldiers are on their way," I said.

"I'll send a message to find their location. We can join. We can help." Vanth glanced at Ryvin and I watched as he inclined his head, giving the shifter unspoken permission.

As soon as Vanth was gone, I looked at Laera and Ryvin. "We haven't lost yet."

Laera sighed. "Fine. Maybe those dragons have an idea. It's their city. I suppose there are worse things than taking out as many of our father's men as we can before we meet Hades."

Ryvin lifted a brow. "Willingness to work with the dragons? Who even are you?"

She gave him a rude gesture, then turned and walked toward the ladder.

4

The library was musty and dark. Dust covered most of the books, a testament to the fact that librarians rarely lasted. Now, I knew it was because my father drained them of their blood and disposed of the bodies.

I shivered. The horrors that man committed without any of us knowing were going to haunt me for the rest of my life.

Light flickered around us as Sophia lit additional lamps and I spun in a slow circle, taking in the space. My father had never encouraged me to come here. Ara did on occasion, but looking up information on my own was never prioritized. Now that I had time to consider it, I think it was discouraged.

Makes sense. There was a lot that was hidden from me. Considering he was planning to live forever, there was no reason to teach me things that might make me question too much.

"This is the painting?" Sophia asked, standing in front of the hidden books.

I nodded, moving to join her.

Working quickly, I liberated the books from their prison. Sophia and I carried them all to a table situated between two chairs. The books were fragile. The leather was cracked and some of the pages were in danger of falling out completely.

"I wonder how old they are," Sophia asked.

"I think some of them came here when the city was founded," I said.

She lifted one to her lap, carefully brushing her fingers across the brown cover. There wasn't a title, but that wasn't unusual. Many books lost the paint on their covers over time. I just hoped the pages inside were still legible.

"What have I missed?" Aunt Katerina called as she entered the room with a pile of documents, books, and journals.

"We just got started," I said.

"Are those the ones Istvan sent?" Sophia asked.

She nodded, then set them down on the small table before finding a chair and dragging it toward us. "There should be some information in these to help you." Aunt Katerina offered a smile to Sophia.

My sister's cheeks turned pink. "I'm sorry we have to do all this work because of me."

"Don't you dare," I snapped. "You didn't choose your parents. None of us did."

"I know I should miss him, since he was my brother," Aunt Katerina started, "but he was awful, even when we were children. I'm not sorry he's gone. I am sorry for what he did to all you girls."

She reached for the top item, a small leather journal with a fraying sewn spine. "We're going to get through this."

I went back to the book I was looking through, hoping I'd find anything that might help. I wasn't even sure what I was looking for. While information about half-vampires would be beneficial, I knew there had to be other things that might give us a chance. There had to be more about Athos that we didn't know.

5

ARA

IT WAS dark when we waded onto shore, our ship already leaving Drakous behind. It was risky enough with the Fae King's armies being so large. Wrapped in shadows, we were concealed well, but we didn't know exactly what the king's powers were. Nobody had known he could create dragons with his magic. What else could he do?

Weapons drawn, we trudged across the beach in tense silence. I shivered, my wet clothes clung to my skin.

A bird called in the distance, the sound making the hair on my arms stand on edge. Or maybe that was from the chill in the air.

"I've got it," Laera said from nearby. Even I couldn't see where any of my friends were. The shadows concealed us from each other just as well as they did from the outside world.

I caught movement as she breached the veil of our dark cocoon, but she was swallowed by the night almost immediately.

The bird sounded again, the call forlorn and haunting in the darkness. Even though I knew to expect the Dragon's liaison to make the noise, I didn't trust it.

"We're good," Ryvin suddenly said. "Laera confirmed it."

I didn't want to know how he knew that information. There was a lot I still didn't understand about Laera's magic.

The shadows dispersed, slowly fading away until we were able to see each other again. I crept forward, staying close to Ryvin and Vanth as we made our way to where Laera was waiting with a uniformed man. We left the sand behind, climbing onto the rocky shore, each step getting more difficult to navigate.

"Your highness," the man inclined his head.

"Not necessary," Ryvin said, "I'm Ryvin, this is Ara, and Vanth. You already met Laera."

The man's jaw tensed, looking uncomfortable at the familiarity, but he nodded. "I'm Rashid. I'll take you to our camp."

We followed him silently, continuing to make our way over the rocky terrain. Loose rocks rolled away, clattering down. I glanced backward and realized we'd climbed higher than I thought.

It was getting a little harder to catch my breath as we continued the incline, but just as I was wondering if I'd need a break, we reached a trail.

It wasn't a road, it was flattened plants and shifted rocks that told us a large group had been through here. I frowned. "Not exactly hiding this location, are you?"

Rashid looked over his shoulder. "We have five hundred dragons gathered in one place. There's not a lot we can do to fully hide."

"Good point," I conceded.

Ryvin gave my hand a quick squeeze. "The Fae King isn't going to come for us here. He wanted the city. And he's vain enough to think that he can wait for them to attack him. He's got the advantage where he is. If he leaves, he loses that."

"That's what we're counting on," Rashid said.

We walked so long, my trousers were nearly dry and I was no longer shivering. The sky turned a faint pink, the early signs of dawn approaching. I glanced toward the sunrise, a twisting sick feeling making me uncomfortable. Was I ever going to be able to appreciate a sunrise again?

As we crested the top of another hill, I caught the sight of simple tents and figures moving around. A few more steps and I could see the whole thing. My lips parted as I took in the sight of so many soldiers gathered. We'd seen their camp in Athos, but somehow, it looked larger and more impressive on the top of this mountain.

"You really don't think the king will come here?" It was impossible to hide this many dragon shifters.

"He can try," Rashid said.

My brows lifted in surprise and I glanced at my friends. Ryvin shrugged and Vanth didn't even seem fazed by the dragon's confidence.

"They have plans," Laera said with a smirk. "Well, I suppose we go find their king and figure out the new way we tempt the fates."

I shuddered as I recalled Morta's words. I felt like all I'd been doing the last few weeks was tempt fate. It was impossible that I was still alive.

"This way," Rashid gestured, then led us through the tents.

Shifters watched us, not bothering to hide their stares. Many of them had been on the shores of Athos not long ago, and now we were at theirs. We traded one battlefront for another.

My shoulders slumped as I realized how little progress we'd made. It was difficult not to feel defeated.

I recognized Bahar seated on a large boulder, surrounded by a group of men and women. They were hanging on his every word as he gestured toward a large paper that looked like a map.

A couple of the people around him noticed us and turned their attention in our direction, causing Bahar to stop speaking. He stood, then faced us, a smile growing on his face immediately.

"You found us," he said.

"Your message was thorough," Ryvin commented.

"Our father is in your throne room. He's already killed your entire council," Laera announced.

"Subtle," Vanth murmured.

Laera glanced at him out of the corner of her eye, but didn't seem bothered by his comment.

Bahar's hands balled into fists. "What else do you know?"

"They've got the princess. He's holding her hostage," Laera added.

Someone charged us, but Bahar interfered, dropping the attacking shifter to the ground before I even lifted my blade. The man's head made a sickening crack when it hit a rock. Blood poured, turning the earth crimson. Empty eyes stared up at us. A knife lay near the dead man's hand.

Gasps and whispers sounded, but nobody else made a move for us.

"Anyone else have a problem with our guests?" Bahar asked.

A woman stepped forward, chin high, posture strong. She lowered her eyes to look at the fallen man and her upper lip curled in momentary disgust before looking at her king. "If you say they are allies, they are allies. But I want to know how the witch knows this information."

Bahar looked at Laera.

The princess rolled her eyes, then let out an exaggerated sigh. "I'm not sure if I'm more insulted at the insinuation that I'm a spy or the fact that my reputation wasn't enough."

"She's got a unique gift," Ryvin said.

"She can read minds, is what you're saying," the woman accused.

Several of the dragons standing behind her shifted their weight uncomfortably. One of them covered their ears with their hands as if that would keep Laera out.

Laera shrugged. "If you say so."

"It's considered impolite to ask fae what their magic can do," Bahar said. "Even their own parents don't know. Which in this case, benefits us."

The woman grunted. "Stay out of my head."

"I don't waste my time on useless drivel," Laera said with a dismissive wave of her hand.

The woman tensed, and for a moment, I thought she might attack Laera, but she relaxed, then returned to the group.

"Come on over," Bahar said. "I have a feeling you three will be able to help us with this plan."

We listened as someone explained the drawing of the tunnels and I tried not to think about the last time I'd been underground. The wild magic had nearly killed me, but we weren't facing that. This time it was crumbling, ancient tunnels that hadn't been used in so long, they weren't even sure if they were still intact.

"You don't think these entrances are monitored from the inside?" Vanth asked.

"The only people who knew about them are all dead or here with us," Bahar replied.

"Who's dead?" Kabir asked. He was limping, and one side of his face was angry and red. The prince must have been injured in the initial attack on the city.

Bahar rose and rushed to the newcomer. "You're up, thank the gods." He embraced the man in a curt manner that made the other man grunt.

"Careful, Nissa says I'm fragile now. Or at least I will be until I heal up a little more." He nodded toward me. "Princess," then at Ryvin, "Your highness."

"I am also royalty, but please, continue to ignore me," Laera said smugly.

"None of us need the titles," Ryvin cut in.

Laera huffed. "Speak for yourself."

Kabir walked over to where Laera was sitting and he took her hand, lifting it to his lips. I stared in shock as he kissed her hand. "I'll call you anything you want me to, Your highness."

Laera's cheeks flushed and her lips parted. For a long moment, she was speechless. Then she seemed to collect herself and tugged her hand away. "Now, how hard was that? Why can't the rest of you behave that way?"

"Because you're more likely to rip someone's arm off, then allow them to touch you," Vanth supplied.

Laera glared at him.

"Well, you seem to be feeling much better, Brother," Bahar said.

"I should be able to join you if you're just crawling around some tunnels," he said.

I lifted a skeptical brow. He was limping. We could all see that.

"We'll discuss that before we leave," Bahar said.

"What was that about dead?" Kabir asked, returning us to the original conversation.

"The Princess of Konos can see things," the woman from earlier explained. "She said the entire council is dead and Tatiana is a prisoner."

Kabir paled, then he turned to Laera. "Is she alright? Have they harmed her?"

Laera shook her head. "The princess is unharmed for

now. But I don't think they like keeping her around. She's almost escaped twice. She's going to get herself killed."

Kabir growled and his eyes flashed dangerously. It was the first time I saw that he was just as deadly as his brother and all the other warriors around us. His playfulness was gone.

"We're going to get her out," the woman said.

"Yes, we will." Kabir looked at his brother. "Any word on Zayn? Is he also a prisoner?"

"I haven't seen anything about the prince," Laera replied.

"He would have tried to fight, but it's possible he got out," Bahar said. "We'll find him," he slapped his brother on the shoulder. "Don't worry. We'll get both of them to safety."

6

ARA

THE TUNNELS WERE WORSE than I expected. Laera and Ryvin sent fae lights ahead, illuminating the crumbling path, but it only highlighted the instability of the dirt around us.

Holes had been eaten into the tunnels, burrows and nests for various creatures that I didn't want to think about. Something crunched under my sandal and I looked down before I could think better of it, wincing when I realized I'd crushed a small skull.

"Are there any animals we should be mindful of meeting?" I asked, trying not to think of the massive serpent that almost killed me.

"It shouldn't be anything dangerous," Bahar said.

"We encountered a few angry badgers," Kabir said.

I noticed he was walking more naturally now. I had to admit, dragons really did heal quickly.

"You forgot the part about how we were poking their homes with sticks," Bahar added.

"Yeah, but we didn't do anything to upset the bats. Or that lynx," Kabir added.

"That was one time," Bahar defended.

"I think we could handle some badgers or a lynx," Vanth said under his breath.

"With all this chatter, we'll tip off my father's men before we even arrive," Laera hissed.

The joviality of the conversation ceased and we all descended into silence. Our footsteps crunched over rocks and bones, and the sounds of something skittering through the holes in the walls occasionally followed us. We paused at a massive spider web that spanned the entire tunnel and even though I wasn't the one to tear it down, I still felt like my skin was crawling with insects when I walked through the space it had occupied.

Our little procession continued, with Bahar and Kabir in front, followed by the scribe carrying the map. Laera was in front of me with Vanth and Ryvin taking the rear. I couldn't explain it, but I could tell when they traded places. I could always feel when Ryvin was the one directly behind me, even if I didn't turn to see him.

We reached an intersection, the tunnel we were in continuing, along with four other tunnels that branched out in different directions. We'd come to turns before, but never with this many options. Two of the tunnels were collapsed, rocks and dirt blocking our progress.

"Which way?" Bahar asked the scribe.

He examined the map he'd drawn, and I watched as the wrinkles in his brow deepened. A bead of sweat rolled down his temple. "I'm not sure. I don't recall this on the maps I studied. All the other tunnels were intersections of three or four, I never saw one with more choices."

"Maybe one of these was never a finished tunnel," Bahar offered. "It wouldn't go on a map if that were the case."

The scribe shook his head. "I saw dead ends listed. The entire system was done in an organized grid. It's why I thought I could navigate us. But if the maps I saw weren't accurate..." His whole face glistened with sweat and his bronze completion took on a green tint. "What if they were wrong? What if I got us lost? We could be trapped here forever."

His voice was high-pitched and terrified, his breathing rapid. He was in full panic.

"Then we'll kill you before you starve to death," Laera said with a shrug.

"Nobody is killing anyone," I stepped forward, putting myself between Laera and the scribe.

His wide eyes were locked on the princess as he backed closer to the dirt wall behind him.

"We'll figure it out," I said. "Where do you think we are on the map? We'll make a guess. That's all we can do. We had no promises that the tunnels we needed were even going to be accessible. We could have encountered collapsed tunnels at every turn," I reminded him.

He finally looked at me, then swallowed hard. The map was in his grip at his side.

"Go ahead, Doren. Nobody is upset, we're going to be just fine," Bahar said, his voice calm and comforting.

Doren nodded, then lifted the map, taking a long moment to review it before looking up at the rest of us. "I think we should be using that tunnel, but it's not accessible." He pointed to the far right tunnel, one of the two that was caved in.

"So we take the one next to it," I suggested.

He shook his head. "I think that one might lead to an underground river. But I can't know for sure."

"Which tunnel then? Just tell us where to go. I'm getting bored down here," Laera said.

He pointed straight ahead. "We continue on our path and take the next tunnel we see on the right."

"Good work." Bahar slapped the smaller man on his back. "I knew we could count on you."

I fell into line behind the others as we continued forward, but each step had me feeling more unease. "You sure this is right?" I whispered. "Something feels wrong."

"I feel it too," Laera said.

"Do you think it's a warning?" Vanth asked.

"I think we need to turn around," Laera said.

"I agree." I couldn't explain it, but there was something disturbing about this tunnel.

Suddenly, the ground gave way and I plummeted, falling into darkness. I screamed into the void, fear making my insides turn to ice. Almost as quickly as I fell, I hit the earth hard, knocking the breath from my lungs. Stars exploded in my vision and my head spun. My entire side was aching from the impact, but I was lucky I'd landed on my shoulder and hip instead of my head.

Scrambling to my feet, I looked up, and thankfully, I could see the flicker of fae lights above me. Too far above me.

Anxious cries reached me, all my friends yelling for me at once. "Ara?" Their voices were a panicked cacophony.

"I'm alright!" I hollered, hoping they could hear me. I started reaching out around me, feeling for anything I could use to climb out of the hole. Loose dirt sprinkled down from each attempt. I was trapped.

"Ara, we're going to get you out of there," Ryvin yelled down.

From somewhere behind me, I heard something hissing. I wasn't alone. "Hurry, please. There's something else down here."

I reached for my necklace, brushing my fingers over the cool metal for comfort, when I remembered the other item I was wearing around my neck. Attached to a leather cord was the small pouch my mother gave me. There were times I obsessed over what it could be, and times I forgot about it completely.

I wondered if this was it, the time I was supposed to open it and find out how it could help me.

Then I felt the shadows wrapping around me, tightening their grip like an embrace. I made a surprised startled sound as my feet rose from the ground. Staying impossibly still, I held my breath until I was up, free of the hole.

As soon as the shadows released me, Ryvin's arms were around me, a large hand weaving into my hair while the other held me tight around my waist with a possessive grip.

"I'm safe," I assured him. "You got to me in time."

"I thought I lost you," he whispered.

"I'm alright. I promise. Just a few bruises."

"Can we leave this tunnel now before anything else happens?" Laera demanded.

"I think that's a good idea," Vanth said.

"The shifter is agreeing with me. That tells you that nothing good can come from us staying here," Laera snapped.

Everyone murmured in agreement and we backtracked to where we'd come from. We could see the opening for the tunnel when suddenly, the ground shook and rocks and debris began to rain down on us.

"Run!" Someone yelled.

I didn't wait. Grabbing Ryvin's hand, I raced forward, all of us sprinting toward the exit.

Rocks pelted from above, and I lifted my arm over my head to protect myself. Dust rose in clouds, making it harder to see where we were going, but we were so close to the exit. As soon as I emerged from the tunnel, I dropped Ryvin's hand and wiped my eyes before turning to see if everyone made it out.

The entire group was gathered just beyond the collapsed entrance, everyone panting and covered in dirt. Vanth coughed, then shook out his tunic. Laera was scowling as she wiped the dust from her arms and face.

Bahar and Kabir were glaring at the tunnel as if it had personally attacked them. I suppose, in a way, it had.

Dread surged. "Where's Doren?"

Everyone glanced around before we all turned our attention to the pile of rocks and earth that had been the entrance to a tunnel just moments ago.

Bahar and Kabir started to dig. Vanth joined in. There wasn't enough space for anyone else to join them, so Ryvin, Laera, and I watched. I think we were all holding our breath.

With each pile of earth they tossed aside, more fell from above to fill in the gaps. It was endless, the piles of dirt and rocks continuing no matter what they did.

Just when a weight of hopelessness settled into my gut, I saw a foot. They dug faster and Ryvin stepped forward, pulling on Doren's leg as the others continued to dig him out.

When they finally uncovered the rest of him, my heart sank. We were too late. He'd likely been crushed before we even started digging.

Bahar and Kabir knelt next to the fallen man and the two of them began whispering in a language I didn't recognize. Bahar closed the man's eyes, then Kabir placed a coin on each eye. They might be from Drakous, but our traditions in death were so similar.

"Very interesting," Laera said.

I shot her a look, trying to tell her to be more sensitive with my expression.

She shrugged. "We're all thinking it. It was a trap, clearly. You set something off when you fell in the hole. It probably triggered the collapse. It was designed so that if you could climb out of the hole, you'd still be stuck in the tunnel."

I glanced at the other two collapsed tunnels. "You think that's what happened to the others?"

"Probably. If so, it means there's likely only one way out of here." She sighed. "I'd rather not die buried underground."

"Nobody else is going to die," Bahar said as he stood. "You." He pointed at me, then moved closer.

Ryvin stepped in front of me. "Careful, dragon."

Bahar stopped moving. "She could feel it." He pointed to Laera. "You did too."

"He's right," Vanth agreed. "Both of them felt like something was wrong right before Ara fell."

"So?" Laera demanded.

"So, you can help us choose the right tunnel. And if either of you so much as get an inkling that something is off, we flee," Bahar said.

"Maybe it's their magic," Kabir suggested. "Something they can sense."

"I don't have any magic," I blurted automatically.

"Well, you've got something. Maybe it's like the human oracles, or the priests that occasionally see the future," Kabir replied.

"Ara, you felt something. Whatever it was, it was a warning," Ryvin said. "You too, Laera."

"Why is it always up to the princesses to save the day?" Laera rolled her eyes. She grabbed my upper arm. "Come on. Let's go see if it's safe for the big warrior men."

I fell into step beside her and we walked toward the nearest tunnel. We paused in front of it, then waited. After several long moments of awkwardly standing there, I looked at her. "What am I supposed to do?"

"Do you feel anything unusual?" she asked.

"No."

"Me neither."

"That must be the correct tunnel, then," Kabir said.

"Hold on," Vanth interjected. "Let them try the others."

It felt ridiculous, but Laera and I went and stood in front of each tunnel, waiting to see if we felt anything. None of the tunnels gave us the same sinister feeling we'd gotten from the first one.

"Maybe they're all safe," I suggested, not believing it myself.

"Maybe we need to take a few steps inside," Laera grumbled.

"No, not happening," Ryvin said.

"We'll turn around if we feel anything strange," I said. "It'll be easier for the two of us to get out in time. Besides, if something happens, you can dig us out."

Ryvin crossed his arms over his chest. It was clear he didn't like the suggestion, but he didn't argue when Laera and I took a few steps into the nearest tunnel.

"Anything?" Laera asked.

I shook my head, then left the tunnel. We silently walked to the next one, and with a glance at each other, we knew there was nothing wrong with this one, either.

"I'm not sure this theory works," I said. "Maybe we felt the immediate danger when we triggered the trap."

"Probably," Ryvin agreed.

"Try the last one, and if it's the same, we'll just guess," Bahar said.

Laera and I exchanged skeptical looks before stepping into the final tunnel. We were only a few steps in when the shaking started. Eyes wide, I launched forward, grabbing Laera's hand and tugging her along with me.

As soon as we were free, she yanked her hand from me. "I'm perfectly capable of taking care of myself."

"Sorry." I coughed, then brushed off the fresh layer of dirt.

Ryvin was next to me in a second. "No more going in without me."

"We were fine," Laera snapped. "She's alive, isn't she?"

Ryvin's jaw was tight, but he didn't respond.

"Oddly, I didn't get any bad feelings so that theory is invalid. We're going to have to guess," Laera said.

"Or we split up," I suggested.

"No," Bahar said. "That's a terrible idea."

"The point is to sneak up on the king and try to end him," I replied. "Isn't it?"

"We need strong magic to make it happen," Vanth explained. "I watched so many fail to kill him."

"He can't withstand dragon fire," Bahar said.

"And Ryvin's got the power of two gods," Laera said. "Plus, I might be able to get into his head and delay his reactions."

"So we stay together," I conceded.

"This way," Bahar said. He had the abandoned map in his hands.

"I thought he said that was the wrong way?" I asked.

"We have to try something," he countered.

"Let's go. But if anyone gets any urges to flee, we all run, got it?" Laera said.

"You can stay close to me, Princess," Kabir said in a seductive tone. "I'll watch out for you."

"You couldn't handle her," Vanth warned.

"I like a good challenge," he quipped.

Ryvin laughed. "Go for it, we're probably all dead after this, anyway."

"I'd rather take my chances with the badgers," Laera said before marching into the tunnel.

7

ARA

THE TUNNEL WOUND AND TWISTED, making more turns than the others we'd traveled down. Bahar was trying to use the map to make note of where we'd been and where we were, but after a long while of traveling, the map was down at his side, abandoned.

"We're going to die in here and be food for the badgers, aren't we?" Laera asked from behind me.

"Worst case, we backtrack and find our way out." I sounded more optimistic than I felt.

I could hear the rattle of disturbed pebbles and the increased cadence of our breathing. The fae lights flickered and glowed, moving with us as we traveled through the endless darkness.

I was getting very tired of tunnels and mazes.

The line halted, and I realized I'd been so in my head I

hadn't noticed we'd come to another fork in our path. This time, the tunnel we were in continued and another one branched off to the right.

Without waiting, I moved forward, getting closer to each entrance. As soon as I stepped deeper into the tunnel we were occupying, a rush of nausea overcame me and I stumbled back.

"What is it?" Bahar asked.

"You're sensing something," Ryvin commented.

"I don't know. I suddenly don't feel well." My face was damp with sweat that I didn't think had been there before and my head felt like it might float away from my body. Nausea continued to roll through me until I had to stumble away and empty the contents of my stomach.

Bahar and Kabir started to retch as well.

"Everyone to the other tunnel!" Vanth called.

I worked to contain myself, standing up straight and swallowing down any rising bile. My stomach was still rebelling as Ryvin and Laera gently pushed me toward the other tunnel, the others following behind us. We moved as quickly as we could, and after taking a few steps in, the sickness faded. Swallowing hard, I wiped the sweat from my face and the vomit from my mouth.

"What was that?" I asked.

"There must be something in that tunnel. Some other kind of trap." Bahar still looked a little green. "We should continue, put some distance between us and whatever that was."

Everyone nodded in agreement, and we continued on.

With each step, the nausea faded and it wasn't too long before it was gone completely.

"We have to be getting closer," Kabir said. "The tunnels didn't expand too far beyond the city."

"I hope so," Laera said. "I don't have much light left in me."

That sent a jolt of fear through me. "We'll have to do this in the dark?"

"Don't tell me you're afraid of the dark, Princess," Laera teased.

Ryvin placed his hand on my lower back. "I can make more light. Laera's just better at it."

"Must be all the shadows," Bahar said.

"Stop talking," Kabir hissed. He held out his arm and stood frozen in place.

We halted and listened. It was so loud, I wondered how I'd missed it. From somewhere nearby was the unmistakable sound of rushing water.

"Keep quiet," Bahar instructed.

We all moved ahead slowly and silently. Even our breathing was quiet. The cave widened, and light appeared. Real light. Not magically created light.

I could smell the damp earth and feel wind on my face. The tunnel opened to a cave, the dirt walls becoming stone.

"We did it," Bahar whispered. "We're in the walls."

Relief made me let loose a long breath, but I knew we were just walking from one danger to another. Surviving the tunnels was bad enough, but now we were inside an occupied city.

"Wait here." Bahar crept forward, nearing the mouth of the cave. We watched as he peered out, then cautiously stepped beyond the confines of the stone archway.

After several heartbeats, he returned, then gestured for us to join him. I nearly cried when I saw the sight outside. Hills and trees dotted the landscape. In the distance, I saw the unmistakable form of the towering wall that surrounded Drakous. We were inside its borders. A few small homes sat in the pasture lands below us to the right. To the left, I saw the palace. It was so small from this distance, but we could walk there in less time than we'd been in the tunnels.

"We should rest until nightfall," Ryvin suggested. "It'll be easier to get to the palace under the cover of darkness."

Wordlessly, we all retreated into the cave. It wasn't comfortable, but with the view of the outside world and the occasional gust of wind that found us within the confines of our stone surroundings, I felt better. Hopeful even.

We had Ryvin's shadows, and Laera's ability to manipulate emotions. We had two dragons and a wolf. My stomach twisted a little as I realized that I was, once again, the weakest member of the group. While I could tap into Ryvin's magic, I still worried I'd deprive him of his full strength.

No, I wasn't going to allow myself to downplay my abilities. Balen's words returned to me, reminding me to use my weaknesses to my advantage. The Fae King knew what Ryvin did. He would see me as nothing more than his son's human plaything. I wasn't worth the effort to fight. And that might work to my advantage.

Despite taking turns at watch, I don't think any of us actually slept. There was too much at stake. Too much adrenaline and anticipation. Too much of everything. My whole body felt like it was on alert, flinching and reacting to even the smallest sound.

Ryvin rubbed my shoulders gently, the touch soothing. "You have to find a way to ignore the stress. I know it's difficult, but you have to keep calm, or you're going to make mistakes."

"How do you do it?" I asked quietly. "How do you all charge into battle knowing you're going to take lives and remain so composed?"

"Practice," he replied. "We trained for this, then we fought. Over and over. Until it was second nature."

"I need that. I need that ability to turn it off and fight." I thought about how I'd found my way there outside the Opal, but those deaths still haunted me. Even now, as I prepared for more destruction, their faces still occupied my mind. They'd wanted me dead. Tried to kill me. And I still felt guilty for my response.

Ryvin kissed my forehead. "No, you don't. Keep as much of yourself as you can. Let us take this burden for you."

"I don't want you to have my mistakes added to yours," I said.

"They're not mistakes. And even if they were, I'd gladly take them all to lighten your load. That's what you do for someone you love." He pressed his lips to mine and I relaxed into him, letting the safety of his arms wash away all the anxiety of the moment.

He jolted and pulled away, an annoyed look on his face. I followed his gaze and found Laera staring down at us. "Can you maybe not while the rest of us are in here?"

"Leave them be. They deserve a moment together before we face what might be our death," Bahar said.

"I didn't think you'd be the hopeless romantic type," Laera said, wrinkling her nose.

"He wasn't before. I think it's that mating bond. Makes you soft," Kabir said.

"I'm glad I don't have that problem." Laera sighed, then crossed her arms over her chest. "Is it about time to go kill my father? I'm not sure these two will keep their clothes on if we stay here much longer."

"It was just a kiss," I said, but I could feel the need burning low in my belly. Ryvin had a way of making me forget about everything else and crave him, even when it wasn't the ideal time for those kinds of distractions. Maybe a mating bond really wasn't always the best thing.

Ryvin stood, then offered his hand to help me up. I accepted, then brushed the dirt off my trousers. "Let's get this over with."

"Careful what you wish for, Princess," Kabir said.

Vanth and Ryvin both growled.

"I wasn't threatening her," Kabir replied.

"They get that way sometimes, despite the fact that I try to remind them that Ara can take care of herself," Laera said.

"Again, I'm right here. I can speak for myself. And yes, I

can take care of myself." I hated when they did that. At least the lust was extinguished. "Can we stop discussing me and focus on why we're here?"

"Right." Bahar moved closer to the rest of the group. We all formed a circle and my insides twisted with anxiety as reality hit. We were actually doing this. We were actually going to breach the palace and assassinate the Fae King. There was a part of me that was excited at the prospect. I wasn't sure what that said about me, so I shoved the rising glee away, focusing on Bahar's words.

"We'll enter through the lower kitchens. If there's staff still alive, they won't say a word when they see us. It will give us access to the rest of the palace from there. Any guards will be killed quietly and quickly as soon as we find out where the Fae King is in wait."

"He's in the throne room," Laera said.

Everyone looked at her.

"What? Isn't that part of why you want me here?" She shrugged.

"What else do you see?" Kabir asked.

Laera's expression slackened, her eyes going glassy and dreamy. I could tell she wasn't aware of her body anymore at all. Whatever skill she was using was risky. If she did this around people who wanted to harm her, she'd be in serious danger. I also knew it was the skill that made her such a useful spy.

When her vision returned to normal, her face paled and she wore an expression unlike anything I'd seen from her. My heart thundered in my chest. She looked worried. Or scared. I didn't think that was possible for her.

"Most of the fae are gathered in the throne room. There's a spectacle they're gathering to witness. It'll mean less obstacles for us to get there, but a lot of threats once we reach the king. He's going to have a lot of people around to defend him," she said. "We might be better off waiting until he's retired for the evening. There's too many guards."

"What's the spectacle?" Rvyin asked carefully.

She glanced at him, then swallowed hard. Her face returned to its normally bland expression. "It doesn't matter."

"What is it?" Bahar asked.

She looked over at him. "It doesn't matter."

"It does."

"It's a distraction. And it's bait. For us. He must know we're trying to reach him. It also could mean he knows exactly how much I can see." She looked around at the group. "To be honest, it might mean we're about to fail spectacularly if we go now."

"What is the distraction?" Bahar demanded.

She sighed, a resigned sound that was so different from her usual confidence and disregard for others. Her mouth tightened, and she looked like she was at war with herself.

"What is it?" I asked softly, moving a little closer to her.

She glanced at me, then turned to the dragon shifters who were staring at her, unblinking. I could feel the weight of their anticipation around us like a heavy cloud of dread.

"They've been torturing your sister," Laera announced. "And they all gathered to watch her execution."

8

Ara

The roar that exploded from the dragons was so intense the ground shook, and debris fell from above. I covered my ears with my hands, squeezing my eyes closed to keep the dust away.

It crashed around us, like a wave breaking against the cliffs, before receding into an echo, a ripple of pain so enveloping that I felt like my own heart was breaking.

When I released my hold on my ears, I looked up and found both dragon shifters were already on their way out of the cave.

"Stupid shifters," Laera mumbled as she walked after them. "This is why I didn't want to tell them. They're going to charge in there and get themselves killed."

I followed her, then grabbed her shoulder, pulling her

toward me. "You said this is bait. That means your father knows what you can do and knows you're watching."

Vanth and Ryvin were chasing after the dragons, trying to stop their progress. I left them to it while I stood there with Laera. "They're waiting for us. We've lost all element of surprise. We have to change the plan."

"What are you suggesting?" Laera lifted her chin toward the dragon shifters. "They're not going to wait."

Ryvin and Vanth had managed to calm the dragons enough to get them to return to where we were standing outside the cave. They were both so tense I was certain they were holding their dragon forms in by sheer will. And I wasn't sure how long they'd win over the beasts within.

"You have an idea, Princess?" Bahar asked through gritted teeth.

"You're still a king and the Fae King has allies based on treaties and protocols and expectations. He can't lose face in front of the others or he'll lose his army," I said.

"So?" Bahar asked.

"I think I know what you're getting at," Ryvin said. "I think it could work."

"What could work?" Kabir asked, his tone clipped.

"You go in publicly. Let your people see you arrive. Let all the Fae King's allies see you arrive. You go in with the intention of creating a treaty. An alliance. He would put everything at risk if he took you down if you went peacefully. He'd show his allies how untrustworthy he was and risk them turning on him."

"You want us to surrender to the fae?" Bahar looked incredulous.

"I want you to get your sister out," I clarified. "And see if you can get close enough to end him."

"This could work," Kabir said. "He won't expect us to come in level-headed. He's expecting fire and brimstone. Proof that the dragons are as uncultured and dangerous as he's told all his allies."

"Lying bastard," Bahar snarled.

"He's not going to let me and Laera near him. We're traitors," Ryvin said.

"Not if you return with me as your prisoner and an agreement with Athos for their submission to him," I countered.

"This isn't going to work," Vanth said.

"You have a better idea?" Laera challenged.

"No. But I figure there's a good chance we're dead no matter what we do, so I'm in. Whatever the result." He shrugged.

I hated how defeated he sounded. "The difference is that they're expecting us to come at them with an attack. It'll throw them off, challenge their plans. That gives us an advantage. It lets us get two dragons up close and personal with the king. If we can keep the guards off them long enough for them to shift, we could end this with minimal bloodshed."

"And if we fail?" Bahar asked.

"At least we tried. We know that we have little chance of beating him on the battlefield right now." I sighed. We'd been so optimistic that we'd defeat him in Athos. Between his magical dragons and whatever extra hidden magic he had, it seemed impossible that we could ever win. "We can try now, or we can wait until he comes for us in Athos again."

"Alright," Bahar conceded. "It's time to kill the Fae King."

I CAUGHT sight of faces peering through windows, illuminated by the flickering light of candles and lamps. It was late, but the dragon shifters who lived near the castle must have been holding vigil for their city.

As we passed them, it didn't feel like fear or condemnation or judgment. It felt like awe. Or maybe I was imagining it. Marching down the street with my hands tied behind my back wasn't exactly how I imagined visiting Drakous for the first time.

The cobblestone streets were even and clean, showing obvious care in their construction. The buildings were strung together into long rows, attached in series of eight or ten long before another road interrupted them. Each building appeared to have shops on street level with homes above. They spanned three or four stories high.

There were so many people living here. All those windows, all those faces, all those flickering candles were people. Families, even. So many who were in serious danger with their king deposed from his throne.

I wanted to learn more about this place where humans and dragons and vampires all lived together. It wasn't the rough and tumble city I'd been told about.

I let my head drop along with my shoulders as I gave myself a moment to mourn how much was taken from me with the lies told in Athos.

Soldiers in the red tunics of Konos headed toward us, marching in unison, balls of fae light floating above them.

"It's time," Laera mumbled.

Ryvin had been walking alongside me, but he moved in front of me. I knew it was to shield me from the oncoming soldiers. Laera remained by my side, gripping my arm, leading her prisoner forward. Vanth dropped back, taking up the rear.

We halted as soon as we reached the group of soldiers. They paused, standing in front of us with unreadable expressions.

Bahar took a step forward. "I have come for an audience with the Fae King."

One of the soldiers, a gruff looking male with fair hair and ruddy cheeks stepped forward. "And you are?"

"Bahar Nasrul, King of Drakous."

The soldiers glanced at their companions and a few of them shuffled their feet. I had to hold back a smirk. We were right, they weren't expecting this.

The guard who'd addressed Bahar nodded once. "Come with us."

We were surrounded by the fae guards, the soldiers quickly moving into position around us, marching along the road with us as we made our way to the palace.

Every time I caught one of them staring at me, I had to steady my hands. Their gazes were far too hungry. They wanted bloodshed. I could practically feel their hatred and rage, their desire to fight. They'd likely come here with the promise of war. And if the city peacefully surrendered due to lack of soldiers, they didn't get the bloodshed they wanted.

I glared at them, meeting their stares with malice behind my own. I hoped each and every one of them got the end they deserved.

The castle was a large, solid stone building. There weren't open air colonnades or columns holding up the various levels. It was heavy and stern. The opposite of the airy and light palace I'd grown up in.

Windows were vertical slits, evenly spaced around the upper floors. The lower floors had no windows at all.

"Dragons are allergic to sunlight?" Laera asked.

"It's built for protection, not appearances," Bahar said.

"Bet you're regretting that decision now," Laera said.

Kabir chuckled. "We didn't count on our enemies getting access to it."

"Then you weren't spending enough time in your war room," Laera shot back.

"No more speaking," one of the guards called.

It didn't matter anyway, because we were at the front doors. Dozens of guards stared as we walked through, our escorts remaining around us as we crossed into the dark, chilly interior of the castle.

The stones under our feet were polished with age, cracked in a few places, and uneven in their placement. While the city appeared better constructed and planned, this building didn't have the same care. It had to be old. Far older than the other buildings we'd passed.

Tapestries lined the gray walls, showing faded scenes of dragons flying against what was likely once a blue sky. The color had been leached from most of them, diminishing the typical opulence found in a castle. It was definitely more about function than aesthetics, as Bahar had mentioned.

I tried to ignore the stares of the countless guards we passed as we walked down the hall. Interestingly, I noted that they weren't all clad in red. There were greens and blues and golds mixed in with the occasional red tunic. These were the allies. I wondered where all the men from Konos were stationed and what their actual numbers were compared to the allies they'd added.

We paused in front of a massive iron door. Dents and divots indicated that there had been multiple attempts at knocking it down over the years. The flecked remains of paint were bright gold. It must have been quite impressive once.

The guards fanned out away from us as the doors opened, then repositioned with half of them in front of us, the other half following behind our group.

Heat radiated from the space as we entered the throne room. It was a large, dark stone chamber lined with flickering torches and overflowing with people. I was certain the number of bodies crammed into the space was the cause of the warmth. It also contributed to a very unpleasant smell that made me wrinkle my nose.

The Fae King was seated on a simple wooden throne atop a stone platform. The queen stood behind him, like a statue clad in emerald. Next to her, a silent sentinel, stood Selena.

"Traitor," Vanth hissed under his breath.

We were prodded forward, the gathered crowd making approving sounds and whispers. They wanted a show and with us joining, they were getting exactly what they wanted.

"What do we have here?" The Fae King bellowed. He rose from the throne and walked to the edge of the platform, pausing right in front of the steps. "My wayward children and a fallen king."

The gathered sycophants laughed too loudly. It was a nervous sort of sound. Forced rather than approving. Maybe they weren't as desperate for a show as I thought.

"Father," Laera shoved her way past the guards, then dipped into a low bow with practiced grace. "I come to beg for forgiveness. I was blinded by pride, but have seen the errors of my ways."

Ryvin moved to join her, and I nearly reached for him, not wanting to stand here without him by my side.

"Can you forgive a son for being blinded by the call of his mother?" Ryvin asked, dropping into a bow of his own. "A goddess is difficult to resist. I was weak and I made a mistake."

"We brought you a gift," Laera added. "An offering to our most noble father."

I resisted the urge to roll my eyes. Laera was going to ruin our plan by overplaying this.

Vanth grabbed my upper arm and roughly dragged me forward. "Come on, Athos trash."

I let myself stumble and whimper as he pulled me forward.

"You brought the Athos princess back?" The king looked pleased.

"She nearly stole your son away from you, but we were able to prove her deception. I think he's seeing clearly now," Vanth said, his head in a low bow.

"Very good, very good." The Fae King descended the stairs. "And I see you've also secured additional offerings?"

"We're here to negotiate a truce," Bahar said. "King to king, we need to do what is best for all our people."

"You are no longer a king," The Fae King snarled. "Unless you're here to bow to me, you have no business in this kingdom. It is mine."

I swear Bahar looked like he was going to explode right there. My heart raced as I waited for the shift.

Any second, a pair of dragons would explode. My fingers twitched, ready to pull off my bindings the second I could be of assistance.

But nothing was happening. Time dragged by, and we waited. Something was wrong.

"Bring out the prisoner," The Fae King yelled.

A smaller door on the opposite side of the room opened and a pair of guards dragged a semi-conscious woman through. Her long red hair hung in dirty tendrils, hiding her face. Her bare feet dragged on the floor behind her.

"You monster!" Bahar growled. He moved toward his sister but froze as soon as a group of guards drew their weapons and turned them on the unconscious woman.

"How dare you!" Kabir bellowed. "How dare you treat a member of the royal family this way. Release her now!"

The Fae King moved closer to us, his steps slow and deliberate. "I don't think you're understanding what's going on here. Your household is meaningless. You are no longer in charge or Drakous. This kingdom is mine. And Athos will be next."

9

ARA

THE DRAGON SHIFTERS ROARED, each of them charging toward the Fae King, but they came up short, freezing in place in front of him. Wearing bewildered expressions, they glanced back at the rest of us.

"Why didn't they shift?" Vanth asked.

The Fae King held up his hand, a purple stone gleaming and sparkling on his middle finger. "It's nice, isn't it? A gift from a friend of mine." He turned his attention to his children. "You might have stolen your mother's magic from me, but I found alternatives that might be even better. I don't even need the power of the gods. With this magic, even they can't defeat me."

He walked to the dragons, then shoved Bahar with an unnatural force. The Dragon King fell backward, unable to hold himself upright. The Fae King laughed and his audience laughed with him. This time, it felt a little more like they approved of the joke.

"They can't shift. This whole room has been warded. I can't have a dragon sneak up on me and burn me alive." He kicked Bahar just as he was getting up, knocking the king to the ground again. "What a pathetic mess."

Shadows billowed around us, darkness quickly enveloping the Fae King. Vanth charged, his blade drawn. The crowd screamed but made no move for the exit. As I backed away from the fight and the increasing shadows, I noticed that the doors were barred, multiple guards standing at them. None of us were getting out of here easily.

Grunting and the sound of clashing metal told me a battle was underway, but I couldn't see the fight through the thick shadows expanding in front of me.

The dragon shifters were on their feet, but they were only visible for a moment before they were smothered by the darkness.

Laera stood next to me, focused on something I couldn't see, doing whatever it was that she could to aid our cause.

Guards moved closer, awkwardly staring at the increasing dark cloud. I heard them arguing, trying to decide if they should join the fight, or if they'd accidentally harm the king in the process.

"Enough!" The Fae King's voice echoed around the room.

The shadows cleared and I saw Ryvin on the ground, Vanth's blade at his throat. The shifter quickly raised his weapon and turned to find his target. Both dragon shifters were nearby, weapons in their grip. Everyone was breathing heavy.

"Kill the princess," the Fae King said with a dismissive wave of his hand.

"No!" I ran, knowing I was the closest. Guards quickly intercepted me, capturing me and holding me in place.

It was as if everything was moving in slow motion. The dragon princes were running, but they were too slow. Ryvin and Vanth charged forward, even Laera was making her way toward the guards holding the woman captive.

Her head was on the floor before anyone reached her.

The scream of pain from the dragon princes nearly tore me in two. It was as if someone had splintered their very soul. They probably felt like someone had.

"Kill them all!" the Fae King shouted.

The crowd erupted in cheers, the sound deafening.

The guards descended upon my friends and the guards holding me released me so they could unsheathe their weapons.

I pulled a dagger from my thigh and stabbed the first guard in the neck before he knew what hit him. I swept my leg under the foot of the second one just as he pointed his sword at me. He landed with a thud and I didn't hesitate to plunge my knife into his neck.

Bright red blood coated my hands and arms. I could taste the copper tang and I knew I had to be covered in the stuff. There wasn't any time to dwell as more guards charged toward me and I had to fight.

The crowd started throwing things, and I had to dodge as I was avoiding the guards coming after me.

My friends were all surrounded, attacking soldiers wearing tunics of various colors. Ryvin stood out in black, making him the easiest to find. His shadows billowed around him, taking down any fae who was stupid enough to challenge him. Vanth was larger than most of the fae he was fighting, and he was taking out two at a time. Laera had a sword drawn and was holding her own well.

With the number of guards who continued to charge Ryvin, I couldn't bring myself to test out using any of his shadows for myself. I was insignificant, likely not seen as much of a threat as the others. I knew that could work to my advantage and I weaved around the fighters, searching for anyone who was distracted. My kills weren't dignified. Stabbing them from behind wasn't going to get me any accolades, but we were outnumbered and fighting for our lives.

Laera was starting to look worn down, her swings getting slower, her moves sloppier. I moved closer to her and tripped one of the soldiers making his way to join her attackers. He didn't go down like I hoped. Catching himself, he spun to face me, not hesitating before lunging toward me. I dodged, but not before his blade sliced my upper arm.

I bit back a scream, channeling the pain into rage as I swung for him. He was fast and avoided my blade far too easily. I crouched, avoiding his next swing before stabbing my knife into his thigh.

He howled in pain, then kicked me before I could

retrieve my blade. I went down, landing hard. Another kick landed in my side and I braced for another, but nothing came.

I felt the cool caress of shadows and looked up to find Ryvin with murder in his expression. The guard who'd injured me was on the ground, blood pouring from his face as he clawed at his neck, desperate for air.

Ryvin offered a hand, helping me up. As I got to my feet, my attacker fell, his chest going still.

"You alright?" Rvyin asked.

I leaned down and yanked my knife from the man's thigh. Blood oozed from the injury. "I'll live."

Ryvin glanced around, then returned his attention to me. "I'm going to help Laera and Vanth. Get to the back door. Take the dragons with you."

"Got it."

He ran off, and I fought my way toward the fallen princess, where the dragon princes were hacking their way through every guard stupid enough to attack them.

My heart ached and I held in the rising bile as I stepped over her head. It was so fucking disrespectful. She deserved better. I never even met her, but I felt like I owed her more. I had to help get her brothers out.

Dark shadows began to swirl around me, rising from the ground like tendrils of smoke. They were increasing quickly, taking over the whole room in fluid, graceful movements. I knew what Ryvin was doing and I knew we didn't have much time before darkness would consume everything. I sprinted toward the dragons.

I came to Kabir first, just as he fatally wounded his

opponent. The soldier was clutching the gushing stomach wound, staring at Kabir wide eyed. I grabbed the prince's upper arm, pulling him to me, quickly stepping back away from his weapon as he attacked on impulse.

"What are you doing?" He hissed, stilling his blade before it could harm me.

"We gotta go," I said, as quietly as I could. I leaned my head toward the small back door.

He shook his head. "These monsters killed my sister."

"I know, but you already got the ones who did. And we can't win. Not right now." I gripped his wrist. "Please. We have to go. She wouldn't want you to die like this."

Another soldier charged and we both moved forward, causing the guard to hesitate. My knife bit into his side as Kabir sliced his sword across his throat. The man made gurgling sounds as he fell to his knees.

"Brother!" Kabir called.

Bahar spun to face us, then returned to his opponent. He punched the green-clad soldier in the face, then kicked him down before heading over to us. His chest was rising and falling rapidly, his eyes wild. But as soon as he reached us, he noticed the darkness that was quickly making visibility difficult. Even the soldiers were starting to back away, hesitating rather than risk attacking one another.

"It's time to go." I said through gritted teeth. I was expecting an argument, but Bahar glanced around the room, then nodded.

Bahar grabbed my hand, and Kabir grabbed the other, just as the darkness swallowed us. Screams and grunts filled the room. Swords still clashed, but the sounds were less frequent.

We carefully moved toward the door. At least, I hoped we were. I was counting on the dragon's knowing where it was. When Bahar stopped moving, I waited, my skin tingling in anticipation and fear making my chest tight. We were unarmed. The darkness the only thing preventing us from being completely exposed and vulnerable.

It felt like forever before Bahar pulled on my hand and we moved. As soon as we were through the door, I could see again. He closed it behind us and I started to look around for Ryvin.

"I assume this means there's a plan," Bahar said, still gripping his sword.

"We lost in there. You know that," I replied.

He growled.

"Don't growl at me." I glared at him. "Our choices were die in there, or get the fuck out and find another way."

"He can't be killed," Bahar snarled. "We might as well take as many out as we can." He took a step toward the door and I grabbed him, knowing my hold wasn't going to do anything to stop him if he really wanted to leave.

"Becoming a martyr won't bring her back."

He stilled.

"If we can get it so you can shift, you can kill him. We have to get him in the open. That gem can't have that much power," I said.

His jaw tensed and a vein in his temple bulged.

"Where's your prince?" Kabir asked.

My stomach twisted. "He'll be here."

"We can't wait too long," Kabir replied. "I refuse to be ambushed and captured while fleeing." His grip tightened on his weapon.

Ryvin would tell me to run. He'd tell me to leave them behind. "We wait a little longer. Not much. If he's not here, we find our way out."

Every heartbeat was excruciating. Every breath was a reminder that we were waiting in a hallway, unable to help. And giving our enemy more time to notice we were gone and find us.

"Princess..." Bahar said.

We'd already waited too long. I knew they'd given more than enough time. Reluctantly, I nodded. Ryvin and the others were on their own. They'd find their way out. I had to believe that.

We got a few steps down the hall when I heard footsteps behind us. My pulse raced and for a horrible moment, I thought the guards had found us.

It was Ryvin, Laera, and Vanth. All of them bloody and panting as they chased us down the hall.

"Don't stop!" Ryvin called. "Keep going!"

I ran, but my friends caught up to me quickly. All of us were racing down the hall, blindly following Bahar and Kabir. Thankfully, this was their home. They knew every exit.

Down stairs, through rooms, into servant hallways, down more stairs. Finally, we emerged into the kitchen and Bahar stopped, catching his breath. My sides ached and my lungs were burning. Keeping pace with shifters and fae wasn't easy. My legs felt wobbly and I wasn't sure I could sprint like that again.

A few servants stared open-mouthed at us. Then one of them started pushing a table toward the door. It screeched against the stone floor, making me wince. Two more servants joined in, aiding the first in moving the table. When they were finished, they walked toward the chairs and started carrying them to the table, adding them to the top. They were making a barricade.

One of them paused in front of Bahar. "What are you waiting for? We'll hold 'em off as long as we can. Get out of here."

"We'll be back with reinforcements. We will not allow him to hold Drakous," Bahar said.

"We know," the servant said.

Something slammed into the door and we all turned. My heart hammered against my ribs. They found us.

Kabir pushed open the exterior door and we left the kitchen, ending up in a massive garden. Before I could get my bearings, the dragon shifters bolted ahead, then stilled. Their bodies rippled and cracked. Similar sounds came from next to me where Vanth was changing into his wolf form.

Two massive dragons rose into the sky, flying away from the castle in the opposite direction we'd come from.

"They're causing a distraction," Laera said.

"We better use it then," Ryvin said, he looked over at the wolf. "Stay with Ara. Get her to the caves."

"Where are you going?" I was furious he was planning on leaving me.

"Right down the street, for all to see." He grinned, a vicious smile that sent a chill down my spine. This wasn't my Ryvin standing in front of me. This was the dark prince who brought fear and death in his wake. The warrior I'd seen ruthlessly kill his enemies.

"Finally, time to play." Laera pushed her sleeves up, then winked at me. "See you soon."

Vanth made a huffing kind of sound, then impatiently pawed at the ground. I got the message. "Fine. Don't die," I called to Ryvin and Laera.

Ryvin leaned forward and gave me a soft kiss. "Stay with Vanth and don't do anything heroic." He took off at a run before I could respond.

I sighed, hating that I was hiding away while my friends put themselves in danger to draw attention from me. I allowed one more breath of feeling sorry for myself, then started walking, following Vanth toward town.

It wasn't long before we were running again, taking breaks behind shops and ducking between carriages. We cut through alleyways, turning when we heard noise, and hiding behind anything we could find to slowly make our way back through town.

By the time we finally returned to the cave, Ryvin and Laera were waiting for us. I looked skyward, expecting to see a pair of large dragons swoop down to join us. Then I realized how stupid that would be. They'd draw everyone here. "The dragons aren't joining us, I'm guessing?"

"They can find their own way back to camp. Just like us," Laera said. "Now, let's get the fuck out of here before my father's men find this tunnel."

This time, I entered the cave first, with the others behind me.

10

Lagina

"You're going to wear a path into the marble," Argus said.

I shot him a glare, but continued pacing. The waiting was driving me insane. I walked over to my desk where Ara's letter was weighed down with two small rocks. It had been two days since she sent word that Drakous had fallen and she should be here by now.

A knock sounded on the door and I spun toward the sound, my skin prickling as anxiety dripped down my spine. My sisters wouldn't knock. Only one of the guards would knock.

I waited, lifting my chin in a false show of dominance so whoever was on the other side wouldn't see the worry I'd been displaying seconds ago.

Argus opened the door and murmured a gruff greeting to the guard on the other side. He closed it quickly, their exchange too quiet for me to hear. When he faced me, my heart fell into my stomach. I knew that look. "Just tell me. Who is it? Who do we have to mourn next?"

"Nobody is dead," he assured me.

I sucked in a relieved breath.

"The Queen of Konos is here to see you." His face was pale.

My brow furrowed. Had I heard incorrectly? That wasn't possible. Why would she be here? "What?"

"She has requested to meet with you and she came with Selena of the Black Opal," he added. "Selena said the queen comes with pure intentions."

"Do you think it's a trick?" I asked.

He shook his head. "I'm not sure. I'll support you, whichever way you want to take this."

"Where is she?"

"Throne room. Alone."

"Weapons?" I asked, even though I knew she'd have magic she could use against me.

"She's unarmed."

There was a good chance I was already living on borrowed time. "Let's find out what she wants."

The guards outside my study fell into step behind me as I made my way to the throne room. I'd avoided having formal meetings in the space. It was a place my father had enjoyed using to assert dominance. It was also the place he'd died. Devoured by the magical darkness the Prince of Konos could wield.

At first, there was a sense of mourning about the space. Now, I wasn't sure what I felt anymore. The lies and secrets had a way of pushing through the good memories that swirled in my mind. I couldn't think of one without the other. It was too much to sort through with everything else at stake.

I hesitated in front of the doors, the single guard stationed outside them watching me for a signal to let me in. Once, there'd been several guards here at all times, even when it wasn't in use. It was another reminder of how far we'd fallen. How weak Athos was. If everyone else failed, we had no hope.

With that reminder, I nodded to the guard, and he opened the heavy door. If the queen of Konos was sent to kill me, perhaps it would be quicker than the death that was likely waiting for me once this war came to a close.

I swept in with false authority, trying to channel as much of my father's movements as I could. Without turning to face the Konos queen, I glanced her way, taking her in out of the corner of my eye as I made my way to the massive, gilded throne.

She was dressed in a flowing green peplos, a gold circlet sitting atop her silver hair. Her dark skin seemed to glow, that faint, shimmery quality I'd heard some fae possessed. It made me clench my jaw. Someone had told me that if you could see their magic, that was the only warning you'd get before they killed you. It was a sign of power.

The Fae Prince hadn't had that quality, yet he'd leveled an entire battlefield.

What the fuck could this woman do?

I took my time easing into the throne, arranging my

deep blue peplos around me, smoothing the fabric, keeping my gaze down. Finally, when I was settled, I looked up and took in my guest.

She wore an indulgent smirk, as if she knew the game I was playing. With graceful movements, she swept into a deep bow. "Your highness, it is an honor to meet you."

When she rose, I inclined my head in greeting. "Queen Aspasia, to what do I owe this great honor?"

She dropped the fabric she was holding in her hands, letting the dress drag along the floor as she moved closer to me. My guards marched forward, drawing swords. She lifted her hands in submission. "Fine. I'll speak from here."

I waited, keeping my expression impassive, working to maintain neutrality the entire time she moved despite the fear twisting in my gut. I knew she didn't need to be closer to me to end me. Whatever gifts she had, they were powerful. If I was still alive, it was because she truly wanted to speak with me. At least for now.

"Stand down," I commanded my guards.

Slowly, they lowered their weapons.

"Argus, you stay. The rest of you can wait outside. I'll summon you if needed." I waved my hand at the bewildered guards, but they obeyed, filing out of the room with confused backward glances.

Once the door was closed, I stood, then descended the stairs of the dais, moving closer to the queen. She regarded me with curiosity, as if I were something new she'd never seen before. Perhaps I was the first human she'd interacted with.

"You can speak freely in front of him," I lifted my chin toward Argus. "Tell me why you're actually here."

"You're smarter than they give you credit for. Especially for your age. The King of Konos seems to think you'll bend like a reed in a storm. Snapping with ease." She drew out the s, adding a hissing quality to her speech.

"I'm young, but I'm not stupid. We both know how often women are underestimated," I replied.

"That we do," she agreed.

I waited, giving her time to reveal the nature of her visit. Several heartbeats passed before she took another step closer. Argus's hand tightened on the hilt of his sword, but he didn't remove the weapon.

"The King of Konos has taken Drakous," she said.

"I already know that."

"He will come for you next." She made an amused sound. "But it's not his time to shine. It's mine."

I lifted a brow. "Are you threatening me?"

"Oh, no, I'm here to offer an alliance. An actual alliance. Between the humans and the fae. Because when he falls, I will reclaim what I've lost. The Court of Vipers will be the most powerful fae court, and I've been patiently waiting to watch Konos burn."

"I'm listening..." I gestured toward the door. "Would you like some tea? We can continue this conversation in my study."

Aspasia nodded once, then followed me out of the throne room.

The guards silently followed us, doing better at hiding their expressions this time.

When we reached the study, I sent for tea before settling into one of the chairs in the sitting area. The enemy queen sat across from me, looking completely at ease on the couch. She was a stunning, composed woman. Every move she made was precise and graceful. My mother would have loved her.

"I'd love to hear more about your thoughts for this alliance between our kingdoms," I started.

"It's simple, really. You and I are not at war. I have no concern about how humans choose to live their lives, and honestly, you're no danger to us. Unless the magic you liberated begins to show in humans, though even if it does, I imagine we have a long while before it would be a threat." She leaned back against the cushion and crossed her legs.

"I have no quarrel with you or your people. I will not allow more sacrifices or other signs of fealty. You are offering a true peace? Not subjection?"

"I have no desire to waste my time on human politics," she waved her hand dismissively.

I frowned, not missing her derisive tone. We were nothing to the fae. "If you'll be taking over the Court of Vipers, what will happen to Konos?"

"I don't care what happens to them. I have sat by, taking the false title of queen from a man who used me to forge alliances and gain my people's power. After what he did to his mate, I had no choice. The only power I had was to resist the marriage vows. Which means once he is dead, I am no longer bound to Konos, and neither is my daughter."

"What about the prince?" I saw Ara and Ryvin, my chest tightening with anxiety at the thought of anything happening to her. I was still new to the concept of a mating bond, but I knew Ara was connected to him in a way she couldn't control. I hated that for her.

"He won't be a problem. The gods are already coming for him and his stolen magic," she said.

"What do you mean?"

She lifted her brows. "You don't know?"

The knock on the door made us both turn, and the conversation ceased while a servant set a tray with tea and honey cakes on the table between us. Once the door was closed, we sat quietly for a moment, neither of us reaching for the refreshments.

"Explain what you were talking about," I said, finally breaking the silence. "What is going on with the Fae Prince?"

"He stole your sister's magic. If the rumors are true, she was even more powerful than him. And just like his father, he took all that power for himself."

Heat roared, and I could feel my cheeks flush. Ara never told me the details about what she meant when she'd said she had no magic anymore. "More powerful than him?"

"Isn't it always how it goes? Doesn't seem to matter where you come from. Men see us as a threat and find a way to chain us, to dull our shine, to use our gifts for themselves. The king needed me because my court wouldn't rebel against him if I was by his side." She leaned forward and poured the tea into two cups, then slid one toward me.

"Tell me more." I took the offered cup.

She took a tentative sip, then set her cup back on the table. Then she told me how the Fae King had stolen his mate's power. How Ryvin had done the same to Ara. I listened, jaw tense, taking in everything that had been kept from me. How much of this did my father know? Was the power the Fae King held the reason Athos bowed to them so easily?

"Then he set his sights on all the fae courts," she explained. "It was join him or be destroyed. With the power of Nyx, and a son who could kill hundreds without touching them, we didn't stand a chance. I was young, but I knew I could save my people. I agreed to be his consort in exchange for protection. He thought we folded, but we're nearly immortal. We can be very patient."

I was impressed by her foresight. And a little terrified. She was definitely better to have as an ally. "The only problem with this is that it all rides on the defeat of the Fae King. He's already taken Drakous. How could we possibly stop him?"

"For starters, I have allies who will follow me once I give the word. Plus, there's his sorceress," Aspasia said. "You take her down, and everything falls apart."

11

ARA

RETURNING HOME FEELS LIKE DEFEAT. Once I'd have given almost anything to step onto our sandy shores. Now, I feel like the very land mocks me. It's a reminder of how much harm I've brought to my people since I first dared to leave.

The guards recognize us this time, letting us into the palace without hesitation. Or maybe they heard what happened the last time they challenged my friends.

A heavy silence fell around us, sorrow and guilt making me fight against the urge to crawl into a cave so I could hide until everything came to the inevitable end. I wasn't even sure what that end would look like anymore. All of our ideas had failed, and I wasn't sure if there was anything we could do.

The palace was quiet. Guards were few, and I didn't see a single servant. It matched the solemn tone we'd experienced while walking through town. Few were out in the streets, and they stayed away from us as we passed. All of Athos wore the heavy weight of defeat.

Argus walked toward us, a weary smile on his expression. "Welcome back, Princess. I heard the news and I'm glad to see you're alive."

"It's starting to feel like a curse," I replied.

"It's for a reason, we must have faith. The gods will come to their senses," he answered.

I kept my thoughts about the gods to myself. "Where is Lagina?"

"In the study. But you should know, she's got a guest with her." His eyes darted toward my friends before returning to me.

We fell into step alongside him. "What kind of guest?"

"My mother," Laera grumbled.

I stopped walking. "What?"

"Why is she here?" Ryvin asked.

Vanth readied his sword. "Selena's with her, isn't she?"

Laera rolled her eyes. "Put it away, shifter. Yes, she is. But they're not here to harm us. I'm not sure why she's here, but I know it's not a threat."

"Everything your mother does is a threat," Ryvin countered.

"Everything my mother does is for her own benefit," Laera corrected. "Killing us doesn't help her. We're powerful. If she's here, that means she's decided it's finally time to show her true colors and walk away from Konos. That means she needs allies."

I could see the tension in Vanth's shoulders. I touched

his arm. "Let's find out what she wants, then we can decide if we're going to kill her."

Ryvin chucked. "When did you get so murderous?"

"Probably around the time I met you," I replied.

"He has that effect on people," Laera said.

I started walking again, the others following me as we made our way toward the study. With each step, exhaustion began to weigh more heavily. There was something about being in Athos that made my body feel a little safer. I could drop my guard just enough to start to acknowledge how tired I was. I shoved the thought away, blinking a few times to send the sting away from my eyes.

We passed a few guards, all of them straightening as soon as they saw Argus approach. At least they were alert enough to react to him. Not that they'd help us if any of the fae in our palace decided to turn against us.

The guards stationed outside the study parted to let Argus through, and he opened the door for us. As soon as I saw the Konos Queen, I froze. Even though I'd expected her, seeing her here, with my sister, was a complete shock. Both queens rose from their seats and moved toward us. Selena sat on a couch nearby, flipping through the pages of a book, seemingly unbothered by our presence.

"Ara, I heard what happened. Are you alright?" she crossed to me, her brow furrowed with concern.

The Konos Queen stood in the center of the room, her hands clasped in front of her. Her expression was one of indifference, not unlike what I'd see from Ophelia when she was bored.

"I'm alright. But we're in trouble. The Fae King has

more magic than we realized. Something extra; a gift that's making him untouchable. We'll have to lure him into the open to have any chance of taking him down," I explained.

"That won't be enough," the Konos Queen said.

"What exactly are you doing here?" Laera moved past me, marching right to her mother, then stopping in front of her.

Ryvin stood so close to me, I could feel his body against mine. Vanth took a couple of steps into the room, his fingers resting on the hilt of his sword. It was clear neither of them trusted the visitor.

"Aspasia came to offer her assistance," Lagina said. "She knows where to find the sorceress who holds the key to taking the Fae King down."

"You knew?" Laera glared at her mother. "You knew he had this kind of power and you did nothing?"

"What would you have me do? Show my hand to a man with the power of a goddess and a sorceress?" Aspasia asked. "I waited until I could actually win."

"How did he hide that from me?" Laera's voice wavered in a way I'd never heard before. She clenched her jaw, regaining her composure. "How did he know how to hide it from me?"

"I don't know. I never told him anything I suspected of your full abilities. But he's got eyes in as many places as you do. I fear we underestimated him," Aspasia said.

"We didn't underestimate him. We fell into his trap and we blinded ourselves," Ryvin added. "But I'm more inter-ested in what you're really doing here than I am in what his plans were. He's always been clear on his goals. He wants to rule everything and everyone. What are you after?"

"You know what I want," she said, her tone almost playful.

Ryvin narrowed his eyes. "Don't try that on me. Your seduction doesn't work with me."

She hummed. "It would have made my plans come to fruition sooner if it had. But you aren't as easily manipulated as your father." With a chuckle, she turned her attention to me. "Don't worry, he's all yours."

Ryvin wrapped his arm around my waist and I realized I'd moved in front of him protectively without even knowing.

"Mother, don't provoke her. She's far more powerful than you think," Laera stated.

"That's good, then. Because I'm counting on your little group to do my dirty work for me." She shrugged.

"You said you had allies for us. And information," Lagina cut in. "Whatever this pissing contest is, it's done. You help us, or you leave."

Aspasia smiled, and I noticed that Selena was standing now, watching us with an expectant expression.

"Thebes has never been in your father's pocket," Aspasia said, directing her attention to Laera and Ryvin. "They've agreed to fight for Athos."

"What? Why?" I asked.

"Those creatures can't come here. I'm trying to keep my people alive, not feed them to more monsters," Lagina snapped.

"Hold on," I stepped away from Ryvin, "give her a chance to explain."

Aspasia cocked her head to the side, studying me briefly before turning to Lagina. "Is my information incorrect? Is your youngest sister not a vampire herself?"

"Half." Lagina glanced at me accusingly, as if I was the one who'd handed this information over. "And we all know what the vampires in Thebes are like. They were so out of control they covered the entire city."

"That's certainly not true," Laera said. "There's humans living there as well. How did you not know that?"

"What's it like?" I asked, finding myself easily believing Laera. I wasn't sure if it was because I was trusting Laera or if I was getting so used to discovering that most of what I learned was a lie.

"It is largely populated by vampires," Laera conceded. "And many were changed aggressively in the early days. But those who enjoyed preying on others were harshly punished. They haven't allowed anyone to turn a human without their consent in a century."

"Are there not murderers and thieves among humans?" Aspasia asked.

An image of the angry mob coming after me outside the Opal flashed in my mind. All of those people would have cheered to see me dead. They wanted to do even worse than that. Humans. Not fae. Not vampires.

"Why would they help us?" I asked.

"Because they want food," Lagina said darkly.

"Many of them have family and friends in Telos or Athos. They've been prohibited from travel by your kingdom and by Konos. They're prisoners in their own city," Aspasia explained.

"Just like you humans," Laera added. "Except you seem to like that."

"We don't like it." I'd always dreamed of getting out. Of more than what Athos could provide. I knew I wasn't alone.

"Does he know?" Ryvin asked.

Aspasia turned to the prince. "No. He believes they're on their way to Athos to join him."

"They're already on their way?" Lagina asked.

Aspasia nodded.

"That's not going to be easy to explain," I said. "The people here don't trust anyone who isn't human."

"They had no problem sharing all their darkest secrets with me," Selena said.

"They didn't know you weren't human," I replied.

"They won't know a vampire, either," she said.

"We can't lie to them," I replied.

"They didn't want me there, but nobody complained. They welcomed the dragons to save their own lives," Vanth said. "Get your aunt to talk to them. They'll come around."

Blinding light suddenly filled the room, making me squint against the intensity. I shielded my eyes with my hand. "What is that?"

The door opened and the light fractured into a prism of colors, forming dancing rainbows on every surface. I spun to see bewildered guards blindly reaching, trying to move, but seemingly frozen in place.

Ryvin was in front of me, sword drawn, Vanth by his

side. Both men yelled as their weapons were pulled from their grip and thrown across the room. They landed with a clatter on the floor.

"That's no way to greet someone who saved your mate's life," a booming female voice echoed through the room.

The door slammed, then the colors faded. After blinking away the brightness lingering from the light, I recognized the newcomer. "Iris?"

"Shit. More gods," Laera groaned.

"*The* Iris?" Lagina asked.

"Yes, yes, messenger for the gods and all that." Iris waved her hand dismissively.

Selena and Aspasia were both backing up, moving away from the newcomer. I touched my necklace, recalling how she'd gifted me the item that allowed me safe passage across the sea.

Ryvin lowered his head. "I'm sorry for how I reacted. Thank you for the gift you bestowed on Ara."

"Please accept my apology as well, gentle lady," Vanth said.

"The gift was from her mother, but I do accept your apology. Had you tried to stab me, we'd be in a different position right now." Iris nodded to Vanth, then moved closer to Lagina.

My sister looked like she was going to pass out. Her eyes were wide, her mouth open, all color drained from her face. Finally, she blinked a few times, then closed her mouth, swallowing before regaining some control. "Welcome to our kingdom." She curtseyed.

"You have nothing to fear from me, Queen of Athos. The gods have no quarrel with you," Iris said.

Lagina let out an obvious breath of relief.

"They do, however, have issue with your sister." Iris turned to me. My insides twisted and my pulse raced.

Ryvin moved closer to me, and I gave him a warning look. This was my problem to solve. His jaw tensed, but he took a step back, giving me a little space.

"Do you have a message for me, then?" I asked, surprised I was able to keep the shaking of my hands out of my voice.

"I do. And you will do well to listen." She moved with such grace I wondered how I'd missed that she wasn't human when we first met.

"The gods know you are able to access your magic." She glanced at Ryvin, then turned her attention back to me. "And they know that your mate used it as well."

"I will face whatever consequences they require if they leave Ara out of this," Ryvin said.

"This isn't about you, Prince," Iris snapped. Her voice softened, "They have decided that you are too dangerous to live, but too important to die. You have come to represent all of Athos, not just yourself."

"What does that mean?" Laera asked.

"It means that your fate will be determined by one of their own." Iris handed me a scroll tied with a piece of twine.

My heart was pounding so loudly in my ears that I was certain the others could hear me.

Carefully, I opened it.

. . .

Ara,

I have the great honor of deciding your fate. Let's find out if you, and your people, are worthy of life. I'll be waiting for you on Naxos.

Nyx

I THINK I STOPPED BREATHING.

Somehow, I managed to hand the letter over to Ryvin. I stood in silence as the message was passed around the room. Nobody spoke.

Finally, Iris broke the silence, "She's already there. Awaiting your arrival."

I swallowed hard, then looked at the messenger. She'd once delivered an item that saved my life, now she was delivering something that might very well end it.

"You'll go to Ceto's island," Ryvin said. "Nyx can't touch you there and your mother said you can live there."

"She can't spend her life locked away on an island," Laera snapped.

"Ara would die if she was isolated that way," Lagina added.

I looked at my mate, the concern in his expression made my heart ache. I knew if it were reversed, I'd ask the same of him. "You know I can't do that."

He cupped my cheek. "I know, but I also know what Nyx is like. What she's capable of."

"If anyone can survive her, it's the woman who freed her. She's got that going for her," Laera said gently.

I lifted a brow as I turned toward the princess. I'd be less concerned if she was her typical, snaky self. "Don't go writing my eulogy yet."

"Well, this is good," Aspasia cut in. "I had wondered how we'd account for Nyx. Now, Ara will be distracting her."

"She hasn't agreed to go yet," Ryvin said.

"She's going," Vanth said. "You know that already."

"We'll go with her, then," Ryvin declared.

"We can't. This is Ara's task." Vanth was speaking to Ryvin, but looking at me.

"She can do this, Brother," Laera added.

"She invited me. And they're right, I can do this. What-ever she throws at me, I can handle it. What I can't do is find the sorceress or defend Athos. I need you to help my people," I pleaded.

"I don't care what happens to Athos," Ryvin said. "The whole world can burn. None of it matters if you're not in it."

"As charming as your mating bond charged confessions of love are, you are losing the bigger picture," Laera said. "You have a chance to get the gods off your back. Both of you. Nyx can save you both. Well, Ara will be doing it, but you know what I mean."

"She's right." I held up the letter, which had found its way back to me. "It says she gets to determine my fate. If I can prove myself to her, we don't have to worry about running from the gods or finding a way to eliminate my magic. If we win this war, we can just live."

"She's not going to go easy on you," Ryvin said.

"What's to stop her from simply killing Ara the second she arrives in Naxos?" Lagina cut in. "You're all standing around arguing the merit of a half-human woman challenging a goddess as if she has a chance."

"She has a chance. Nyx is honorable. Unlike you humans," Iris said.

I'd almost forgotten she was there.

"Nyx owes Ara," Laera said. "If she wanted her dead, she'd already be dead. This is Nyx giving her a chance."

"It's the best one she's going to get," Aspasia added.

"You have to trust me." I clasped Ryvin's hand. "I'll come to you as soon as I can."

"I'll have a ship here by morning to take her to Naxos," Iris said, then she turned and left without another word.

"Ara, is this what you want?" Lagina asked quietly.

I nodded. "I can do this."

"Get some sleep, Ara," Laera cut in. "You look like you're almost dead."

I shot her a look.

"What?" Laera asked. "It's true. And she needs to be in top form for her visit with Nyx."

"Come on," Ryvin squeezed my hand. "I'll walk you to your room."

As we left the study, I didn't hear a sound. It was as if everyone behind me was already saying their goodbyes.

12

THE DOOR WASN'T EVEN CLOSED before we started tearing at each other's clothes. I gripped Ryvin tightly, digging my fingers into his strong arms while I desperately clung to him. His kiss was hot and fiery and everything I needed.

We were moving, my legs wrapping around his waist as I refused to take my mouth from his. He held me tight, his hands sprawled on my back, supporting me as he carried me toward the bed.

His trousers were undone, but still around his hips. I pushed them down, then pulled him on top of me. Words weren't needed; this was pure desperation. I knew if we spoke, we'd have to address the possibility that this was goodbye. I pushed the thought from my mind and focused on the feel of Ryvin's skin under my fingertips, the taste of his kiss, the feel of the stubble rubbing on my cheeks, the ache of my swollen lips, the growing need low in my belly... So many sensations, so many distractions.

He nuzzled into my neck, kissing down to my shoulder, then up again until his nose was against my ear. His mouth returned to mine and this time, our kiss was heartbreakingly gentle.

It was the type of kiss I could never share with anyone but him. I could feel everything between us in that kiss. The obsession, passion, and adoration I knew he carried with him since the day he met me. My tongue darted into his mouth and he massaged it with his own. The kiss deepened, growing so intense I had to break away.

Staring at him with wide eyes, I reached for his face, pressing my palm against his cheek. "This isn't goodbye."

He kissed my forehead and when he looked at me again, I could see the pain in the depth of his swirling gray eyes.

"Don't do that," I warned.

"I don't want you to go," he confessed.

"You don't get to make that choice," I replied.

"I know," he said.

"You know I have to do this." I reached for his other cheek with my free hand, holding his face between my palms. He was stunningly handsome. His face was carved for me in my dreams, I was certain of it.

He dipped his head, resting his forehead on mine. "I love you, Asteri."

My throat was tight, making the words difficult to say without crying, but I managed to get them out, my heart nearly shattering as I said them, "I love you, too."

All I wanted was the time to love him and be loved by him, but the gods themselves were working against us.

He sat on his knees, then stared down at me, his brow furrowed. I propped myself up on my elbows. "What is it?"

"I want you to know something."

My pulse raced and my mouth went dry. I couldn't speak, so I waited.

"I once told you that Athos meant nothing to me. That I didn't care what happened to the humans who lived there —let me finish—" He forced a smile, and I closed my mouth. "But it matters to you. Which means, it matters to me."

I smiled and sat up more and reached for his hand, giving it a gentle squeeze.

"That means that if something happens to you, I will not abandon Athos. I will fight for your sisters, and your home, as if it were my own."

I didn't think it was possible to love him any more than I already did, but my heart felt like it was going to explode. Tears rolled down my face and I threw my arms around him. He caught me, pulling me into an impossibly tight embrace.

He eased up, then wiped the tears from my cheeks. "So you go and you focus on staying alive. I promise you; I will do everything in my power to save your home. You don't spend even a single second worrying about us here, you got that?"

I nodded. "Thank you."

He kissed me softly, his thumbs brushing against my cheekbones as he moved his hands behind my head. We held each other, living in the moment of the sweetest kiss.

Gently, he guided me to my back. His hand slid between my breasts, skimming my stomach until it reached lower. I parted for him and he adjusted so he could dip between my thighs. I gasped as his fingers began to tease.

The fear of what morning brought faded until all I could think about was the way I felt under his expert touch.

He moved in slow circles, making heat build in my lower belly until I was lifting my hips in encouragement. I needed more. His lips grazed over my hip bones, then he kissed my stomach while continuing the slow progress. Everything felt so good, but it was so slow and steady, I started to whine, "More."

He hummed along my lower stomach, the vibrations making my breath hitch. "Was that begging I heard? It's been a while since I had you begging me."

"I'm not begging," I told him. "I'm demanding."

He laughed and I leaned up and reached for him. He adjusted and our lips crashed together. I pulled him on top of me, his hips settling between my thighs. I needed him as close to me as possible. I needed to feel all of him, taste all of him, breathe him in until I wasn't sure where he started and I began.

Our tongues clashed and his hands were in my hair, then sliding down my neck to my breasts. His palms were rough, but I arched to meet him, encouraging more. His lips moved to my chin, then my jaw, then my neck. I moaned as I leaned my head back, reveling in every sensation.

I could feel his hardness at my entrance, sliding and teasing. My hips rose and fell, impatient for him to be inside me. When his mouth found my nipples, I gasped. His tongue flicked and swirled while his hands caressed and squeezed. Moving from one breast to the other, he increased his cadence. I ran my hands along his back and when I reached his hips, I pulled him closer as I wrapped my legs around his waist.

He took the invitation and thrust into me in one quick moment without slowing the sensations with his mouth. I cried out, arching my back in response to the sudden increase in pleasure.

I kissed every part of skin I could reach, pressing my mouth to his shoulders before drawing his head back to me, recapturing his lips. He moved slowly inside me, the sensations intense and euphoric. I knew I'd never get enough of him.

His kiss was intense and claiming; there was a desperation there that I'd not felt before. I returned it ferociously, using my body to reassure him. He responded, meeting me with the same force as he increased the speed of his thrusts. I gasped for breath, and my hips moved in time with him, struggling for air as pleasure built in a crescendo. I had to pull away, my head tilting back, eyes closed as I moaned. Gripping the sheets, I gave in, letting the ecstasy wash over me as I climaxed.

Catching my breath, I opened my eyes, then cupped Ryvin's cheek. He'd stopped moving and was looking down at me with a pleased smile on his lips. "You're so fucking beautiful when you come undone."

If my cheeks weren't already so hot, I might feel a flush creep in. "Your turn."

He laughed. "I'm not done with you yet." He wrapped his arms around me, lifting me as he sat up, taking me with him. My legs were around his hips and I was sitting on his lap with him still inside me. I inhaled sharply, my eyes widening at the sensation of the new position. He smirked.

He wrapped his arms around me, pulling me so close our chests were pressed together. Moving so my knees were on the bed, I began to ride him and this time, I got to watch as his eyes widened. He moaned, his eyes closing as I increased speed.

After a few moments, he wove his fingers into my hair and pulled my head to him. Our lips collided and we devoured each other. His hands moved over my skin, caressing and kneading my breasts, moving down to grasp my ass, ghosting over my back. His touch left a trail of tingles wherever he went, making all the sensations even more intense.

I dug my fingers into his back as I held on, struggling to stay focused on my movements while all the sensations collided. I was quickly reaching my limit, desperate to continue until I could give Ryvin a release of his own.

His breathing was rapid, and I could sense that he was just as close as I was. I broke from our kiss, moving my mouth to his neck. I licked and sucked and brushed my lips against his skin, tasting the salt of his sweat. He leaned his head back and his hands stilled, sprawled out on my lower back for a moment before he wrapped his arms around me and pulled me even closer. The sensation of losing myself in his embrace pushed me over the edge. My back arched and I let out a series of cries as release coursed through me, emptying my mind of all but pleasure as oblivion overtook me. Ryvin's fingers dug into my back and he groaned, finding his own release.

I leaned my head on his chest, breathing him in as I caught my breath. He leaned down, his cheek against the top of my head. We stayed that way for a long while, so close that we were almost one person.

Then, he turned with me still in his arms, until my back was on the bed. He glistened with sweat, but he had a relaxed, calm smile on his lips. "I'm not finished yet."

I lifted a brow in silent challenge before grabbing him and pulling him to me. After a few more rounds, I fell asleep wrapped in his arms. I dreamed that I was walking through fields of wildflowers on a cliffside overlooking the sea. It was the first time in a long time that I slept soundly and dreamed of something beautiful.

13

I SET the book down at the sound of footsteps and was surprised to see Cora entering the library. She glanced around nervously, as if concerned that someone was going to jump out and attack her.

"We're alone," I called, hoping to help calm her.

Her hands were clasped in front of her, her body tense. "Good." She walked into the library, then hesitated in front of the chair next to me.

"You can sit. You're welcome to join me," I offered. We'd invited her to help, but she'd been avoiding everything that had to do with the war. "Sophia and Aunt Katerina just went to get something to eat. They'll return shortly."

"I know. I saw them in the breakfast room. It's why I

came now. I wanted to talk to you," she said as she settled into the chair.

I turned so I was facing her. "What can I help you with?"

"The alliance with the dragons is the only thing that might save us, isn't it?" she asked.

I knew where she was going with this. "I'm sorry, Cora. If I could offer myself in your place, I would. You know I would."

"I'm not asking to get out of it." She blew out a long breath and I noticed that her hands were shaking. "I'm asking to have the wedding now. Before the fae arrive."

My brows furrowed. "You want to marry the Dragon King now? Is it the mating bond? Are you feeling things for him?"

She shook her head. "Not really. He's attractive, sure. But no, it's not that."

"What then?"

"I want to ensure the dragon's loyalty to us. What will encourage them to help us while their own city is under siege? They could easily walk away from us. Let us all die. Athos can't do this without them, I know that," she said.

"You *did* hear about Drakous," I said with amusement. "I thought you were staying out of all of it."

"I've been keeping up," she admitted. "Sophia gives me updates."

"So you know Ara returned and that she's leaving in the morning," I said.

"I know. I'd rather she be here for this, but I understand if he can't arrive in time. I'm sure she'll understand," Cora said.

"Are you sure you want to do this now? What if he dies in the fight? You might never have to marry him," I said.

Her jaw tensed. "I'm certain. Can you send a message?"

"Alright," I agreed. "I can't guarantee he'll leave Drakous to do this now."

"He'll come," she said with more certainty than I'd ever heard from her. "We should plan for a wedding."

"Cora." Sophia's tone was pure delight. "Come to join our research?"

"I was wondering when you'd leave your room," Aunt Katerina said.

"I wasn't feeling well, but I'm better now." She reached for a stack of papers that was bound with twine. "What are we looking for?"

"Anything about half-vampires or about magic in Athos," Aunt Katerina said.

"I found an old letter that was talking about how a farmer had too many crops back when we first settled here," Sophia said as she grabbed a book and made herself comfortable the floor. "I think the magic might have once benefited us."

"We do use it to warm our water," Cora said.

"Think of what else we could get it to do," Sophia added.

It was nice to see Sophia so invested in helping us. I think it was a distraction to prevent her from thinking about the change she went through. She was getting animal blood dropped at her door daily, refusing to let anyone see her drink it. One of these days, she'd need to work through it, but it wouldn't matter if none of us lived through this.

Cora leaned over, then lowered her voice. "Don't forget what I asked."

"You're certain?"

She nodded.

"You can take my chair," I said to Aunt Katerina. "I have something I need to tend to."

My aunt took my seat and I left to find a hawk. I wasn't sure if I wanted Bahar to come and marry her now, or if I wanted him to delay things. Cora was right, a marriage vow would more publicly bind him to our city. It would be impossible for his people or ours to deny our alliance. But I knew how much she didn't want to wed him. I had hoped they'd get a longer engagement.

I turned the corner toward the scribe's rooms and found Laera and Vanth standing in the hallway, speaking in hushed tones. They stopped talking when they noticed me.

"I thought you were all resting until tomorrow," I said.

"I don't do well with rest," Laera replied. "I think you're the same, aren't you?"

I ignored the question. "Is there something I can help you with?"

"You can inform your scribes that we're not here to harm them. We just need a couple of maps to confirm the sorceress's location," Laera said.

I lifted a brow, studying the princess. I knew she had

abilities to manipulate others, even if I didn't understand it. "Your magic isn't working?"

"I have been informed that we don't use magic to coerce our allies," she said, her tone irritated.

"It's not what Ara would want," Vanth said. "If we are successful, we'll want to maintain a good relationship with Athos."

"I appreciate the optimism," I replied as I walked toward the door. There weren't any guards outside the door. The scribes preferred to govern their own space. It was one of the few areas of the palace I had yet to explore or assert my new role over. They'd been responsive when I'd asked for materials and I'd given them their space. It was my way of hoping to keep them on my side through this transition.

I opened the door and noticed that only one scribe was in the room. "Hello?"

He bolted up from his chair, then dropped into a low bow. "Your highness." As soon as he noticed the others behind me, his eager expression darkened. "You have the outsiders with you."

"They are allies," I explained. "They need your help finding some maps."

"They are not my allies," he said.

"You heard what happened in Drakous, I'm guessing?" The scribes always knew. Even before I sent anyone to formally tell them. It was something I was going to have to figure out eventually if I ever wanted privacy.

"I'm not sure how this impacts us. The Fae King got

what he wanted. Athos is of no consequence. Even if he is irritated with your sister," the scribe said.

"You're clearly a terrible scribe," Laera said.

The man glared at her.

"How can you not see that he's not going to stop, ever?" Laera asked.

The scribe scowled.

"I need to send a message to the Dragon King," I said, changing the subject. "Can you assist me with that?"

He reluctantly looked away from the Fae Princess. "Yes, of course."

"Then I will need you to assist them with the maps they need," I added.

He frowned, but nodded before leading me toward the back of the room where a large cage housed a beautiful hawk.

It didn't take long to scrawl a short message for the king. The scribe helped me attach the message to the bird's leg, then we opened the window and released the creature into the warm afternoon sun.

"You really think the Fae King will come here?" The scribe asked me quietly.

"I do," I said. "And him coming to us might be our only hope at getting him unprotected enough to destroy him."

He glanced over at the shifter and Fae Princess. "You think you can convince the sorceress to help us?"

"We don't have a choice," Vanth said.

"Don't worry, Ryvin and Vanth can be very persuasive," Laera said.

I wanted to ask for more details, but I wasn't sure I needed the scribe to know any more than he already did.

"Tell me what you need," the scribe said.

"We need whatever maps you have for the Isla Chamenos," Vanth said.

I bit down on the inside of my cheek to keep from reacting at the name. The scribe didn't hide his surprise. His eyes widened and his brows shot up. "Chamenos? You're certain?"

"That's what the queen told us," Vanth said, looking over at Laera.

"She wasn't lying," Laera assured him.

"You know what they say is hidden on that island," the scribe pressed. "So many have attempted to find it, none have succeeded."

"Everyone knows the stories," I cut in. "They will have to let us know if they are true when they return."

"Very well." The scribe walked to a shelf and removed a few rolled scrolls. He passed them to Laera. "This is everything we have on the island. Nobody has ever charted it. Just sailed nearby, but nothing too close. Anyone who gets too close doesn't return."

She lifted the scrolls. "Thank you. We'll return them if we can."

He nodded. "Good luck."

I walked out of the room with them and as soon as the door was closed I turned to face them. "You really think you can do this?"

"We'll get it done," Vanth said.

"Just the two of you?" I asked.

"Ryvin and Vanth will go. I'm staying here," Laera said.

Vanth growled. I took a step back, startled by the sound. I knew he was a shifter, but I hadn't ever heard a sound so animistic coming from someone who appeared human.

"We didn't want Ara to know," Vanth added. "We don't want her to worry while she's with Nyx."

"I understand. I won't tell her," I agreed.

Laera lifted a brow. "You'd lie to your own sister?"

"She's not going to ask me and I'm not going to offer the information," I clarified.

"Maybe you and I aren't so different," Laera said.

I wasn't sure I liked that thought.

"When will you leave?" I asked.

"As soon as Ara's ship is out of sight," Laera said.

"What about the city? What can I do to prepare if they don't return before the fae arrive?" I asked, surprised at myself for saying my concerns out loud. But Ara trusted them, and we needed the help.

"That's what you have me for," Laera said. "Worst case, I can help you get everyone out."

"Lagina!" Cora was sprinting toward me and my heart stopped.

"I just sent it. Should I see if I call it back?" I should have waited, I should have known she'd change her mind.

She was panting when she stopped in front of me. "No, not the letter. The letter is fine. I found something." She looked over at Laera and Vanth. "Maybe one of you can help. I think I found something big."

She held a book up for us to see. Laera and Vanth

moved closer, and I moved enough so we could all see. As I skimmed the ancient writing, the pounding in my chest accelerated. Not from fear, but from hope. I glanced over at Laera. "Is this possible? Is this real?"

"It might be." She grabbed the book and studied it, her eyes darting back and forth across the page. We all watched, waiting. Finally, she handed the book back to Cora. "If this is true, and you used to have a magical barrier, you might be able to repair it. It won't be enough to keep the fae out forever, but it could buy you some time."

"How do we find out?" I asked.

"Where is the oldest building in your city? The first thing they ever built?" Laera asked.

"The temple to Athena," Cora and I said in unison.

"Take me there," Laera said.

14

ARA

THE SHIP WAITING in the harbor was like night against the early morning sun. Black sails waited to be expanded from black masts. The body of the ship was painted like midnight, complete with a dusting of stars along the bow. It was both stunning and terrifying.

I released Ryvin's hand so I could go to embrace each of my sisters. Unshed tears stung the back of my eyes, but I wasn't going to give in to them. I wanted to appear strong. I wanted them to think I was confident and unafraid.

"You can do this, Ara," Lagina called.

"You'll be back before you know it," Sophia added.

"We'll keep the war warm for you," Cora said playfully.

I'd seen Nyx take lives without remorse. I watched as she made the tributes seem like nothing. The people I swore I'd protect were taken right in front of me and there was nothing I could do. I was so tired of feeling helpless, and I would fight, but if Nyx wanted me gone, I was going to be just like those I'd failed to protect.

"We'll be here when you return," Vanth said as he pulled me in for a giant hug.

When he released me, I was facing Laera. She looked furious. "Don't die on us." To my surprise, she hugged me. "I'm serious. I won't be responsible for the consequences of Ryvin's behavior if you die."

I smiled, knowing her words were demonstrating true concern in the best way she knew how. "I'll miss you, too."

She scoffed. "I'll be far too busy to miss you."

"You should go," Vanth said. "Before one of us drags you back to the palace."

I nodded, then returned to Ryvin, who'd been waiting patiently. I reached for him and he clasped my hand. Wordlessly, we walked toward the black plank that stretched over the water to the shore.

We paused in front of it. "Please, don't be a hero," he said. "Do whatever you have to so you can come back to me."

I threw my arms around his shoulders and kissed him. His arms went around my waist, pulling me in close as he deepened the kiss. It was over too quickly, both of us stepping away, but breathing heavier. "I'll see you soon."

"Come back to me, Asteri." He kissed my cheek softly. "I'll be waiting for you."

He released my hand, then took a step back. I knew I

had to go now, or I'd lose my nerve. Before I could talk myself out of it, I stepped onto the plank.

After a few steps, dark shadows rose around me and my heart raced. I turned to look back at my friends, but they weren't visible in the darkness.

Panic rose, making my chest tight. I couldn't even see the plank under my feet. Carefully, I moved forward, my hands extended in front of me, blindly reaching for anything that would indicate that I'd made it onto the ship.

The shadows dissipated and I could see that I'd stepped onto the ship. Quickly, I turned and saw that the plank was gone. A black railing blocking the opening that had once been there. The ship had changed, locking me in like a prisoner.

The shadows floated beyond the ship, masking any view of the shore. I couldn't wave goodbye. I couldn't watch my family and friends fade from view. I couldn't watch as my city grew smaller.

Nyx had already cut me off from everyone and everything I loved. The same way she'd been when she was in that cave, alone.

I swallowed over a lump in my throat. What was I sailing into? She said I was to go to Naxos, but would Dion be there? Would she even be there? What if my test was to isolate me the way she'd been isolated? Would I ever see my sisters again? Would I see Ryvin again?

My whole body felt too heavy with grief over something I couldn't control. I had no idea what I was heading toward.

I looked over the edge of the railing, hoping for a glimpse of the sparkling blue sea. I'm not sure how long I stood there, but it wasn't until my neck was aching from staring downward for so long that I finally watched the shadows ease.

White foam billowed atop sparkling blue water, the waves a playful companion alongside the dark ship cutting through the sea.

Sails full, we raced ahead. My hair whipped around my head and water sprayed my face. I embraced it all. The smell of the sea, the feel of the wind and water, the taste of the salt. I was not going to let Nyx defeat me.

I would play her game. And I would win. Because back in Athos, I had things waiting for me that were worth fighting for.

Glancing around, I looked for any signs of a crew. When I didn't see anyone, I explored the ship, hoping for any company as I made the journey. There was nobody aboard. Somehow, Nyx was in command. I wondered if my mother was involved. The sea was part of her domain, and traveling through with her own daughter as a captive was likely risky, even for another god.

I returned to the railing and quickly found evidence that I wasn't as alone as I anticipated. Several sea serpents swam alongside the ship, and beyond them, I caught sight of the occasional dolphin fin. It made me feel a little less alone, but none of the tension eased.

Too soon, we were pulling into Naxos, and the plank appeared again. Accepting whatever my fate was, I walked ashore just as someone appeared through the trees.

"Welcome back," Dion said.

"I wish I could say it was good to see you," I replied.

"That's fair." He sighed, then gestured toward the path I knew led to his house. "I'll show you where you're staying."

I fell into step behind him. "I'm surprised she's letting you interact with me. The ship was empty."

"It was my condition for allowing the use of my island," he explained.

"She actually asked permission?"

"This is my home. My sovereign space. I alone can choose who stays here and who must leave."

"Why Noxos?" I asked. "Your home is beautiful, but why would she choose this?"

"I'm sure she has her reasons, but she didn't share them with me."

"What about your Maenads? She won't harm them, will she?" My thoughts went to how she'd used the Athonian tributes to revive herself.

"She swore an oath that all who lived on this island before you arrived would be safe," he said.

"Before I arrived," I repeated.

He looked over his shoulder. "I tried, Ara. I did. She would not guarantee your safety."

I swallowed hard, trying to shove away the rising anxiety. I knew before I even stepped foot on the ship, but hearing it from Dion made it more real.

He stopped walking, then turned to face me. "You have overcome greater odds. You're not even supposed to be alive. I heard the story. I heard how the fates wanted you dead. Remember that when you face her. You've already overcome more than you should. There's no reason you can't continue to defy the odds."

"Unless it means I'm running on borrowed time," I said.

"Prove them wrong, Ara. Like you always do, and you'll be fine." He offered a small smile, then resumed walking toward his home.

"I never thought I'd be friends with the great Dionysus," I said playfully.

He laughed, that bubbly infectious sound that made me feel lighter. "I knew there was a reason I liked you." He looked over his shoulder. "You know, that offer still stands if things don't work out between you and the dark prince."

I opened my mouth to reply, but the figure standing in front of us made me freeze.

"You actually came," Nyx said, her voice deadly calm with a sharp edge.

I inclined my head. "Nice to see you again, Nyx."

She hummed. "I wish I could say the same about you. But I suppose you could impress me. You did kill the minotaur and free me from my prison, after all."

"You'd think that would have earned her some affection," Dion said.

Nyx gave him a sidelong glare that would have terrified a mortal. Instead, the god laughed it off before walking past the goddess. "Ara, your room is ready whenever you are."

"She won't be retiring to her room just yet. I have something else we must attend to first." She looked at Dion, her expression stern. "Leave us."

To my surprise, he didn't argue. He simply turned and walked away. I wanted to shout after him, beg him to stay. At least Dion was familiar, even if he was unstable.

Nyx gestured for me to come alongside her.

I obliged and tried to keep my expression neutral to mask the fear and anxiety twisting my insides.

"Let's see if your mother made a mistake by letting you live." Nyx reached out and yanked the serpent necklace from my neck, then tossed it on the ground.

My hand went to my neck protectively, then I moved toward the fallen necklace. Nyx's arm blocked my progress. "No magic from anyone else while you're here."

Her gaze dropped to my chest. "Give me the other one."

I covered the small leather pouch that was hidden under my peplos. "No."

She smirked. "No?"

"No. These were gifts from my mother." I wasn't sure what the pouch contained, but if there was ever a time I might need to use it, it was while I was trying to prove my worth to Nyx.

The goddess sighed, then leaned down and picked up the broken necklace. She dropped it dramatically into her other palm. "I will return both items to you once you've completed my tasks."

I stared at the broken chain in her palm, already feeling the loss of the necklace. When I looked up at the goddess, her expression was calm and reserved. Her beautiful face was free of lines with high cheekbones that could have been chiseled from marble. Her eyes were the same as Ryvin's. Swirling, endless pools of silver. Like they were made of the very stars.

"I have your word?" I asked.

Her brows lifted. "You doubt a goddess?"

"I've known too many gods to trust any of you," I snapped.

She smirked. "You might be smarter than I realized."

"Your word."

She nodded. "You have my word. I will return both items if you successfully complete my tasks."

"I want to know how many tasks before I give it to you," I replied.

She looked like she might laugh. "Yes, you are smart."

I waited, giving her time to argue with me.

"There will be three. You complete the assigned tasks, and I will return your items," she explained.

I nodded, then lifted the leather cord over my head. It took me a few breaths before I could talk myself into depositing the leather pouch into Nyx's waiting hand. I had a feeling I was going to need that item to save my life sooner rather than later. It had been a comfort to carry it with me, and losing it felt like I'd been stripped of a layer of protection I'd come to depend on.

Nyx closed her hand and the items vanished.

My eyes widened and I sucked in a startled breath. I wasn't sure I'd ever get used to the various powers the gods held.

"We begin now," she said. "You must get Obsidian to deliver you to your next task."

Nyx vanished.

I raced up the path, trying to chase the goddess, hoping for another clue. As soon as I broke through the trees, I halted and my heart fell into the pit of my stomach.

Standing in front of me was the largest and most beautiful horse I'd ever seen. No, not horse. Pegasus. It stretched massive, black feathered wings from its body, making it look even larger than it already was. "You must be Obsidian."

It reared up on its hind legs, then landed, its hoofs stomping into the dirt, kicking up clouds of dust. The creature grunted and snorted, clearly irritated at my very presence.

I held my hand out, hoping to calm the huge pegasus. The horse swung its head and stomped its massive hoofs, moving closer to me with each step. I had to back up so I wasn't trampled.

My heart raced and I knew he could sense my fear. All animals could feel it, couldn't they? I didn't even know if he had any additional magic, aside from being a flying horse.

"I'm not going to hurt you," I said, trying to mask the fear in my voice.

The horse exhaled through its nostrils, as if annoyed. I frowned, then crossed my arms over my chest. How was I to ride this creature if it wouldn't even let me approach it?

With a sigh, I dropped my arms to my side. Then I slowly lifted one arm, reaching for his muzzle. Obsidian backed away from me, shaking his head in a way that made his dark mane swish from side to side.

"Are you Nyx's horse?" I asked.

Obsidian stomped, then shook his head, snorting with indignation.

"Alright, so you don't belong to the goddess," I said. "Maybe you don't belong to anyone?"

The horse was still. I took that as a good sign.

"I need your help. Nyx says I'm to tame you and get your help. I think she intends for me to ride you," I said.

The pegasus backed away, flapping its wings in irritation as it did.

"Alright. You don't trust me yet, but I'll earn your trust." Even as I said it, I had no idea how I was going to do so.

For a moment, I considered trying to call on my magic, but I didn't think it could help me here. A pegasus isn't exactly a monster. And there's not much I could do with Ryvin's shadows, even if I could summon them while I was this far away from him.

Growing up, I'd always had stable hands to help assist with the horses. While I appreciated the animals, I hadn't spent much time around them unless I was actively riding. Now, I wish I'd joined Sophia in the times she'd spent brushing and caring for the horses alongside the stable boys. She'd always had a soft spot for them and they adored her.

A smile made my lips curve. "I know what might help." I glanced around, realizing that for this to work, I was going to need to hope that he would stay here while I left. "Will you wait for me?"

The pegasus didn't respond. Instead, Obsidian simply stared at me, as if I was little more than an insect crawling through the dirt.

"I'll be back." I hoped leaving wasn't going to cause me to fail. If Obsidian wasn't there when I returned, I wasn't sure what my next steps were. I couldn't fail the first task. I had to follow through with this and complete everything Nyx threw my way.

15

Ryvin

Vanth was sitting on a crate against the railing of the ship. His elbows rested on his knees, his head lowered as he stared at the floor. I took a few steps toward him, then paused to look at the crew. They were busy, talking with each other, or doing their work, oblivious to me or the shifter in their midst.

We'd promised unrestricted access to Konos and Telos to the merchants who owned this ship upon the defeat of the Fae King. I think they were already imagining what they could do with the wealth they'd access through such open trade. While we'd allowed the occasional human vessel in, it was rare in Telos, and even more rare in Konos. Plus, I might have alluded that I'd put in a good word with Ceto to help their crossing be less dangerous. I'd figure that out if we survived.

I continued on, stopping in front of Vanth. He glanced up. "I'm getting a little tired of ships."

"I don't think we're quite done with them yet," I replied as I sat down next to him.

"It has to end eventually," he said. "I'm just hoping when I meet my end, my feet are on solid ground. I don't want a serpent's teeth as my last view of the world."

"I'm not sure a sea serpent would touch you, given how much time you've spent around Ara," I pointed out.

"I'm not the one with the gift from a goddess." He nodded to the gold circle around my wrist.

"You have enough of her scent on you," I said, my tone harsher than I expected.

Vanth laughed. "Trust me, if I wanted your woman, I'd have made my move already."

I tamped down the jealousy that clawed at my chest. "I know."

The shifter turned to look at me. "Do you? You finally conceded that I am not a threat to your mate?"

"I don't always control my responses." I hated admitting that, but it was true. "But I know you're a good friend to Ara. She's lucky to have you. And so am I."

We sat there for a long while, listening to the chatter of the crew and the roar of the waves. For the first time in a while, I felt myself relax just a little.

"Why'd you do it?" Vanth asked.

My brow furrowed. "Do what?"

"Save me. Why didn't you send me to the executioner's block?" His expression was deadly serious.

I shrugged. "I'm not sure."

"You're lying," he replied.

My brow furrowed.

"I know you well enough to know your tells. Your fingers tensed."

I looked down at my hands, then made myself relax. I didn't even realize I was tensing. "How long have I been doing that?"

"I noticed it about a year after we started working together," he said.

"And you tell me now?" I shook my head. How many others figured that out?

"I wasn't about to give that information up. It kept me alive," he said.

"You thought I'd harm you?" I hadn't ever considered killing the shifter, which was a decidedly strange thing now that I was thinking about it.

"No, but it helped me react and made me realize you weren't as bad as people said you were," he replied.

I laughed. "Not as bad? The only one with a death roll as long as mine is Hades himself."

Vanth shrugged and we fell back into silence again.

"I knew it would anger my father," I blurted out.

"What?" Vanth looked confused.

"Keeping you alive, promoting you." I shrugged. "It was a childish move to make my father mad. It wasn't benevolent, or particularly thoughtful. It was petty."

Vanth laughed, the sound infectious. "All this time, I thought there was a deeper reason. But it was just childish rebellion?"

I joined in the laugher. "Yep. Nothing more than a pissed off kid."

"Well I'm grateful, no matter the cause. I don't think I've ever told you that," Vanth said after he caught his breath.

"You owe me nothing." I set my hand on the shifter's shoulder. "I'm the one who owes you my thanks. You've always had my back. And you have Ara's. I am honored to call you my friend."

He nodded, then turned his attention to the distance, where we could see a tiny speck that would grow to be our destination.

I stared at the tiny landmass. It was so small that it wasn't even recorded on most maps. If Aspasia's information was accurate, we were close to showing up uninvited at an incredibly powerful sorceress's home.

"Do you think she's loyal to my father?" I asked Vanth.

"No. Your father has never done anything to earn true loyalty in his entire life. She's either afraid of him, or he gave her something she really wanted," Vanth said.

"I guess we have to figure out what she might want more," I replied.

"There's always something. Those with power always want more," Vanth said darkly. "My concern is the problem we might create if we give her what she wants."

The island looked like a mountain rising from the sea. A peak bathed in shrubs and trees that grew from the water itself.

Glittering scales reflected in the distance as we neared

the shore. The monsters were just out of reach, staying away from our vessel, for now. I wasn't sure how long they'd be able to wait for us before the creatures decided to attack. I had to hope there'd still be a ship waiting for us when we left this island.

The rocky shore was nearly all cliffside, with one area that was lower. A narrow sandy beach gave way to rocks before giving way to shrubs and trees at the base of the mountain.

There were no signs of life as we waded through the water toward the sand, but I could feel the magic. It was cloying, almost sweet. It hung thick around us, making the air feel like it might explode with a single touch. It was powerful, but unstable. We had to be in the right place.

"Where now?" Vanth asked when we came to the base of the mountain.

Something shimmered, creating a rainbow suspended from nowhere. I reached for it, my fingers making the rainbow distort. There was something here, some kind of magic ward. I'd read about these but hadn't seen any in use. We had no need to ward things in Konos.

Carefully, I pushed my hand forward and it vanished behind the ward, making it look like my hand was suddenly missing.

Vanth made a startled sound.

I pulled my hand back, showing him that it was intact. "There's a shield here, but it's letting me through. I think we're supposed to go through it."

"Why would she have a shield, but then allow visitors to just walk through it?" Vanth asked skeptically.

"She wouldn't," I replied. "Which means she's expecting us."

Pulling my sword from its sheath, I stepped through the shield before Vanth could object.

16

The temple was empty of visitors. Acolytes moved quietly around the space, some of them staring at us with suspicion.

We walked deeper into the temple, pausing at the large statue of the goddess in the center. I set a vat of olive oil at the statue's feet. "We mean no disrespect with our visit, Athena. We want to save our home. Our people. If there's any help you can offer—"

"Your highness," A female voice called.

I turned to see an acolyte lowering her head in a bow. "What an honor to have you here."

"We don't have time for ceremony," Laera said sharply.

"It really is a necessary visit," I insisted.

The acolyte lifted her head. "I'm afraid the Naos is

reserved only for those who have dedicated their life to the goddess."

"Athena will understand," Laera said.

"What our friend means, is that this is an emergency," Cora said, surprisingly diplomatic.

"I'm not sure any of you have the authority to speak for the goddess," the acolyte replied.

"I'm trying really hard to be nice to you," Laera said. "But it won't last much longer."

"And you are?" The acolyte asked.

"This is the Princess of Konos," Sophia said.

The acolyte's eyes widened slightly, but she quickly lifted her chin and relaxed her expression. "I'm happy that our visitor has an interest in the goddess, but I really must ask you all to leave."

"Adina, please return to your duties," a woman dressed in a deep blue peplos said. The acolyte bowed, then walked away without objection.

"I'm sorry, she's very devout. I'm Daphne, the head priestess here. To what do we owe the great honor of so many royal women?"

"I don't know how quickly news travels to you," I began. "But we're in serious danger and there may be something here that can help us."

"The rumors are true then?" Daphne glanced at Laera. "Even the ones about working with the royals of Konos?"

"Not all the royals," Laera clarified.

"I see," Daphne said. "I must admit, you aren't the first from Konos to come here."

My stomach twisted. "What do you mean?"

"We caught someone on the grounds during the Choosing. A vampire. He didn't come into the temple, so we didn't report it. Most everyone thought he was hoping to find someone who strayed for him to feed on, but I didn't agree. I was outnumbered," Daphne said.

"What do you think he was doing?" Cora asked.

"I think he was searching for something. Perhaps whatever it is you are looking for." The priestess gestured toward the entrance. "Perhaps we should speak outside, where it's less crowded."

I noticed that all the acolytes were now standing around and watching us. As soon as they saw me watching, they scrambled away, quickly pretending to work on other tasks.

Our group followed the priestess out of the naos and down the steps to the large garden outside the temple. There were no acolytes out here, only carefully manicured cypress trees and colorful flower beds. Large vats of oil burned on either side of the entrance, the heat making me feel a little nauseous.

I moved away from them, finding a shady place near a grove of trees. The others followed.

"Tell us what you think he was looking for," I said.

Daphne seemed nervous, her eyes darting from side to side as she spoke, "The previous priestess told me there were times when suspicious individuals came and wandered the grounds. Sometimes they vanished as soon as anyone spoke to them. She suspected they weren't human."

"But you didn't find out what they were after?" Laera asked.

She shook her head.

"So how are we supposed to find it?" Cora asked.

"I think it's going to be up to me and Laera," Sophia said. "In the caves, I could feel magic."

"Magic?" Daphne whispered.

"An ancient shield of some kind, we hope," Lagina said. "Something that might help us keep Athos safe."

"It would be old. Something dating back to the first Athonians," Cora said.

Daphne's eyes widened. "I think there's something you should see."

She led us back into the temple, shooing away the curious acolytes with a wave of her hands and a stern look that would have made my mother proud. My chest tightened. I didn't let myself think of my mother often and I still hadn't had a chance to mourn her.

I mouthed a few words asking for my mother's peace as we passed the statue of Athena. I think the goddess would have liked my mother.

The back of the statue was just as polished and gleaming as the front, but it was difficult to see the details with the limited light. The way it was set up made it obvious that nobody came behind the statue. The acolytes and few who were permitted near it must only view it from the front.

Daphne took a torch from the wall and lit a smaller vat of oil that was sitting near the feet of the goddess.

"Well, that's interesting," Laera said.

I followed the princess's line of sight to a break in the marble at the base of the statue. "It's a trapdoor."

"What's down there?" Sophia asked.

"We were warned to never open it," Daphne admitted.

"Great. We get to crawl into some dusty, spider-infested hole where we'll probably be eaten by some monster," Cora said.

"You really think there's a monster down there?" Daphne asked, her voice tight.

"Honestly, it wouldn't surprise me," Laera said.

"I hate monsters," Sophia murmured.

I glanced over at my sister, knowing she'd seen and done things that I never would have dreamed her capable of since discovering her true identity. I didn't want her to put herself in any more harm's way.

"I'll go," I offered. "There's no reason for all of us to venture down there."

"Oh, no you don't," Cora insisted. "I have no interest in becoming queen."

"What does your future husband think of that sentiment?" Laera asked.

"Not the time," I snapped.

"I never asked to be queen of Drakous," Cora retorted.

"You're marrying the Dragon King?" Daphne asked, not bothering to hide the surprise in her expression.

"Yes. Yes. Gawk at the woman who has to bed that beast," Cora said sarcastically.

"I heard he's very handsome," Daphne quickly added.

"He is," Sophia said sweetly. "And I think he's kind.

He'll be a good husband. And if he's not, I'll tear his throat out."

All of us turned to stare at Sophia. She smiled sweetly, as if she'd simply offered a compliment.

"We're wasting time," Laera said, breaking everyone's silent surprise. "I'm going down there. I need someone with magic to accompany me and I need someone to stay up here just in case."

"I'll go," Sophia volunteered.

"No, you'll stay with your sister. I'll go. If you hear us scream, come down and kill whatever it was that made us yell, got it?" Laera asked.

Sophia's shoulders dropped and I couldn't tell if it was relief or resignation. "Alright."

"We don't have any weapons, in case you missed that detail," Cora pointed out.

"I'll be right back." Daphne darted away.

"They keep weapons at the temple to Athena?" Cora asked.

I shrugged. "I'm not sure."

The priestess returned, breathless, with a few torches tucked under her arm and a satchel over her shoulder. "These might help."

I took the torches from her and passed one to Laera while the priestess set the satchel down on the floor. I caught the glint of metal inside the bag. She rifled through it, producing several daggers of various sizes and construction. Most of them were adorned with jewels and glittered with a shine that told of ceremonial display rather than battle.

"Are any of them sharp?" Laera asked.

"Yes. We do use them," Daphne said as she stood. "Take whatever you need."

I knelt and selected the simplest looking dagger. It had a short blade and a longer handle, making it easier to grip. It reminded me of the ones I'd used in the past.

"I've got my own weapons, thanks," Laera said.

The priestess looked at Cora and Sophia expectantly.

"I don't know how to use those," Sophia admitted.

Cora picked up a long dagger with an amethyst studded hilt. It looked heavy. "I suppose you just shove it in the offending party."

"Something like that," Laera mumbled.

Sophia picked up a blade that was inlaid with gold. "Hopefully nothing comes out of that hole that we have to use these on."

"Only one way to find out." Laera was tugging on the small bronze handle. She grunted as she tried to lift it. "I could use a hand."

I set down the items in my hands, then dropped to my knees so I could help pull. The two of us struggled, yanking on the aged bronze with all we had.

Just as I thought we'd need to inquire about help from someone stronger, the door lifted, nearly throwing the two of us across the room as it released.

A cloud of dust billowed up from the opening, making us cough. When it cleared, Laera and I stared down into the darkness. I could see the first few rungs of a ladder against what appeared to be a stone wall, but beyond that, it was too dark to know.

"I'm getting really tired of being in tunnels underground," Laera said.

I tucked the abandoned dagger into my waistband, then grabbed the torches from the ground. I lit them both in the fire of the oil, then passed one to Laera. "Come on, before I come to my senses about how stupid this is."

"Be careful, Gina," Cora called.

"We'll be listening if you need us," Sophia said.

"May Athena watch over you," Daphne added.

I wasn't sure any of the gods bothered with us. Maybe Athos was a forgotten land. A place where the gods didn't wander. Perhaps that's why we were in this position in the first place.

I climbed down carefully, holding the torch with one hand while I used the other to ease down each rung. Mercifully, the ladder held our weight and we made it to the bottom.

By the light of the torch, I looked around the room as I waited for Laera to join me. It was a dark, damp space lined with stone bricks against the walls. Whatever this place was, it had been created very intentionally.

"What is this place?" Laera asked, her torch adding more light to the dark space.

"I'm not sure." I walked a few steps forward, quickly reaching the end of the room. It wasn't a tunnel; it wasn't much of anything. Dirt floors and walls made of gray brick. "Maybe it was just a storage room. Probably for wine or meat. Something they wanted to stay cool."

"I don't think so."

I spun to find Laera standing at the opposite wall. Her

torch illuminated it, showing dark stains I hadn't noticed before. "Is that..."

"Blood," Laera finished. "Lots of it, from the looks of it."

"Could have been for sacrifices before they built the temple," I suggested.

Laera moved her torch, revealing another portion of the wall that was free of the bloodstains. In the center of the wall was a strange, circular brick.

I walked over to where she was standing. "Look at that."

Laera noticed the odd addition and reached for it, pressing her palm to the stone. The whole room shook as the wall began to move.

17

"Dion!" I started shouting as soon as the house was in view. "Dion, where are you?"

I didn't stop running until I burst through the door into Dion's house. Several women were lounging on the couches where I'd sat with my friends not long ago.

They squealed, then scattered in a frenzy of gauzy peplos and petals, flowery crowns falling as they fled.

"Sorry!" I called. "I didn't mean to startle you. I was looking for Dion, have you seen him?"

They were gone before I even finished asking. Frustrated, I cursed, then turned, nearly colliding with the god. I jumped, making a startled squeaking sound.

Dion laughed. "You act like it's a surprise that you found me after all that screaming."

"I thought maybe you left the island."

"I wouldn't be a very good host if I did that, now, would I?" he asked.

"I need help," I said.

He frowned, an expression that made my stomach turn. I wasn't sure I'd ever seen anything other than a smile on the vivacious face.

"I can't assist you. This is between you and Nyx," he explained.

"I just need to know if you have stables here. Supplies for horses."

His brow furrowed slightly, as if considering if my request was a violation. "Are you planning to flee? We're on an island, you realize."

"I know that. And no, I'm not going anywhere. I just need some things for taking care of a horse."

He pressed his lips together and looked like he was thinking. Finally, after what felt like forever, he tilted his head. "Go through the other door. You'll see the stables."

I could have kissed him, but I caught myself, knowing that he'd take the gesture too far. Instead, I gave him a quick hug, something that was also probably too much considering his incessant flirting. "Thank you."

I didn't stick around long enough to allow him a snarky response. Instead, I was running again, hoping that by the time I found what I needed, Obsidian was still waiting for me.

To my relief, the pegasus was there when I returned, though I could swear he was glaring at me with annoyance. I slowed to a walk, trying to catch my breath. "You know, I've never seen anyone with as much of an expressive face as you."

Obsidian shook his head.

When I stopped near him, I started to remove the items in the bag I'd filled, setting them all on the ground. Out of the corner of my eye, I watched for the reactions to each. As I suspected, Obsidian was carefully studying each thing as I set them on the ground.

When I produced an apple, his ears seemed to relax, pointing slightly forward. His tail swished and he lowered his head before taking a step closer.

I held the fruit in my open palm, then extended my arm, careful not to move too quickly. "Do you want this?"

He moved even closer, then quickly leaned down and grasped the apple with his lips, taking it from my hand. He backed up and I could hear the crunching of the fruit as he chewed.

As soon as he was finished, he looked at the bag expectantly. I dug inside and removed another apple, repeating the process of feeding the pegasus.

I had no idea how or why Dion had an entire crate of apples in his stable, but I was grateful they'd been in there when I went to look for a brush and some food. I expected hay or grains. The apples were a welcome treat.

After feeding him all six of the apples I'd brought with me, I showed him the empty bag. I could read the disappointment in his eyes.

"I'll bring more later," I promised.

Obsidian eyed me as if he wasn't sure if he believed me. I was starting to feel a little strange for reading so much emotion and response in a horse, but this wasn't a normal horse. His size alone would have been enough to classify him as special, but adding the wings was a whole other level. I had no idea what pegasuses were capable of or how much he could understand me. As far as I could tell, he was completely aware of every word I spoke.

I crouched and picked up a brush. "Would you like me to brush you?" I wanted nothing more than to get on with the tasks so I could return home, but I knew I couldn't rush this. At least that's what I kept reminding myself as I fought against the rising anxiety reminding me that the Fae King could be on his way to Athos right now.

Obsidian lowered his head, then stepped closer to me.

"I'll take that as a yes, but if you want me to stop, you simply tell me, alright?" Internally, I was hoping he didn't knock me down and trample me.

Slowly, I reached for his neck, then ran my hand along his hair. He was free of dirt and felt clean. I knew I'd made the correct choice to go right to the softer brush. I began carefully, going easy until I felt more confident to work to a more steady cadence.

His coat was already shiny and well cared for, but he seemed to appreciate the methodical motions of the brush. I took my time, brushing one whole side before moving to the other. He was patient and seemed relaxed while I brushed him.

Sweat rolled down my temple. I forgot just how much work this was and Obsidian was easily twice the size of the horses I was used to.

Finally, I finished. Stepping back so I could face him, I

lifted the brush, then showed him I was setting it down on the ground. "All finished. Would you like me to attend to your mane?"

He nodded. An unmistakable, obvious nod.

"Great." I picked up the comb and approached with caution. "I'm going to get started."

My arms were aching, and I was starting to feel worn down from all the effort of caring for the massive horse, but I was determined to win him over.

Just as I finished his mane, Obsidian nuzzled me, nearly knocking me down. I startled, jumping back in surprise.

The pegasus's eyes widened in response.

"I'm sorry, I wasn't expecting that." Worried I'd insulted him, I moved closer, then extended my hand. "You're much larger than the horses we have in Athos. Far more beautiful and intelligent as well."

He made an annoyed snort.

"I'm serious. I'm not trying to flatter you. You actually understand what I'm saying." I waited, with my hand outstretched, nearly touching Obsidian's muzzle.

After a few heartbeats, the pegasus leaned closer, brushing his muzzle against my palm. I stepped closer, then stroked him. "You're a sweetheart, aren't you?"

He snorted as if to disagree with me, but nuzzled closer. I laughed. "I like you, too."

Suddenly, he turned away from me and his ears flattened against his head.

"What is it?" My pulse kicked up in response to the perceived threat. "What did you hear?"

When he returned his attention to me, he lowered his head, then bent a front leg, almost like he was bowing.

It took me a moment to realize the intention. "You want me to ride you?" My heart was racing for another reason now. Climbing onto this creature was the plan the whole time, but now that I was faced with it, I was having doubts.

I wasn't the most talented rider, and I'd be doing this without a saddle. He was so large, it was going to be difficult to even mount him. Then there was the whole aspect of the fact that he had wings. Was he intending to fly with me on his back?

He whinnied impatiently. I knew it was possible this was the only chance I'd get. Plus, I couldn't risk insulting him.

"Thank you," I said as I moved to his side. I set my hand on his back, then stilled. How was I supposed to get up there? I didn't have a stool or anyone to give me a lift. A quick glance around let me know there weren't even any large rocks or tree stumps. I wondered if Obsidian would follow me to the stables.

Then, an idea struck me.

It was insane. Absolutely impossible. Yet, what if I could make it happen?

Closing my eyes, I reached for that dark place within. The place where I found my magic in the past. Only this time, I wasn't searching for mine. I wanted to borrow some of Ryvin's.

I wasn't sure if it would work being so far away, but I had used it when he wasn't next to me with success. Taking steady breaths to keep myself calm, I rested one hand on

Obsidian's side. "I need a little help getting up, but I promise I'm not going to harm you."

Closing my eyes, I reached deeper, calling Ryvin's shadows to me, letting myself feel the magic building. It came like a soothing caress, and I opened my eyes to see the shadows wrapping around me in fluid, graceful spirals.

I nodded to them, encouraging them to create a cloud under my feet. The swirling gray and black shadows obliged, churning in a way that reminded me of waves as they wound together.

Obsidian nickered, tossing his head. His ears wiggled. I stroked his side, whispering calming words while I instructed the shadows to lift me.

To my surprise, I rose from the ground and was able to finally mount the pegasus. Weaving my hand into his main, I held fast. "Good boy, Obsidian. Good boy."

The pegasus reared and I held on, having to call the shadows around me to keep me from falling. Thankfully, they were woven around me now, anchoring me to the massive steed.

As soon as Obsidian's hoofs hit the ground, he took off, racing across the island. My eyes watered as the air blew past me, whipping my hair around my face. I could hardly make out where we were going at this speed and if not for the shadows, I wouldn't still be holding on.

Obsidian shot into the air. I swallowed the scream I almost unleashed and fought to keep the shadows around me. The pegasus dipped and dove, spun and twisted. The movements so intense and unnecessary that I knew he was trying to throw me. Then, he tucked his wings to the side and we went into free fall, heading right for the rocky ground below.

I tugged on his mane. "Pull us up, Obsidian! Pull us up!"

The pegasus seemed unconcerned about our impending doom.

This was not how I died. I refused to let this be my end. Anger surged and I fought back, reaching into the depths where that dark spark that reveled in chaos lived. The part of me that wanted to rebel. The part of me that I never fully allowed myself to access.

With a roar, I let it out. I let it all explode like a flash of lightning. Shadows billowed around me, expanding into the sky like thunderclouds. I could feel the darkness in my veins, the familiar buzz of magic, the rush of power that I had held back.

Obsidian righted himself, his wings fully extending, catching us on a gust of wind, just before we'd have crashed to the ground. He flapped a few times, then landed, as if nothing strange happened.

I half-leaped, half-tumbled off his back, then distanced myself from the insane creature. Heart racing, I shoved my wind-blown hair away from my eyes and glared at Obsidian. "What was that for?"

The pegasus started eating some of the plants growing between the rocks where we'd landed, not even bothering to look up at me. Thunder rumbled in the distance and I looked skyward, taking in the heavy, dark clouds. We were about to get a whole lot of rain.

"How the fuck are you alive?" Nyx's voice cut through the wind and thunder.

I turned to see her staring at me, an annoyed look on her face.

"You should be dead." She gave Obsidian an angry, sidelong glance. "Even if you managed to mount him, he should have tossed you."

"I'm sorry to disappoint you," I deadpanned.

"How did you survive?" she asked.

"I don't see how that matters," I countered. Any hope I'd had of being friendly with the goddess was gone. She wasn't going easy on me. "What is the next task? I want to get the fuck off this island."

She moved closer to me, then studied me with narrowed eyes. After several heartbeats, she retreated, then a wicked grin curved her lips. "You used magic."

"So?"

"I won't make the mistake of allowing you to do that again," she replied.

"You'd take my magic?" I balled my hands into fists. "I did free you and help you regain yours."

"You forget your place, child," she hissed. "I am the one who determines your fate. If I say you must perform without magic, you will have your magic stripped."

I glared at her. "All you gods are the same, aren't you?"

"I wouldn't worry about the gods just now. You're here to prove to me that not all humans are the same. Your people are the ones who forgot about me. They allowed me to be buried and trapped under your city while they went about their lives. I gave you darkness, night, starlight... and how did your kind reward me? By using the cover of night to perform their misdeeds. By forgetting my name. By telling stories of my terrible power and ignoring all the gifts I bestowed.

"So answer me this, Princess, are all humans the same? Because if that's the case, I will simply end all of you right now."

I swallowed hard, realizing that I'd pushed too far. In my anger, I did the same thing she accused the others of. I'd forgotten just how powerful she was. "We are not all the same."

"Then prove it if you can." She winked. "Don't worry, when you fail, I'll let you watch me destroy your people before I kill you."

18

RYVIN

ICY COLD CRASHED AROUND ME, and my breath caught. The feeling was sharp, but brief, fading suddenly as I emerged on the other side of the shield. The scent of pine and dirt assaulted my senses as a sprawling forest came into view. It was as if we had traveled somewhere else entirely.

Massive pines stretched toward the sky, creating a canopy that only allowed for dappled sunlight to poke through the numerous branches. Their trunks were so large I couldn't wrap my arms around them and they stood so high, the thought of scaling them made me nervous. I'd never seen anything like them in all of my travels, and I was certain they didn't belong on this island.

"Where are we?" Vanth asked.

"I'm not sure." It was possible we'd gone through a

portal, but there was something about the landscape that felt off.

I took cautious steps forward, mindful of the fact that the woods were eerily silent. There was no movement from the wind in the branches, no sound of animals skittering through the underbrush, nothing flying or jumping along the branches. No sounds at all.

"No birds." Vanth said, staring up and scanning our surroundings.

It was unsettling enough to walk into a forest that didn't belong on an island like this. The addition of no life solidified that there was a good chance that none of this was real. I didn't think we crossed through a portal. "Maintain your guard. I have a feeling we won't be alone long."

Vanth was already tense, his grip tight on his hilt. "I'm not sure this sorceress is going to listen to us easily."

Suddenly, the ground rumbled and the trees began to melt. "What the..." I stepped back, wanting to give myself some distance from the massive trees as they drooped. Brown and green ran down their trunks like thick dollops of gooey paint. The branches wilted, sagging toward the ground until they fell off the trees entirely.

"What is this?" Vanth asked, backing away until he was right next to me. "This island doesn't want us here."

We couldn't leave. We had to find this sorceress and figure out how to destroy the gifts she'd given my father. I slid my sword back into its sheath and marched toward one of the melting trees. When I reached out to touch it, my fingers went through it. "It's an illusion."

Vanth grunted, then approached another tree. His

hand went right through the melting trunk. "She's trying to scare us away."

"Then we're getting closer to her." I retrieved my sword again, then continued forward. Vanth was behind me and the two of us fell into familiar habits of assessing the space around us, pausing on occasion to give a longer look. We'd been in so many battles together over the years that we didn't need words. Even if I didn't want to be here doing this, I was glad he was the one by my side. I probably trusted him more than I even trusted Laera.

Something screeched, making the hair on my arms stand on edge.

"That wasn't you, was it?" I asked the shifter, trying to diffuse the tension.

He handed me his weapon. "I think it's time I change forms."

I sheathed his sword so I could hold it for him, then covered him while he shifted. The huge gray wolf next to me bared his teeth, releasing a growl. His superior senses were catching something I missed. "Show me."

He took off, and I followed at a run, charging toward whatever was waiting for us in this sorceress's playground.

We wove around the melting trees, even though we could likely charge right through them. As we moved, the forest began to flicker and fade. Some of the trees were transparent, giving away their false nature.

Just as the trees vanished completely, leaving us on a shrub covered rocky surface, a beast came into view. With an ear splitting roar, the monster swept in. Its enormous body and leathery wings were reminiscent of a dragon, but its head was that of a giant eagle. The monster cried out, the sound making my bones vibrate.

The creature flew at us, snapping its sharp beak and flapping its enormous wings. Vanth reached it first, not hesitating to attack. He launched himself at it, digging his claws into its scales and clamping down on the elongated neck.

It twisted, throwing Vanth like he was nothing more than a nuisance. It charged at me and I attacked, dragging my sword along its chest. The monster seemed irritated, but wasn't injured by my steel. The dragon scales were protecting it.

Scrambling back, I knew we'd have to be smart about the way we defeated this beast. This creature shouldn't exist. It was an abomination. Either bred or magically created.

"Distract it," I called to Vanth.

The shifter moved with precision, charging toward our foe. He growled and snapped, attacked and fled, before striking again. The monster was turning in circles, trying to bite or claw at the smaller threat. Vanth was faster. And he was practiced in battle. He was so much deadlier than the monster realized, but he needed help.

I called my shadows, easily bringing them to the surface until they twisted and swirled around me. They flowed and undulated, a familiar part of me that obeyed my commands. For years, I'd hated the dark power I commanded. There had been too many accidents when my magic first manifested. It was a risk to even be in my presence for nearly a decade. If my emotions got the better of me, everyone paid the price.

Eventually, I embraced the fear I commanded. With that confidence, I owned my shadows. And I used them in horrific ways to ensure my father's power. I was the monster everyone accused me of. And I enjoyed it.

Now, I reached for that depth. That slightly unhinged part of me that wanted destruction. The part that reveled in the fear I could command.

"Run!" I screamed, trusting that Vanth knew what I meant.

The shadows exploded from me just as the wolf passed me, taking shelter behind me.

Darkness consumed the monster, the shadows weaving around the creature in an impossible web of death. It cried out, but quickly turned to a strangled, gurgling sound as the shadows tightened around my enemy. Soon, there was no sound at all, and the shadows flattened, having destroyed everything in their wake. A soft breeze blew, causing the shadows to move and flow like smoke from a fire. They skimmed over the rough ground, killing anything green and growing before they faded away completely.

The space where they'd been was barren. The monster was gone. The plants were gone. A dark stain on the rocks remained as a reminder of what was.

"I forgot you could do that," Vanth said.

I looked over to see the shifter pulling on his clothes. I retrieved his sword and handed it to him. "I used them in Athos. The day they attacked us."

"They weren't the same kind of shadows. Those were targeted. You spared all our men and Ara. What you just did would have taken us out."

"It was necessary," I said, my voice clipped. I could still feel the lingering anger making all my muscles tense. The place I had to reach to use those shadows was dark, even for me. It came at a cost.

"You shouldn't do that again," he warned.

"I don't recall asking your permission, shifter," I spat.

"Be as pissed at me as you want, but you bring this Ryvin home to Ara, you might as well be saying your good-byes," he warned.

Ara. Her face appeared in my mind, a reminder of what I had to lose if I ever returned to that place I'd occupied for so long. It had been a battle to bring myself out of that place. To find my own identity after being my father's weapon.

I looked at Vanth, then nodded. "Let's find this sorceress so we can get home. Ara is going to be waiting for me."

"She will." He started walking. "I caught a scent over here."

I followed him to a well-hidden path. If not for his keen wolf senses, we might have missed the minimal signs that someone had walked here. They'd been careful, but a couple of the sparse plants were broken in a way that couldn't be done by the wind. And considering the lack of wildlife, it couldn't be blamed on a rodent.

We continued along a path that got more obvious with each step. As if the person who'd traveled it dropped their guard the higher up the mountain they climbed. The path slowly became a ledge, circling the mountainside. The drop got higher with each footfall, but we continued, the signs of travel too obvious to ignore.

Finally, we could see the end of the path leading us right into a cave. Vanth and I glanced at each other, silently judging the fact that this mysterious sorceress lived in a cave on top of a mountain. It was a little unoriginal. Though, I had to give her credit for the guard we'd slayed. It would have prevented most trespassers.

We slowed as we approached the cave, taking cautious steps until we reached the opening. Slowly, I peered into the mouth of the cave, expecting to see some indication of a home.

Instead, I saw only death.

The entire ground was littered with human skulls.

19

Lagina

We were in a tiny, hidden room with recessed shelves full of ancient books. Spiderwebs filled the corners and our feet shuffled across a thick layer of dust.

"I wonder how long this has been here," Laera said, brushing her fingertips over the spine of one of the books.

I reached for one and it crumbled in my grip, the worn leather falling apart in my fingers. I gasped, then set it down, trying not to disturb the other tombs. "They aren't much use to anyone anymore."

"I don't think that matters," Laera said. "Look at this."

I turned and noticed that Laera's torch was on the ground, smoke rising from the extinguished flames. Several balls of glowing light hung around her, illuminating a wall covered in paintings. "No wonder they kept everyone out."

I joined her at the wall, my lips parting in surprise as I took in the images. While the books were decaying, the paintings were as clear as if they had been applied this morning.

The entire wall was covered. Showing the topography of Athos, the temple we were currently standing under, and the palace. There were lines that I guessed were the future streets, long before anything else in the city was built.

There were people with glowing hands around the buildings and walking around the empty city. Then, there was a very clear burst of something bright that came from this temple, forming a gold bubble around it. There were two similar symbols near the palace. One in the area, I think, was now housing the stables, and the other in the space where the orchard now grew. An arch of gold spanned from each of them, covering the entire palace in a warm light.

"The shields," I said in awe. I had to admit, I didn't believe it was actually possible. There was a part of me that still wondered, but I'd seen magic. I'd felt it when they freed the magic under the city. There was so much I didn't know. Why not a shield that could protect us?

"This whole time, you've been sitting on so much magic." Laera shook her head. She traced her fingers over the lines and I noticed several of them converged at each bright point. They weren't roads. "What are they? The lines?"

"Ley lines. Natural veins of magic that flow in the earth. There's a lot of them in Athos." Laera turned to face me. "I don't know how they got those shields to work, but I can take a look. Do you think you can find these locations?"

I returned my attention to the map and guessed that the source at the temple was in the back, behind the temple itself. It was a good place to put it. Nobody went around to the back. The way the temple was designed made it so the front faced lush vegetation and the back was near a cliffside of craggy rock. Very little grew back there.

"We should go," Laera said. "Just in case there's anything else down here."

I didn't need to be asked twice. With a nod, I turned and left the chamber. As soon as we stepped past the sliding door, it rattled and began to move, sealing the room from prying eyes.

Chills ran down my spine when I realized the door could have closed at any moment while we were in there. Suddenly feeling very claustrophobic, I stepped toward the ladder, ready to leave the darkness behind.

"Are you alright? No monsters?" Sophia asked as soon as she saw me climb through the trapdoor.

"No monsters," I assured her.

"Thank the gods." Her shoulders slumped in relief.

"Did you find anything?" Cora asked.

"We did," I said.

Suddenly, Laera was in front of me, then she had the priestess in her grasp, a weapon drawn, the blade pointing at the woman's throat.

Daphne gasped, her eyes wide with terror.

"What are you doing?" I cried.

"Let her go," Sophia pleaded.

Cora approached slowly, taking in the weapon and the terrified priestess. "What'd she do?"

"Cora," Sophia hissed.

"What did you write in the message?" Laera demanded.

"Message?" I stared at the priestess, my brows furrowing in confusion.

Daphne smirked. "So you really couldn't see what was on that scroll? How very interesting."

"You'll tell me or I'll send you to the Underworld," Laera promised.

"You'll send me to the Underworld anyway," Daphne said.

"No, she won't. She can go to the dungeons. Await a trial," I said.

"I don't answer to you," the priestess hissed. Her body contorted, slithering and undulating, growing larger. She shoved Laera away, knocking the Fae Princess to the ground. The knife landed with a rattle before sliding across the marble.

The priestess's peplos was torn, shredded fabric falling to the floor as wings emerged. Her beautiful face remained, despite its increase in size, but her body was now that of a bird.

"It's a harpy," Sophia whispered.

The creature screeched, then flapped her wings, rising higher inside the temple before swooping down toward Sophia. I shoved my sister aside, landing on top of her.

When I rolled off of her, I saw Laera chasing down the

monster. Cora raced over to where I was sitting with Sophia. "Are you two alright?"

I looked at Sophia, who was pushing herself up to standing. She smoothed out her peplos, and I turned to Cora. "We're fine."

I retrieved the dagger that was still in my waistband, grateful that it hadn't stabbed me when I landed. As soon as I took my first step, Sophia moved in front of me. "You two stay back. I've got this."

"You can't be serious," Cora retorted.

I took Cora's hand in mine, then dragged her out of the way. Sophia was stronger than she used to be and she'd seen things when she went to free the magic. I'd had minimal training to fight and I certainly wouldn't pretend I could hold my own against a harpy.

"She's going to get killed." Cora looked at me, her expression pleading. "You have to stop her."

I held onto her hand tighter, hoping she wouldn't run after our youngest sister. "You have to trust her."

Cora's fingernails bit into my hand as she tightened her grip. Her gaze was fixed on the battle in front of us, her face pale. Her concern for Sophia made her tense, but I wasn't going to let her charge out there. She'd never shown any interest in combat, and I wasn't sure if she'd even held a dagger before.

A high-pitched cry drew my attention back to the fight, and I gasped as Sophia dodged a swipe of the harpy's talons. Laera attacked from the other side, slicing her knife through the beast's side. The creature twisted, using one of her enormous wings to knock the Fae Princess down.

Sophia rallied, charging at the monster. To my horror, she leaped onto the harpy's back, clinging to the feathers as the creature thrashed. It twisted, trying to dig its pointed claws into my sister. I could see Laera standing behind the monster, her gaze unfocused, her posture stiff. She was doing something with her magic and, whatever it was, she wasn't in a position to fight.

"They need help," I whispered as I released Cora's hand. I tightened the grip on the blade I was still holding in my other hand. "Wait here."

"Oh, no you don't," Cora said with a huff. "I'm coming with you."

I didn't argue as I ran toward the monster, waving my hands and yelling to get its attention. The creature locked its eyes on me. They were so strangely human, but not. I ignored the hair standing at the back of my neck and the chill running down my spine.

Gripping the hilt the way Ryvin had taught me, I raced toward the monster. She spread her wings wide, as if she was going to take off with Sophia still on her back. I couldn't let that happen. I jumped, then drove my knife into one of the wings, dragging it along. The harpy let out a howl of pain, then swung her other wing around, knocking me down. I hit the marble floor face first and tasted blood immediately, but didn't let myself wonder what I'd injured.

Scrambling to my feet, I caught sight of my weapon still lodged in the harpy's wings. Blood poured from the wound, leaving a thick trail of crimson on the white floor. The bird-woman was screeching so loudly I winced.

"Here." Cora was standing next to me, a knife in her grip. "Finish her."

I accepted the weapon, but just as I was considering where to attack, I saw Sophia reach the harpy's neck. She impaled the monster in the fleshy area above where her feathers began.

Blood sprayed and then began to run from the monster's mouth. Her eyes went glassy and she spun in a strange, wobbly circle. Sophia jumped from her back, then ran to Laera. She guided the still unfocused princess away just as the harpy hit the ground.

A ruby pool spread from the place the beast lay until it started to drip down the still open trap door.

I wrinkled my nose. "That's going to be awful to clean."

"That's what you're thinking about right now?" Cora asked. "How terrible it will be to clean?"

"No, that's what I'm letting myself think about," I informed her. "I'm not quite ready to think about what just happened."

Sophia's peplos was stained red, her arms, hands, face, and hair were splashed with crimson. Her cheeks were flushed, her eyes wild. She looked more alive than I'd ever seen her.

"Thank you, Sophia," I said.

"You did good, too," she replied.

"I'm not sure I know either of you," Cora said, a touch of awe in her tone.

"Just wait, it'll be your turn soon enough," Laera said.

She looked like herself again as she scowled at the

fallen monster. "I'm sorry I didn't help. But I must say, I'm impressed."

"I had to break into the harpy's mind. Thankfully, I got the information before you all sent her to the Underworld."

"What information?" I asked.

"The letter she sent. It explained it all to my father." She glared at the harpy and I got the sense that if she could kill her again, she would.

"This monster already destroyed the shield here, but she didn't get to the ones at the palace yet. She let my father know she was going to destroy them all so he could send his new dragons to take us down. He'll be here soon. He's eager to finish his war."

"But we can use the others, then?" I asked.

Laera was staring at the harpy with such disdain, I was growing concerned. "Was there something else?"

She looked up at me. "She planned to eat us. I saw it in her mind. Her fantasies of how she was going to do it. In my opinion, we didn't make her suffer enough."

"I think I want to learn how to fight now," Cora cut in. "I will not be dinner for some crazy priestess."

"Laera said she'll keep teaching me if we all survive this," Sophia said. "You should join us."

Cora mumbled a noncommittal response. I caught the words, *duty* and *marriage*. She was already preparing for her life to change as soon as Bahar returned.

"We need to get back," Laera said. "I don't know if anyone else working for my father knows about this."

"That picture didn't show the shield covering the whole town," I said.

"It doesn't," Laera confirmed.

I looked at my sisters. "We have to evacuate the city. Get everyone up to the palace grounds."

"That's impossible," Cora said. "We don't have space for everyone."

"We'll have to find a way to make it work," I replied.

20

ARA

NYX'S SMILE WAS A WARNING. I knew whatever she had coming was going to be far worse than a pegasus trying to kill me. I glanced over at Obsidian, wishing he could give me a clue as to what to expect. Or maybe information about how to survive.

"In there." The goddess pointed to a cave, that same disturbing smile on her lips.

Reluctantly, I walked toward the small opening. Another cave. Another dark space. I was never going to allow myself to enter anything like this if I survived this war. I'd live in an open home with billowing curtains as my walls and the sound of the sea in my ears. A reminder of the wide expanse of freedom the water promised anyone brave enough to traverse her depths.

I watched Nyx, keeping my expression impassive. I

wouldn't give her the satisfaction of knowing how tightly wound my insides were.

The cave opening was lower than any I'd ventured in before, and it was shallow. I could see the entire thing by standing in the entrance. I looked around, noting that it was a completely typical cave. Dirt and rocks covered the floor, light entered through the mouth, walls were covered in moss. It didn't seem to have any tunnels or crevices I could explore. I turned in a slow circle, certain I was missing something important.

When I returned to facing the cave entrance, I intended to ask Nyx for clarification, but she wasn't there. Naxos wasn't even there.

My heart leaped as I stepped out of the space to find myself standing in Athos.

How was this possible? The cave must have been a portal. But it didn't look like the portal on Konos and I hadn't even felt the magic. Maybe it was Nyx herself who sent me. I didn't know the full scope of her power, but I knew it was great.

I was on the outskirts of the city, near the temple to Athena. It would take me some time to walk to the palace, but I wasn't sure that was the best use of my time. There was no way Nyx had sent me here for a visit with my family. I hadn't even been gone that long yet. If they saw me, they'd think I was finished and that I'd survived her tasks. I didn't want to get their hopes up only to leave again.

If a visit wasn't the reason for my return home, it had to

be something else. What task would I need to complete in Athos?

I started walking toward the temple, looking around as I did in case there were any clues. I expected to see acolytes and priests walking around the grounds, tending to the garden. Or catch glimpses of them inside the marble building, completing their duties to the goddess. Instead, it was empty.

The lack of other people was making my fingers tingle in anticipation. Something wasn't quite right. Though, nothing had been right for a long time. Had they evacuated the city in the time I'd been away?

I knew I wasn't supposed to enter the temple, but I couldn't help but take a few steps in to confirm that I was truly alone. Flames danced and flickered on vats of oil, burning faithfully despite the lack of attendants.

"Hello?" I called.

My echo was the only response.

A lump in my throat made swallowing harder. Even in times of battle, the priests usually stayed in the temples. They were sacred spaces, meant to be off limits in war. Where would they have gone?

I exited the space, then began walking toward town. If the temple wasn't the destination for this task, maybe it was in the city. Or at the palace. Or maybe I was supposed to go to where Nyx's new temple was being constructed. Did she want me to do something about making her more loved by the people?

What if I never figured it out? Would Nyx help me

figure it out or was she going to let me wander forever unaided?

The city was as empty as the temple and everything looked more run-down than it had last time I'd walked through. Was this because I'd last seen it in the dark?

Paint was peeling on every surface. The blue roofs were chipped and had blotches of color that didn't match. The roads seemed even more uneven and were littered with loose stones that I had to avoid. A group of stray cats peered from the darkness of an alleyway, their eyes glowing as they observed me.

It was so still. So quiet. So empty. Like death had already come for Athos.

Goosebumps rose on my arms, and I rubbed them to send away the sudden chill. I wasn't sure if I should keep walking out in the open or if I should avoid being seen. I'd never felt this unsettled here.

When I reached the Black Opal, I was startled to see that the courtyard was exposed, the wall that used to block the entry was completely gone. The building itself was destroyed. The roof had caved in. The once pristine black top of the building had made it iconic among a sea of blue. Now, it was crumbled remnants. The entire structure sagging under its weight.

The people must have found out that Selena was fae. It was the only thing I could come up with to explain such complete destruction. It would have taken a massive group to do something like this.

Unless it was a monster or some other kind of attack. My pulse raced and I started to run. I no longer cared what my task was, I had to get to the palace and find my sisters. Things were very wrong in Athos.

There were no guards waiting for me. Nobody stood outside the palace gates. The gates themselves were parted, a gap between them indicating that they weren't even closed, let alone locked. Anyone could access the palace.

My lungs were still burning from sprinting here, but I ignored the discomfort as I pushed the gates open and raced toward the front steps of the palace. The front door was missing, leaving a wide opening anyone could walk through. How had so much happened while I'd been away? What if I was on that island longer than I realized? What if the battle ended, and the fae won and everyone I loved was already dead?

"Lagina?" I yelled as I ran down the empty hall. "Cora? Sophia?" I went from room to room. Nobody in the breakfast room or the throne room. Nobody in the study or the library. Even their bedrooms were vacant.

Tears streamed down my face, and I burst through the back doors into the garden beyond. Ryvin was standing there, as if he'd been waiting for me this whole time. I cried out in relief, then ran to him, but he stepped back, avoiding my attempt to wrap my arms around him.

"What is it?" I asked. "What's going on? Why are you moving away from me?"

"We don't have time," he said. "The sea is angry. Ceto is going to take the city."

My brow furrowed. That didn't make any sense. "Why would she do that?"

"I don't know. But if you don't stop it, all of Athos will be destroyed. You must come with me now." He extended his hand, and I hesitated. There was something wrong with all of this.

"Is that why everyone left?" I asked.

"Yes, they're getting to higher ground," he confirmed.

Some of the tension eased. It was going to be alright. The people had fled, which could also explain the destruction at the Opal. They'd probably pillaged it for anything valuable. I was going to have to leave that out when I saw Nyx again. It didn't help her view of humans to know how destructive they could be. But it wasn't like the gods were any better.

"But how can I stop the sea?" I asked.

"Your magic. We'll both channel whatever we can and we'll send the rising tide away from the city," he said.

"Your mother, she took my magic," I said. "At least she said she was going to. I can't help."

"We have to calm the sea or everyone's going to die," Ryvin said.

"You can do it. You can use my magic," I said.

"I need you with me, you can help me. Tell me what to do." His jaw was set, his expression serious. "I think if you're closer to me, I can channel more of your magic. I'm not sure I'm strong enough on my own."

I nodded. "Alright. Together."

"Why is Ceto sending the water?" I asked as we made our way out of the palace grounds, the two of us jogging to move faster.

"She thought the city turned on you when they sent you to Nyx," Ryvin said.

"But I went on my own." I glanced at him and noticed the pained expression on his face. "I need to tell her. She can spare the city."

"It's too late," he said. "She knew they fled to the site of Nyx's new temple and she's sending everything there. She's going to kill everyone."

My heart thundered in my chest and I picked up my pace. "We have to stop her."

Suddenly, Ryvin grabbed my arm, pulling me to a stop. "I have to tell you something."

My breathing was coming in rapid breaths. His expression alone was enough to break my heart, and I braced myself. "What is it?"

"It's your sisters," he said.

My chest felt tight. "Tell me."

"Ceto took them. They're on an island that shouldn't exist near Nyx's temple. If we prevent the water from reaching Athos, your sisters will die."

"No." I shook my head. "No, that's impossible. How could she do that?"

"I'm sorry. You'll have to choose. We might be able to save them, but it's not a guarantee. The monsters could get to us before we reach them. But if we try to save them, everyone who lives in Athos will die." He squeezed my hand. "The choice is yours."

I felt like I was dying already. How could anyone expect me to make a choice like this? Everything I'd done was to help my sisters; to keep them alive. It was how I ended up in Konos. It was probably the reason this stupid war was even happening. I couldn't let them die.

But if I attempted to save them and failed, I'd lose everything. All the humans who called Athos home were counting on my family to keep them safe and my father had done nothing but harm them. He'd sent their children to their deaths, he'd kept a goddess locked away. He was the reason we were in this situation in the first place.

"Do you think we could save them?" I had to ask, even if I was already trying to find a way to say goodbye.

"We might. But we have to decide soon. We can't do both. There's no way we could do it ourselves. Splitting up would mean we both lose." He rubbed his thumb across my hand soothingly. "Whatever you choose, I'll support you."

Lagina wanted to be a great queen. She wanted to serve her people. Sophia had been angry when I sacrificed myself in her place. Even Cora seemed to be coming around to helping Athos rather than only thinking of herself.

They'd never forgive me if I saved them and then returned them to a ghost town. While I knew there were other humans living in Drakous, they were few. Athos was the greatest hope for humans to survive.

I felt like I couldn't breathe.

I knew what I had to do, but dooming my sisters was impossible. It was all impossible. Tears blurred my vision. "How am I supposed to do this?"

"You do what you think is best and no matter what, I'm here by your side," Ryvin replied.

I knew what he'd choose. I knew if there was a chance to save me and damn the rest of the world, he'd choose me.

But I wasn't him. I couldn't do it.

Please forgive me.

I knew they'd understand. I knew they'd encourage me to save our city, but it broke everything inside me to turn to Ryvin and tell him my choice. "We save Athos." The words barely came out. My throat was so dry, my tongue too large. My heart a million slivers that I'd never rebuild. I knew I'd never recover from this, but it was what I had to do.

He nodded, then silently, the two of us raced toward Nyx's temple.

21

Ara

An ornate doric temple stood on a hill overlooking the palace. Neat rows of cypress trees lined the pathway, leading to a lush garden overflowing with flowers. I stopped, then looked over at Ryvin. "How is the temple complete?"

His brow furrowed. "Are you feeling alright, Ara?"

I bristled a little, unused to hearing my name on his lips. When was the last time he'd called me by my name, and why did it feel so off? "Exactly how long was I in Naxos?"

"We can discuss that later," he replied, his attention fixed on the sea in the distance.

We could see the city from here and already the water had covered the harbor and was washing up against some of the buildings down below. It would destroy everything if we didn't appease it.

"Let's go." I would figure this out after we'd calmed the sea.

As we continued along the pathway in the garden, I couldn't shake how strange everything felt. Nyx's temple shouldn't be finished. And why would Ceto come after Athos? What had happened with the fae?

Before I could ask any additional questions, I saw the citizens of Athos nestled among the gardens. Some were bundled in blankets or sitting on cushions they'd brought along. They crowded together, wary looks on their tired faces. I passed crying children and shivering elderly couples. There were people filling every space as far as I could see. Thousands all crammed into one place.

"Up here." Ryvin led me closer to the temple. We were standing at a cliffside, looking down into the churning sea below.

The sea was an angry, steely gray. The waves crashed against the cliffs with brute force that sent fear creeping through me. I'd never seen it this destructive. I could practically feel the urge of the water to destroy everything in its wake.

Suddenly, I heard cries and shouts coming from nearby. When I turned, my heart stopped and I couldn't breathe. My sisters were calling to me from what looked like a large, flat rock in the middle of the churning water. The waves splashed over the stone, soaking them and making them scream. They were huddled together, the three of them soaking wet and shaking, holding on to each other through their last moments.

"It's getting worse," Ryvin shouted. He pointed toward town, the opposite direction from my sisters, where the water was now filling the streets. Homes were being crushed by the waves, sending debris and pieces of Athos out into the water.

If we were going to send the water back to where it belonged, we'd have to do it soon. Even this hillside wasn't going to be high enough to save the people of Athos if we waited much longer. As it was, already half the city was gone.

"You sure about this? I can go to your sisters instead," he offered.

I looked back at them. They were so far from shore I wasn't even sure we'd be able to get to them in time. I felt like I was dying, like my soul was being pulled from my body. I couldn't sacrifice an entire city for them.

"Send the water away from Athos," I said.

Ryvin nodded, then lifted his arms. "If you've got any magic you can access, send it my way. We'll need everything we can get."

I could still hear my sisters screaming in the distance, but I worked to ignore it. Tears rolled down my cheeks as I searched for that space inside where my magic resided.

The water was already responding to Ryvin's magic. Well, my magic through him. Each rushing wave had less power and stretched less into Athos. It was receding, retiring to where it belonged.

Even as he sent the water away, I fought to find my

magic, to aid him in any way I could. And because I kept hoping that if I was strong enough, if I could make this go faster, then maybe, just maybe, we could find my sisters.

I couldn't hear them anymore. They were silent. A heavy weight settled in my stomach.

"Send me everything you have!" Ryvin shouted.

I shut out my feelings and worked to focus. The magic had to be there, at least a little bit. There had to be something. But it didn't matter how much I struggled, or how hard I tried. There was nothing there. I felt like a hollow, withered shell of myself. Not human, but not magical, either. I lost everything. Myself and now my family...

Ryvin lowered his arms, his breathing heavy. "I think we did it."

I turned, but the rock was gone. And so were my sisters.

I didn't remember falling to my knees, but somehow, I was on the ground. Somewhere very far away, I thought I heard the sound of cheering. They were celebrating, but they didn't know the cost.

Inside, I died. Inside, I was defeated.

I closed my eyes and leaned down until my forehead was resting on the cool grass. I'd given everything for Athos. And I felt like I had nothing left.

SILENCE HUNG HEAVY AROUND ME. The sound of the cheers dissolved. The roar of the sea faded. I could only hear my breathing and the pounding of my heart.

The scent of something sweet filled my nostrils, and I forced my eyes open. It was dark, and I was shivering. My forehead was resting on dirt and I could feel the sting of a few small pebbles that were embedded in my forehead and palms.

I pushed myself up until I was resting on my knees, then looked around. A single fae light flickered in front of me, illuminating the gray, rocky walls. I wasn't in Athos. I was in a small cave.

My eyes stung and my cheeks were still damp from tears as I stood. I exited the cave, walking into the darkness of Naxos. Stars glittered overhead, and the moon shone down on me with its cold, watery glow. I scowled at it, then looked around for the goddess I knew had to be nearby.

When I didn't see her, I began to walk. No Nyx, no Obsidian, just starlight and the sound of waves crashing against the shore. After walking for a bit, I caught the sight of more fae lights glittering in the distance. I had never been so grateful in my life to see Dion's home.

Nyx was waiting for me outside. The goddess was clothed in a sheer sparkling black peplos that was shimmering with gold sparkles that glowed like actual stars. I wouldn't be surprised if she was wearing a piece of the night sky.

She swirled a glass full of ruby liquid, then took a long sip while studying me in silence.

"That was cruel," I said after a long pause.

"You agreed to my terms. The challenges are my choice." She watched me with a pleased feline expression.

"It wasn't real," I said, more to calm myself. There was

no alternative. I couldn't accept that my sisters were actually gone.

"I worried the illusion would give it away, but you didn't start questioning it until you saw my finished temple. Really, when would such a situation ever occur? Your mother doesn't even have that kind of command of the sea."

"You made me leave my sisters to die," I said, my tone accusing.

"I needed to see how you'd respond. You see, I know how selfish humans are. I know they'll choose themselves over others. I thought your sisters were the most important thing in your world. I thought for sure you'd choose them and watch the rest of your kind perish." She frowned. "I hate that you proved me wrong."

"I told you. There are good humans and bad humans, just like the gods. But we're worth saving." My words came out flat. I was too tired and too relieved that it was all a dream to fight her.

My sisters were safe. They were alive. I couldn't allow myself to consider any other alternative. Besides, I was convinced that if anything had happened to them since I arrived, Nyx would revel in sharing that information with me.

Movement made me turn, and I saw Dion coming through the door to join us. He had two glasses of wine in his hands. "She's finished for the day, correct? You assured me she'd be my guest while she was here. And a guest needs a drink, a meal, and a good night's sleep."

The god handed me a glass. "Drink. It's the good stuff."

I accepted the glass, not realizing until that moment how much my hands were shaking. I took a sip, not caring enough to wonder if he was tricking me. My body still didn't know that losing my sisters had been pretend. I could still feel the pain of it, still feel the missing pieces of my soul where they were supposed to be. I wondered how long it was going to take to recover from what Nyx had just put me through.

"You may rest for now," Nyx said as she rose to her feet. She tossed back the rest of her wine in one gulp, then passed her glass to Dion. "I'll return soon for your final challenge."

In a swirl of shadows, she vanished.

I dropped my glass and fell to my knees, my whole body shaking as I broke down. "I can't do this."

A warm hand rested on my back. "You can. You're so close. Just one more task."

I looked up at Dion, sniffing, then wiping my tears with the back of my hand. "Why do you even care? You helped us before and you're helping me again."

He moved his hand away. "I'm not sure. I guess I enjoy watching the gods get what's coming from a half-human who isn't even supposed to exist."

I wasn't sure if that was a compliment or not. It didn't feel like one. "Whatever your reason, I'm grateful."

"Don't go getting soft on me now, Princess. You'll need to find that rage you felt this morning if you want to survive."

I was getting tired of existing in a place of constant anger. "Do you think we have any chance of winning?"

"Who? You against Nyx? Of course."

I shook my head. "No, Athos against the fae. Do we have any hope? Or is all of this for nothing? Should I just retreat? Hide out the rest of my days on Ceto's island?" I knew Ryvin would go with me if I could convince my mother to let him join me. I couldn't deny that it was a tempting thought. It was getting so much harder to continue fighting.

"You'd never be happy there. You'd spend the rest of your life wishing you did more," Dion replied. He stood, then extended his hand.

I accepted his help and began walking with him toward the house.

"The maenads made dinner. You should eat. If Nyx has her way, that final challenge could be your end." Dion winked, then handed me a fresh glass of wine he made appear out of thin air. "If you need any ideas, I'm more than happy to help you make tonight memorable."

"I'm still not going to sleep with you." I gave him a scalding glance but took the wine, anyway.

He grinned. "I'll show you where my room is, just in case you change your mind."

I rolled my eyes and sighed. At least I could count on Dion to never change.

22

Lagina

There was something in the air when we reached the palace. It made my skin crawl and I resisted the urge to turn and walk the other way.

"The air tastes weird," Cora said.

"Is that magic?" Sophia asked.

"It is, indeed. There's a lot around the palace. Like it's drawn here," Laera replied.

"That will be good for the shields, right?" I glanced at the fae princess, hoping to get some optimism from her. Instead she had that ever-present scowl she always seemed to wear.

She shrugged. "One way to find out."

"I'm no help with the magic stuff," Cora said.

"I'm sure we can find a way for you to help," I countered.

Laera raised a skeptical brow and I shot a glare at her. Cora was finally stepping into her strengths and offering support. I didn't want to stop her.

"No, I don't need to be a distraction or get a job to keep me busy. I'm going to town to start evacuating people," she said.

I stared at her, my mouth parting in surprise.

"Don't give me that look. I do care about Athos. I do care about our people," she said.

"I never said you didn't," I replied. "I'm just not sure it'll be safe."

"I know what everyone thought of me. But mother isn't here anymore to tell me my only worth is my body. I'm more than that. I need to do this before I marry. Before I go back to that role of the pretty face." She balled her hands into fists and stared at me with determination.

"A mating bond has nothing to do with your looks," Laera said.

"That's not helpful," Cora retorted. "It's still about me being the prize for someone else based on something I didn't do." She looked at me. "Let me do this."

"I'm coming with you," Sophia chimed in.

"Oh, no," I shook my head. "Have you two forgotten that Ara was nearly killed by our own people?"

Laera set her hand on my shoulder and I turned to her. The Fae Princess was staring at my sisters. "You need to let them go. Besides, if anyone messes with them, Sophia has ways of making them regret their actions."

I hesitated, wondering when my sisters had matured so much. It was like they'd aged years since our father died. I supposed finding out about all the lies we'd been told had a way of forcing us to face reality unlike anything else in our sheltered lives.

"Be careful," I relented. "Remember, you can't force anyone. If they won't listen, move on. We won't be able to save them all."

"You sound like a queen," Cora said, a note of pride in her tone. She smiled warmly. "We'll be careful. You do the same."

I nodded, then held back the tears as my sisters turned and left for the city below.

"Where are the stables?" Laera asked.

I pointed. "I need to tell the guards and servants about what's coming so they can prepare. Then I'll meet you there."

"Go. Hopefully we can get this shield up before my father arrives." Laera took off toward the stables and I walked toward the palace.

Argus was waiting for me at the entry. "How did it go?"

"We found what we needed. The shield exists and we might be able to use it," I explained.

His shoulders lowered and he visibly relaxed. "That's the first good news I've heard in a long time." When he caught my expression, his tension returned. "What's the bad news?"

"We can only shield the area around the palace."

"We're bringing the whole city here, aren't we?" he asked.

I nodded.

"I'll prepare my men. We'll get tents and provisions ready. Anything else?" he asked.

"Have you heard from Ara?" It had been a few days since she'd left for Naxos and I was getting anxious. I didn't know how long the goddess planned to keep her.

Argus shook his head. "Nothing yet."

"Any word from Ryvin about the sorceress?" I had a feeling it was the same as Ara, but I had to ask.

"No."

"What are we going to do if they can't remove that extra power? How long can we keep everyone alive in the shield?" I swallowed hard. Athos wasn't built for a siege.

"I'll find out and let you know," he replied.

"Thanks, Argus. For everything."

He nodded. "Anytime, Your highness."

Knowing he had everything under control, I headed to the stables, hoping that Laera had some good news.

As I got closer, my instincts flared with warning and I broke into a run. Breathless and on edge, I entered the stables. The horses whinnied and stomped as I passed by. They were just as spooked as I felt, but I couldn't find the source of our anxiety.

As soon as I exited through the other doors, my heart fell into my stomach. Laera was on the ground, unconscious, a dark crimson stain on her side. I ran to her then dropped to my knees, pressing my fingers to her neck to feel for a pulse. Just as I found her heartbeat I heard hissing.

Teeth bared, golden eyes locked on me, was a chimera. The monster's lion's feet pawed at the ground, its serpent tail whipped around, hissing and spitting. The goat head glared at me, as if trying to decide which part of me to devour first.

I stood, not taking my eyes from the beast. I needed a weapon. There was no way I could defeat this thing with my hands. It had injured Laera and she was more skilled than I was.

Carefully, I backed up, risking lowering my eyes in a sign of submission. The hissing ceased after I'd taken a few steps so I glanced up to see what it was doing. The monster had turned its attention from me to a large, cylindrical stone. It was circling the gray rock. The goat head opened its mouth and breathed fire on the rock. When the flames ceased, the creature investigated the stone. The snake snapped at it and the paws pushed on it, but the rock looked the same as it had.

It was trying to destroy the shield. That had to be the marker for the convergence point that we needed. I had to stop the monster before it could complete its task.

I continued to walk backward until I was at the door to the stable, then I turned and darted back into the building. There had to be something here I could use.

I scanned the walls, seeing hammers and rakes. There were hoof picks that were fairly sharp and a pitchfork that might work. I crossed the space to the tools, the horses continuing to act unsettled. They could probably smell the chimera.

I shoved the hoof pick into my waistband then grabbed the shovel. It had a slight point on the end and was heavy.

It might do more damage than the pitchfork or rake. Their points looked rather dull.

Satisfied with my choice, I returned to the back of the stable and took a deep breath before walking through the door.

The chimera was breathing fire on the stone. I moved toward it quietly, knowing I'd only get one chance to sneak up on it. Something snapped under my foot and I winced. The creature's head whipped toward me and it snarled, then it returned to lighting up the stone with its breath. I hoped I wasn't too late.

Since it already knew I was there, I ran, shovel over my shoulder, ready to swing. The monster's fire ceased and it turned toward me, lowering its upper body, preparing to pounce. I paused my advance, tightening my grip on the handle.

When it leaped, I swung.

The shovel smacked the chimera in the head with a sickening thunk, knocking the beast to the ground.

My hands were shaking, but I moved toward it and lifted the shovel to strike again. The monster righted itself and just as I pulled back to swing, it attacked, knocking me to the ground. I lost my grip on the shovel when I fell. Claws bit into my chest as the beast pinned me down. It opened its jaws and I knew what was going to happen next.

I grabbed the hoof pick and jabbed it into the goat neck before rolling away. The monster cried out, a horrible sound that was somewhere between a screaming goat and a roaring lion. It set my teeth on edge and made my eyes water. I covered my ears and moved away from it.

The hoof pick was still in the chimera's neck but it wasn't going down. The lion paws swept back, then it lowered, the snake hissing as the lion shaped rear end wiggled like a cat preparing to attack.

I went for the fallen shovel, but the creature reached me first, massive paws landing on my turned back. It shoved me to the ground, digging its claws into my skin. I cried out as sharp pain sliced down my entire back. I'd never felt anything like it. Tears slid down my cheeks and I whimpered as I pulled my legs up to my chest, and covered my head with my arms.

I prepared to be roasted alive, curled up in a pathetic crying ball. I was just glad nobody was here to see how I'd failed.

The heat didn't come. I took a few more breaths, until I was calm enough to lower my arms and open my eyes. The monster was back at the rock, igniting it with everything it had.

I stretched out my legs and turned to push myself to stand but the pain in my back roared to life. I bit down on my lower lip to keep from screaming. Trying another position, I worked to make myself rise, but the pain kept me down.

I couldn't move. I was going to die here. Bleeding in the dirt. I'd be embarrassed if I wasn't in so much pain.

Out of the corner of my eye, I noticed movement and a flicker of hope filled my chest. It was quickly swallowed by fear. "Get out of here. It's too dangerous." I didn't want someone else to meet my same end.

Laera's face appeared above mine. She had dark bruises along her cheekbones and her silver hair was a mess but her eyes were fierce. She pressed her index finger to her lips, then removed a blade from a pocket on her thigh. I noticed she had a blade in the other hand as well.

I made myself shift just enough that I could see the chimera, still focused on its task. When I turned back to Laera, I whispered, "Kill it."

She grinned, then walked away from me. She moved like a dancer. Like she was walking on air. Silent and graceful. The chimera didn't even flinch as she approached.

When she struck, it was a blur. Blood sprayed, the flames died, the creature bellowed in agony.

Then there was Laera, standing over the quivering form of a fallen chimera. Her shoulders rose and fell quickly as she glared down at the monster. She was covered in crimson.

With a roar of her own, Laera attacked again, diving her blade into the softest spots of the beast. When she was finished, the creature didn't move.

Laera returned her blades to the pockets on her thighs, then walked over to me. "Can you get up if I help you?"

"Yes." I didn't care how much it hurt.

Laera grabbed my wrists and pulled. I screamed as pain expanded from my injured back and chest, radiating through my entire body. I grabbed her wrists, forcing myself to get up. She didn't say a word about the tears or the curses coming from my lips.

Somehow, with stars exploding in my vision, I was on my feet. I took a few tentative steps. The pain was intense, but as long as I wasn't moving too quickly, I could walk.

"You'll need to get that cleaned and you'll need the antidote if the snake got you," Laera said.

"I don't think it bit me," I replied.

"That's good." Laera walked back over to the stone, then caressed the rock as she walked in a slow circle around it. "I don't think it was damaged. Chimera fire didn't seem to be enough to erode the stone or the magic. I can still feel it."

"Can you make it work?" I asked.

Laera removed her hand from the stone, then looked up at me. "No."

My heart fell into my stomach. "No?"

"Not alone, anyway. It's been dormant for so long, the spark is buried. I need another magic user," she replied.

"Sophia?" I asked hopefully.

"I don't think she's strong enough," Laera replied. "I'd need Ryvin or Ara, but they've not yet returned."

"What about your mother?" I suggested.

Laera scowled and after a few breaths, she nodded. "I'll ask." She closed her eyes and went so still, I wasn't sure if she was even breathing.

An overwhelming urge to shake her to see if she was alright came over me until I remembered what she'd done at the temple. This was magic. She was doing something with it.

She opened her eyes. "She's on her way. And she's bringing Selena."

"Thank you," I said.

"It still might not work, you know," she said.

"I know. But we have to try," I replied.

"He's on his way," she added. "My father."

"How far?" I asked.

She shook her head. "I'm not sure. He was blocking me out completely, but now I'm getting through a little. It's like whatever he used to keep me out is cracking."

"Let's hope it falls apart completely soon," I said.

"It will." She sounded confident.

"Can you check on anyone with your magic?" I asked.

She lifted a brow and I realized I'd overstepped. "I'm not trying to inquire about your magic. I'm wondering if you can check on Ara."

Her shoulders dropped. "I haven't been able to find her or Ryvin or even the shifter."

"I hope she's alright," I said.

"She's stronger than you realize," Laera replied. "So are you."

"This better be important," a sharp female voice called.

We turned to see Aspasia and Selena emerging from the stables.

"It is if you want to survive the upcoming attack," Laera said.

Aspasia sighed dramatically. "Fine."

"There's a convergence point here with a shield stone. There's another in the orchard. We need to turn them on," I said. "Can you help?"

Aspasia slowly began to remove the bangles on her

wrists. She held them out toward me. "Hold these. Gold isn't the right conduit for this kind of magic."

I took the jewelry and waited while she removed the heavy gold necklace at her throat. She handed it to me, then turned to her daughter. "Let's get this over with. You interrupted my nap."

Selena followed behind the queen, and Laera led them toward the stone. I watched as the three fae women formed a circle around the convergence point. They held hands, then all of them lowered their heads as if in prayer and closed their eyes.

They were silent. There was no chanting or dancing as we'd heard from the stories of how women sometimes used magic. But I knew they were using it. Goosebumps traveled up my arms and a chill ran down my spine. The air tasted like a storm and something seemed to buzz with energy all around me.

Wind whipped around us and all three women's hair rose the way someone's would when they were too close to lightning. I took a step back, heart racing. I was so close to it the hair on my arms stood on end.

The stone began to glow. Brilliant white light lit the rock until it was the same luminous quality as the stars in the sky. It flashed, the intense light making me close my eyes against the brightness. I could see the light through my eyelids, and then it faded.

Carefully, I opened my eyes and saw that the stone had taken on a warm golden glow. I wasn't sure if I was imagining things or if I could actually feel the vibration of the stone from where I stood.

The women released each other's hands and dropped their arms to their sides. "It appears to be working," Aspasia commented.

"Thank you," I said.

She smoothed down her hair, then did the same with her green peplos. "You'll hold my jewelry until we ignite the second one."

It wasn't a question, it was a command. I bristled, resisting the urge to remind her that I was also a queen. Instead, I smiled sweetly. We needed her help. "Of course."

"We'll get the next one turned on and meet you back in the palace," Laera offered. "Thebes has arrived."

$$23$$

Cora

"You don't have to trust me," I said, not hiding my frustration. "You can stay here and wait for the fae if you'd rather take your chances."

"We already defeated the fae once. We'll do it again," the woman said through the crack in her door.

"That was a decoy. Don't you understand? They're going to return with their full forces." I was getting tired of arguing with people who had no sense of survival. Sophia had much better luck than I had. Nearly everyone she'd encouraged to leave had packed their belongings onto their backs and headed toward the palace. Meanwhile, I'd been spit on twice and had a door slammed on my face.

"Fine. Stay here. I don't care what you do." I turned and marched to the next home, hoping I'd have better luck.

The door opened before I arrived, and a timid woman peered out. "Is it true? They're evacuating to the palace?"

"Yes," I confirmed. "Please, please just go. Even if I'm wrong, the worst thing that happens is you go back home in a couple of days."

"I have children," she said.

"Bring them. And bring only what you can carry. There isn't much space," I replied.

"Alright. We just go to the palace grounds?"

"Yes, they'll be waiting for you." A knot in my chest loosened. Finally, someone was going to listen to me.

Suddenly, she let out a yelp and slammed the door on me. I jumped back in surprise, colliding with something behind me.

I spun quickly to find Bahar glaring down at me. "Why are you out here unaccompanied? Where are your guards?"

I crossed my arms over my chest. "I am capable of taking care of myself."

"No, you're not. I asked about you. You have no weapons training, no fighting skills. No diplomacy training. Nothing. You're going to get yourself killed."

"Well, when you say it like that..." I could feel my cheeks heat. I couldn't exactly counter with the fact that I'd been taught how to seduce and lie to get what I wanted. I'm sure that's not what someone wants to hear from their future wife.

I looked at the closed door behind me, then back at him. "You terrified that woman. I was trying to help her."

He rolled his eyes, then knocked on the door. To my

surprise, it opened a crack. The woman squeaked when she saw Bahar.

"My apologies, kind lady. I arrived to accompany my bride-to-be on her tasks to help her people." He inclined his head as if greeting a royal.

The woman's cheeks reddened, and I balled my hands into fists as jealousy flared. I shoved it away quickly, hating the stupid way I reacted to him.

She opened the door wider. "We'll leave as soon as possible."

"Thank you." I forced a smile, hating that I was angry at her for the way she was looking at Bahar.

She closed the door, and I returned my attention to the Dragon King. "Why are you here?"

"I came at your request," he replied.

I started walking to the next home. "I mean why are you in town and not at the palace?"

"I came for you, so I found you," he said.

I caught sight of several people peering out their windows or doors watching the king. "Fine. But you need to stay out of the way. You're scaring people."

"As long as I know you're not out here alone," he replied.

I looked over to where Sophia was speaking with a family across the street, checking that she was doing alright before I moved to the next home. We'd already covered most of the city and had enlisted the help of a few priests to cover other neighborhoods. We'd be finished soon. My stomach tightened in anticipation of what would happen when we returned to the palace.

I shoved the thought away and walked to the next house, knocking before I could think more on my upcoming wedding.

"I THINK we got a lot of people to understand," Sophia said as we walked toward the palace.

The streets were full of people carrying far too much in their arms and on their backs. "I hope so."

"You did what you could," Bahar added. "And I anticipate you'll see more head to your gates when they see the fae ships arrive."

I slowed down, letting Sophia get ahead of me. Bahar matched my pace. "I'm sorry I asked you to leave your people. What's happening in Drakous?"

"The Fae King's men occupy our city, but they won't hold it if we can eliminate the king," he said.

"What makes you think he'll come here himself? He didn't last time," I pointed out.

"Pride. He wants to claim the credit and he thinks he's invincible," Bahar said.

"Is he?" I asked.

"He could be. We have to hope getting him in the open is enough," Bahar admitted.

"Did you know about the sorceress?" I asked.

"Not in time to save my sister," he replied darkly.

I stopped walking, grief washing over me. It was as if I could feel his anguish. "You had to watch it." I didn't know how I knew, but I did.

"He's not going to stop until he destroys anyone who might be a threat to him," Bahar said.

I set my palm on his bicep. "I'm so sorry."

He placed his hand on top of mine. It was warm and the touch was comforting. "You'd have liked her."

"I'm certain I would have."

"Cora? Everything alright?" Sophia called.

I turned to see her waiting ahead, watching us with curiosity. I dropped my hand. "We're fine."

We started walking again and I couldn't help but feel guilty for calling Bahar away from his people. I was so worried about saving my own that I'd left them unprotected while he was here with me. "If you need to return, I understand. I shouldn't have summoned you."

"I belong by your side. Kabir is there in my place. He can handle whatever arises in Drakous while I'm here. And I brought some dragons with me. We can help. When the Fae King arrives, I will fight alongside Athos to ensure your safety." He was staring straight ahead, not looking at me.

My chest felt tight. "I don't deserve any of the loyalty you're showing me."

He glanced over, a small smirk on his lips. "Careful, Princess. You keep speaking like that and I might start to think you actually care for me."

I was silent the rest of the walk to the palace, afraid I'd say something that might scare him away. Or worse, make the warm feelings I was starting to have thaw into something more intense.

There weren't guards stationed at the wide open gates.

People were flooding in, and the few guards I saw were busy directing families to the empty spaces around the palace.

A few of Bahar's men were stationed near the front doors, as if waiting for their king to return. To my surprise, they inclined their heads in greeting but didn't speak to him or follow us inside. They seemed to have taken over spaces usually reserved for our guards. They were already working with us, defending my people, even without a marriage. But what would happen when things got more challenging? Would they even give us a warning before leaving?

We strolled down the marble hallway, past rushing servants carrying bundles of food and fabric. Every resource in the palace was being distributed to the citizens taking over the grounds.

"So, are you ever going to tell me the reason you needed me here so badly?" Bahar asked.

I grabbed his sleeve and tugged him away from the main hallway into the breakfast room. The table was empty, and the room seemed so small without my sisters gathered. I wondered if we'd ever do that again.

"Had to get me alone, did you?" he teased.

"I want us to get married. Now," I blurted.

The playful smile on his lips faded and his brow furrowed. "No."

"What?" I released my grip on his tunic. "I thought you wanted to marry me."

"I do. But not like this. Not because you're afraid I won't help your people," he said.

"Lagina told you," I said.

He shook his head. "Nobody had to tell me, Princess. It's obvious you don't want to marry me, but you care about your city, your home. Don't worry, I'm not going to abandon you just because you haven't given yourself to me yet. I can be very patient."

I crossed my arms over my chest. "I don't have time for patience."

"You don't want to marry me. And trust me, I have no problem getting my needs met elsewhere until you're ready." He shrugged.

I was fuming. "How dare you."

"What?"

"How dare you threaten to fuck other women when you have me right here!" Rage consumed me. There was no way I would ever allow him to touch another woman. "You are an engaged man. You don't get to bed other women. That's not how it works."

"You're free to be with other men, if that's your concern," he said.

It felt like I'd been slapped across the face. I'd been with lots of men, for no reason other than boredom. I'd been with men to learn things for my mother, or to gain favor for my family. Then there was Tomas. The one I thought I was with for love.

None of them mattered anymore. None of them would ever satisfy me again. I grabbed the front of his tunic, low on his chest, then pulled him closer to me. His brows lifted in surprise.

"What did you do to me?" I demanded. "Why are you the only man I can think about?"

"Mating bonds are strong." He pried my fingers off his tunic and stepped back. "You need some time to cool off, before you do something you might regret."

"Why do you keep turning me down?" Nobody turned me down. I simply had to bat my eyelashes and I got any man I wanted. Any man but this one.

"Trust me, it's not easy," he said, his voice a little husky.

I glanced down and noticed the bulge in his trousers. So it wasn't just me. I reached for him, and he caught my wrist. Slowly, he leaned down so his nose nearly touched mine. I was staring into his deep green eyes. "Naughty."

My insides heated until they were molten. I squeezed my thighs together, then pulled my arm away. "You're not as tough as you think you are."

"Neither are you, Princess." He rose to his full height, a confident smile on his lips. The kind that reflected victory.

He thought he'd won.

I grabbed him again, but this time I reached higher on his tunic and pulled hard. He bent unexpectedly and before he could react, I pressed my lips to his.

He tensed, his lips stilled. I dragged my tongue along his lower lip and he groaned, then he wrapped his arms around me, lifting me off the ground. I threw my legs around his waist and dug my fingers into his shoulders to steady myself.

He devoured me like I was his last meal and I returned each stroke with even more intensity.

I won.

He was mine.

His hands found their way up my tunic and let him explore until I could tell he was at the point of no return. Then I released his waist and broke free, quickly distancing myself from him. Panting, I watched as he gazed at me with the frustrated look of a predator who'd just had his meal stolen.

"We wed tomorrow," I managed between breaths. "Then I'm all yours."

"You are my punishment from the gods, aren't you?" he bit out.

I made a show of smoothing my tunic, then freed my messy hair from the tie that had held it back at the base of my neck. My long gold hair tumbled free. "I look even better when I'm naked."

"This is your last chance for a taste of freedom," he warned. "Once I marry you, there's no going back. You're the Queen of Drakous. The mother to the future heir to the kingdom. My queen. My mate. Mine."

The growl that came out with his final word made my knees weak, but I held myself together. "I'll arrange for a priest at sunset." Before I could give in to the urge to tear all of his clothes off, I left the room, leaving my soon to be husband behind.

24

BONES RATTLED AND SHOOK, spilling all over the ground as something emerged from a pile of them near the rear of the cave.

The figure was that of a man. He was three times my size, but still in the shape of a man. I sent an orb of light into the air and it illuminated the space enough for me to get a better look.

"Fuck," Vanth said with a growl.

"Shift. Now," I hissed as I reached for my shadows.

The cyclops roared, spittle flying from his mouth. I wrinkled my nose against the scent of rotting death that came from the monster as it lumbered forward, arms extended.

"I can't shift," Vanth said through gritted teeth.

My shadows weren't responding, either. "I don't have my magic."

Vanth took a step closer so he was next to me, then rolled his shoulders. "Then we kill him with steel."

Jaw clenched, I nodded. We attacked, charging the monster with our weapons drawn.

The cyclops laughed, sending more foul smelling breath our way. I ducked under a massive hand just before it could strike me, then spun, managing to get a slice across the monster's calf.

He yowled, then struck me again. this time, his hand, which was nearly the size of me, sent me flying across the cave. My back hit the wall, then my head hit with a crack. I managed to maintain my grip on my weapon, but getting up took effort. I blinked, trying to clear my blurry vision.

I took a moment to steady myself, knowing I couldn't charge in if I wasn't able to see clearly. Vanth was attacking the monster by stabbing him, then moving quickly, making the cyclops twist and turn in circles to catch the quick-footed shifter.

It was like watching a cat play with a mouse. I swallowed hard at the thought, knowing that in the end, the mouse rarely wins.

I reentered the fight, ducking behind the cyclops opposite of Vanth. I sliced along the monster's ankle, trying to bring the monster down. He roared in pain, but to my surprise, he didn't turn to me. Instead, he grabbed Vanth, then pulled the sword from the shifter before tossing it to the ground. Vanth screamed as the cyclops squeezed.

I shoved my sword into his ankle again, going as deep

as I could. The cyclops let out a howl and dropped Vanth. The shifter landed on the rocky ground like an abandoned child's toy. He wasn't moving.

My sword was stuck, and before I could get it out, the monster had me in his grip. I hissed out curses as I struggled to get free. If I had my magic, this beast would already be dead.

One huge eye stared down at me and I was face to face with the monster's putrid breath. He bared his rotting teeth and I could see the points on them. They were a predator's teeth, sharp enough to tear into flesh.

"Let me go," I demanded.

The cyclopes laughed. "You come into my home and attack me and you want me to release you?"

"You came at us first," I reminded him.

"Anything that comes into my home becomes my dinner," he snarled.

"We're not here for you. We're here for a sorceress," I confided.

"What do you think all those who came before you were after?"

"I need to see her." I needed to keep him talking. There had to be a way to delay my end. A way to get out of this.

I continued to feel for my magic, trying to find even the smallest thread. Where had it gone? How did it simply vanish?

"You're not even enough for a full meal." He frowned, completely disappointed that I wasn't larger.

I tried for Ara's magic, hoping I could find it. She could

connect with monsters in the sea, surely there was something she could do with a monster like this?

Nothing came.

"I suppose I could save you, in case anyone comes looking for you," he said. "A few more your size would make for a better meal."

His hand tightened around me, crushing me so I couldn't breathe. My arms were pinned to my sides so I couldn't grab at him. I tried to push against his squeezing, but my strength was nothing compared to his. I heard my ribs cracking before the pain burst across my chest. He was going to end me, right here.

I failed.

The pain was making my vision fade, but my thoughts went to Ara. She was counting on me. She was with my mother, fighting her own battle for her own life. She wasn't going to give up. I knew that.

This was not how it ended. I was not going to die here and never hold Ara in my arms again.

I leaned down and bit the cyclops's hand.

He yelled and dropped me. I hit the ground, then everything went black.

25

ARA

THE SOUND of the waves crashing against the shore wasn't enough to help me find comfort. It had been two days since Nyx left me with Dion and I was struggling to keep myself from commandeering a ship to return to Athos.

I stared at the water, hoping to find some solace in the foam that washed ashore. It was dark, the ocean before me an endless expanse of black. There was no moon tonight, making it even more ominous than usual.

I turned to see the path I'd traveled, still illuminated by sparkling fae lights that Dion had left to light the way for the goddess. At least he said that was why he lit the path. I wondered if it was because I'd traversed the trail in the dark last night for a moment of peace by the water.

In another life, I might have enjoyed living on this island. It certainly would have been better than serving at a temple. Dion's maenads avoided me, but when I saw them, they seemed happy. I caught them gardening and painting and splashing in a river. They didn't spend all their time catering to the god. They seemed to do it because they wanted to.

Though, I knew there were things I wasn't privy to, and I wasn't foolish enough to think that Dion's reputation was all false. If I learned anything from my time with the fae and the gods, it was that reputations were earned. And they were rarely inflated.

"I thought I might find you down here."

"Don't tell me you can read minds," I said to Dion as he stepped into the soft sand.

He lifted a brow. "Thinking about me, were you?"

"About how different your island is from what I thought it would be," I admitted.

"You're different than I thought you'd be, too," he said.

Neither of us offered any followup and I don't think either of us wanted it. He stood there next to me, staring into the dark sea for a long while. Finally, he spoke, "She's back. She sent me to find you."

I nodded, keeping my attention on the sea.

"She's going to push you harder this time," he warned.

"It is the final challenge." I'd spent the last several days imagining all the terrible ways she could torture me for her own amusement.

"The stories about her are true, you know."

"I know." I glanced over at Dion, hating that his expression didn't hide his concern.

"Do you know that it's alright to do what's best for you? To allow yourself happiness? To let yourself live," he said.

"I'm not sure I know how to do that," I admitted.

"All the things you've done have been brave, there's no doubt about that. But have you ever stopped to wonder if the people you continue to sacrifice yourself for would do the same for you? Do they deserve what you do for them?"

"I can't let myself ask those questions," I said.

"You should. You should always ask those questions. Because everyone else always asks them," he replied.

"The only question I ask is whether or not I can live with myself if I don't help."

"You're far too good for any of them," he said with a sigh. "Come on, she's waiting."

Reluctantly, I followed him back to the house.

Nyx was waiting outside, holding a glass of wine in her hand.

"He'd choose her even if they weren't mates," Dion suddenly said.

I glanced at the god, my brow furrowing.

"I didn't ask your opinion," Nyx replied. "And I certainly don't need you here right now. You may leave."

Dion squeezed my shoulder. "Remember what I said." He walked into his house, leaving me alone with the goddess of night.

"Is that what this is actually about?" I asked. "Not humans or how they treated you, but the fact that you don't think I'm good enough for your son?"

"This can be about more than one thing," she replied.

"I got you out of your prison for him," I reminded her.

"And then he took your magic. Why wouldn't you want revenge on him?" she asked. "You could have left him to find someone else and you could go fuck Dion or find some human to fill your needs."

I wrinkled my nose. "I'm not with your son because of my—needs." Well, not just that, but I wasn't about to explain that to her.

"We'll see about that." She held out the glass. "Drink."

"What is it?" I asked.

"Your third challenge," she said.

I walked over to her and took the glass. I'd agreed to the challenges, so it wasn't like I could decline. If she wanted me dead, she'd have done it already. Or maybe this was it. She had made it clear she was going to try to eliminate me with each of the challenges.

"Go on, now," she encouraged.

"Can I ask one favor of you?" I asked, the glass poised at my lips.

She lifted a brow and gave a noncommittal shrug.

"If I don't survive, tell Ryvin the truth. Tell him what happened to me and the part you played in it." I kept my eyes locked on hers, waiting for her to flinch.

Instead, she smirked. "Tell him yourself when you next see him."

I tried to mask my confusion.

"Now, stop delaying. I'd like to be done with you." She inclined her head, her eyes dropping to the wineglass. "Drink it all."

I'd faced death more times than I could recall at this point, what was once more? Faking greater bravery than I actually had, I took a tentative sip. When nothing happened, I took another sip. Then I knocked back the rest of the glass in a few large glugs.

Nyx took the glass from my hand and tossed it aside. "Time to go."

The ground was unsteady, the world tilting slightly. She was going in and out of focus.

She lifted her arms and clouds of darkness billowed up around her. They wrapped around me, holding me like a bundle of soft cloth. I felt weightless, but I wasn't sure if it was her magic or the wine.

Just as I was almost enjoying the soft rocking sensation of Nyx's shadows, they dissipated. I knew I was on solid ground, even though I was swaying and struggling to keep myself upright.

"It's kicking in faster than I anticipated," Nyx said. "I might have miscalculated the dosage."

Her words hardly registered as I stared in shocked amazement at the portal in the center of the labyrinth. "We're in Konos."

"Where we first met," she said. "Well, at least where you first met me as I am. The emaciated version in the prison didn't ever feel like me."

"What are we doing here?" My tongue felt thick.

"I'm giving you a choice," Nyx said. "I saw you choose your people over your sisters, but it was a situation that would let you live as a hero. You'd be revered, loved, and hold even more power as the new queen on Athos."

"That's why you think I did that?" I stared at her in disbelief.

"Of course. It didn't prove that you were willing to save your city. It proved that you valued your own life."

"That's not what happened." My throat felt tight as I recalled what it had felt like when I thought my sisters were gone. I wasn't sure I'd have survived to claim the title.

"It doesn't matter. I'm not making that mistake again," she said. "This time, you can choose yourself or you can choose your mate."

My eyes widened. "What did you do to him?"

"I didn't do anything. But he's still about to die. You were dosed with a slow acting poison. You have some time before your body starts shutting down."

"What?" My pulse kicked up.

"This portal can take you to the zarchonii fields in Telos, where you'll find the cure by eating the flowers. Or you can take it to where Ryvin is nearing his final breaths. You can't do both," she said.

"You really are a monster. Your own son?"

"What will it be, Princess of Athos?" she asked, the smile on her lips making me feel sick.

"Ryvin." There was no hesitation. No second thoughts. No need to waste time thinking. "Get me there, now."

She lifted a brow. "There is no portal where he is to get you to Telos. No zarchonii flowers to save you."

"You know why you hate humans so much?" I snapped. "It's because you can't love. You can't begin to comprehend that our fragile little lives might be worth it to us because we can find beauty and joy in the small moments and the people around us. You don't deserve the temple they're building dedicated to you in Athos. I hope they forget you and you fade away with all the other ancient gods nobody can remember."

"That would be something, wouldn't it? It's a pity you won't be around to see it happen." She shoved me into the portal.

I stumbled into darkness, landing on my hands and knees. Something sharp dug into my palm and I recoiled when I realized it was a bone fragment. Very slowly, I stood, working to get my bearings through the spinning of my vision.

The space I was in was dimly lit and the stench was making my stomach churn. I was in the mouth of a cave, the only light coming from behind me, where a fire crackled near the entrance.

Carefully, I turned, doing my best to keep my movements slow and silent. I was standing in a pile of bones and every time they shifted, I froze, hoping I wasn't making too much noise.

Then I saw them. Ryvin and Vanth were both hanging from a wall, tied up like insects in a spider's web.

I didn't even try to stay quiet as I raced toward them. Their eyes were closed, but their breathing was steady. I reached for Ryvin, shaking him gently. "Ryvin, wake up."

His brow furrowed and he groaned. I made a relieved cry, surprising myself with the sound. Ryvin opened his eyes, then narrowed them, as if it was painful to keep them open. "Ara?" His voice was hoarse.

"Thank the gods you're still alive. I'm going to get you two out of here." I shook Vanth. "Wake up, come on. Wake up."

"Ara?" Vanth was just as groggy as Ryvin.

"I'm here, I'm going to get you both down." I started working on the knots holding Ryvin to the wall.

"You have to get out of here," Ryvin said. "Please, go. Before he returns."

"Before who returns?" I was curious, but there was no way I was going to leave them in this cave.

"The cyclops," Ryvin replied.

My hands stilled for a moment, taking in the new information. A cyclops. They were impossibly strong and extremely difficult to kill. They were some of the gods' favorite creations. Extremely skilled with making weapons, they'd been given abilities to survive that humans certainly didn't possess.

I returned to working the knots. "Then we better hurry before he returns."

I finished Ryvin's bindings and he fell from the wall, landing hard. "Sorry!" I hurried to help him up, then turned my attention to the shifter.

"You two go, don't waste time with me," Vanth said.

"You know me better than that," I said.

"How are you here?" Ryvin asked, moving alongside me to help with some of the other knots. At least he appeared in relatively good health.

"Your mother sent me to help you," I said, adjusting the truth just a little, so I didn't worry him. If we got out of here safely, I could say my goodbyes and explain more.

"She's lying to you," Vanth said.

"I know," Ryvin agreed.

I stayed silent and finished the last knot on my side,

allowing Vanth to fall from the wall. He landed more gracefully than Ryvin had. The shifter rubbed his arms where the ropes had left red marks. "We need to get away from here."

"We have to find the sorceress," Ryvin said. "And I don't think her pet cyclops is going to let us reach her if he's still breathing."

Vanth leaned down and picked up a long bone that was probably from a leg. "The eye is the only weakness."

"How do we reach it? I can't use my shadows," Ryvin said.

Guilt squeezed in around me. "Was that my fault? I used them."

"No, there's something preventing magic here," he clarified.

I started walking toward the entrance. The fire was still crackling away, and I noticed that a massive roasting spit was positioned above it. It was large enough to support a man. A chill ran down my spine. He was preparing to eat my friends.

"Where are you going?" Rvyin asked.

"I have an idea." I stepped out of the cave, Ryivn and Vanth behind me. My steps were a little uneven and there was a spin on the world around me. I knew I wasn't going to be the best person for the task.

"I need both of you up there." I pointed to the rocky opening of the cave. "When he arrives, you jump on him."

"What are you going to do?" Ryvin asked.

"I'm the bait."

26

I WAITED NEAR THE CAVE, behind a large shrub that mostly shielded me from view. Between the smell coming from the cave, and the fact that cyclops are rarely challenged, I hoped he wouldn't be able to detect me until I was ready.

It felt like forever waiting there. I was getting restless, moving from foot to foot, while giving myself the occasional break to close my eyes so I could have a reprieve from the spinning. My stomach churned and I was starting to sweat. The poison was getting worse. I wasn't sure how much time I had.

Several times, I wanted to leave my spot and check on Ryvin and Vanth, but I couldn't risk giving any of us away. Finally, I heard the unmistakable sound of a lumbering creature. As I hoped, the cyclops didn't care if anyone knew it was coming. At least that meant he was probably the worst monster around. Hopefully, he was the only one guarding the sorceress.

Heavy footsteps came closer, and I prepared to be caught. Swallowing hard, I tried to convince myself that I was going to be fine. That the waves of nausea weren't distracting. That I didn't need the ground to be still to complete my task.

The monster stopped in front of his fire, dropping some wood on it before stoking it. Then he headed toward his cave.

I moved, making the shrub rustle. I shifted so more of me was uncovered, then ducked behind again, as if desperate to stay out of sight.

I couldn't watch the monster anymore, but I heard the steps getting closer.

"Who dares come to my home? Are you here for your friends? I was hoping I'd get a few more of you for my dinner," the cyclops called.

I balled my hands into fists and prepared myself. I knew it was possible this was it for me, but I was already on borrowed time.

Making what I hoped was a believable startled scream, I ran. The monster laughed, giving chase.

I ran until I was positioned in the correct place, then stopped and stared at the cyclops. The fear in my expression wasn't false. He towered over me, his fists larger than my head. The giant eye was locked on me and he grinned at me, his expression full of hungry malice. He was already drooling and I could see the sharp points of his rotting teeth.

"Please," I begged. "Please don't eat me."

He reached a massive hand toward me, and I tensed, preparing to be captured. Instead, he roared and flung his hands away from me, flailing wildly as he tried to get the two men off his back.

Ryvin and Vanth were holding on with everything they had as Vanth climbed on top of the monster's shoulders. He leaned forward, preparing to strike while Ryvin used a blade to poke at the cyclops every time his hands came too close to the shifter.

I turned away just as Vanth shoved the bone in the monster's eye. When I looked back, I caught him slicing his sword through the already injured eye. The bone stuck out, looking impossibly small in the massive eyeball, but the blade had sliced all the way across.

The cyclops screamed, the sound making me cover my ears. Ryvin and Vanth were now attacking the monster, going for his neck while the cyclops was trying to cover his injured eye.

I couldn't watch. I'd killed people, but this was brutal. The monster was so large, it dragged on. It felt cruel, but then I reminded myself he planned to eat me.

When I opened my eyes, I saw that the cyclops' mouth had gone slack. He swayed, then began to fall like a tree that had been hacked down with an axe.

Rvyin and Vanth leaped from his shoulders, landing in the dirt nearby. We all stared at the monster, as if waiting for him to rise and charge us again.

"I think he's dead," Vanth said.

Ryvin returned his weapon to its sheath, then bypassed

the fallen monster to reach me. He pulled me into his arms and I relaxed into him, feeling nothing but relief that I'd saved him. It didn't matter if it cost me my own life. He'd get to keep living, and that was enough.

Thunder rumbled overhead, and I felt the first drop of rain on my arm. Instinctively, I looked to the sky, but with the incoming storm, there were no stars. Raindrops hit with more frequency, making the fire flicker and sizzle.

"We should get inside," Vanth suggested.

Ryvin kept his arm around me as we entered the cave, which helped me appear steadier than I was. My hands were shaking, though, and I felt both too hot and too cold. But he was alive, even if I wasn't going to be for much longer.

"Do you think the entrance is in here somewhere?" Vanth asked, already searching the walls.

"It might be." Ryvin moved away from me and sent several fae lights into the space, brightening it as if we were outdoors under the midday sun.

The walls were splashed with dark dried blood and every bit of the floor was covered in bones. How long had people come here and ended up as a meal for this monster? I didn't even know this sorceress existed before this, but she must have had a lot of people coming to her over the years. Had the Fae King done that? Come here and appease the cyclops somehow so he could meet with the sorceress? Or had she gone to him?

I carefully waded through the piles of bones, trying not to think too hard about how many had died to leave behind this many.

We scoured the walls, brushing fingertips over the stone, searching for any signs of expansion or secret passages. As I moved along, I noticed a breeze that didn't belong. Like someone was blowing at me.

Kneeling, I found the source and passed my fingers in front of the small hole. Dirt fell as I brushed my fingers around it, trying to determine if it might be something of importance.

Suddenly, the room rumbled.

"What's happening?" Vanth called.

"I think I did something," I stood and stepped away from the wall, running into Ryvin who'd already come to where I was.

A gap appeared in the wall as a door slid open.

"Good find, Ara," Ryvin said.

"Let's hope she's home," I replied.

I braced myself for another tunnel but was surprised to find an open space enclosed by tall rocks. A hidden open cave of sorts, buried in the stones. The ground was covered in lush grasses and fragrant flowers. A warm breeze blew past, bringing the scent of salt to mingle with the strong florals.

"What is this place?" I looked around in awe. It was an oasis, a paradise hidden away from view.

It wasn't a large space, but it was big enough for a small home, no larger than the shacks that lined the poorest areas in Athos. Outside the building, sitting on a bench, was a woman clothed in flowing white fabric. She had long, dark hair and a pale complexion that made me wonder if she was even actually here. She might as well be a phantom.

"None of you are supposed to be here." The woman stood, the fabric of her dress moving in opposition to the wind. A phenomenon I'd seen once before.

"You're the sorceress?" I asked in disbelief.

The Fate smiled, her mouth was full of black teeth. I shuddered and took a step back.

Morta had always been intimidating, but compared to this fate, she was a warm and welcoming presence. This fate radiated death and destruction. I could feel it and I knew it wasn't just the fact that I was knocking on the door of the Underworld as we stood here.

"You're not allowed to take sides, Nona. Why would you give my father something of such power?" Ryvin asked.

"Why did Morta help you all those times, Prince of Darkness?" The Fate took a step closer, setting her dark eyes on me. Though she didn't appear to be blind like her sister, she had the same penetrating gaze, like she was looking through me.

"Morta has never aided one side over the other. She's given me advice, mostly in the form of riddles, but never any gifts. Nothing that would sway my path."

"Except for keeping this one alive." She pointed a gnarled finger at me. "She was meant to die."

"Is this your retribution for that, then?" Ryvin asked. "If it is, take it out on me, not on all of Athos and Drakous. My father doesn't deserve the gifts you've given him."

"None of that matters anymore," Nona said. "Ara has

tempted us for the last time. She'll be in the Underworld before any of you leave this island."

Ryvin pulled out his sword. "Threatening my mate was the wrong move."

"No, wait." I ran in front of him, stepping between Ryvin and Nona. "She's not threatening me. She's telling you the truth."

Ryvin lowered his weapon. "What are you talking about?"

"Ara, what are you saying?" Vanth asked.

Nona watched us with a wicked smile on her lips. I looked away from her, not wanting to see her entertained expression. "It was the final challenge from Nyx. She poisoned me."

Rvyin's hands were on my cheeks in a heartbeat. He tilted my face up so I was looking into the swirling silver depths of his eyes. "No. That's impossible. You're fine. You're here, you're talking to us, you saved us in the cave."

I set my hands on top of his and fought against the rising tears. "I made a choice. I could go for the antidote, or I could save you."

"No." Ryvin rested his forehead on mine and I could feel his warm breath on my face. "Please tell me this is some dark lie. Please tell me it's not true."

"I'm so sorry." Tears rolled down my cheeks. "I couldn't let you die."

"I will die without you," he said.

"No, you won't. You promised me you'd look after my family. You promised you'd look after Athos," I said, suddenly remembering what he'd told me. When I made my choice, none of that came to mind, but now that I was here, I remembered everything we ever said. All our stolen moments, all the times we'd been together. It had been far too short, but I wouldn't trade it for anything.

"Touching, really," a new voice said.

I looked over to see another woman standing near Nona. She had the same dark hair and deathly complexion. Her cool green eyes reminded me of the first sprouts of spring.

Ryvin grabbed me, shoving me behind him. "You can't have her. This is Nyx's doing. It's not her time."

"It was her time long ago, Princeling."

Vanth drew his weapon and stood next to Ryvin. "Morta cuts, not you, Decima."

"Morta has been compromised," Decima replied. "Ara was supposed to leave this world as soon as she entered it. She's had more time than she should have already."

"Where is Morta?" Ryvin demanded. "Call her here. I know you two can do that. Get her here now."

I set my hand on Ryvin's arm. "It's going to be alright."

"It will be once I ensure that your thread can't be cut," he said.

There was a popping sound and for a moment, the space next to Decima was blurry. I thought maybe I was imagining things until I saw Morta materialize next to her sister.

"So many calling my name," she said as she floated toward us.

"You can't have her," Ryvin said protectively.

Morta frowned, and I got the sense she wanted to speak but was holding back.

Ryvin and Vanth both moved in front of me and I shoved my way through them.

"You can't fight off the fates." I turned and faced them, then reached for Ryvin's hand. "I made my choice. You can't tell me you wouldn't have done the same thing."

"I can't do this without you," he said.

"Yes, you can. You must." I reached over and took Vanth's hand. "You two are going to win this, then you're both going to find happiness."

A tear streamed down Ryvin's cheek and he quickly brushed it away. I released their hands, then turned to face the fates, focusing my attention on Nona. "You will remove whatever extra power you bestowed on the Fae King."

Nona's sisters gaped at her. "What did you do?" Decima asked.

"What I had to," Nona hissed. "I'm finished being a tool for the gods. I want to control my own fate, not just everyone else's."

"So you gave power to a madman?" Decima asked.

"You know more than us what that outcome will be," Morta said.

"It's the only path that might give us the power we deserve," she shot back.

"You're trading one master for another," Decima snapped. "The Fae King does not share power."

"He stole his own mate's magic and buried her in an underground prison," Morta explained. "He would gladly sacrifice his own children. And you think you'll be the one to stand against him?"

"He's using you, you idiot," Decima spat.

"They all use us," Nona snarled. "We can defeat him. Together."

"Not with the power you gave him." I pulled away from Ryvin. "We were there. We saw the control he has. What do you think will happen once he claims Athos? He's turned everyone into an ally because they fear him."

"And it won't be long before they turn against him," Decima said. "You know I speak the truth. You'll gain your power, but over a world of corpses."

"There will be nobody left but us and the gods," Morta said.

I shivered at the chilling picture.

"You know we speak truth," Decima said gently.

Nona's lower lip was trembling, and I suddenly saw her more like a spoiled child than a grown woman. Let alone a deity who could control and command human lives.

"You're certain?" she asked.

Decima and Morta simply stared at their sister.

I watched them, my breathing growing more difficult by the heartbeat. Fighting against the exhaustion and the desire to close my eyes, I waited.

Finally, Nona nodded. "Fine. I will revoke the gift."

I let out a long breath. "Thank you." Ryvin and Vanth echoed my gratitude, but their tones were muted.

"You will owe me a favor," Nona replied.

"I'd be happy to give you one, but I'm afraid I won't be here to repay it," I said.

She scowled. "You are not meant to die yet."

"I thought I didn't have a path?" I asked.

"You do now," Nona said. "You have changed the stars, Ara of Athos."

"I hate when they do that," Decima said. "I don't like changes."

"How?" I took a step closer to the fates, but my unsteady legs nearly gave way. Ryvin caught me.

"Does this mean she'll pass the poison?" Ryvin asked.

"No, it means someone will have to save her," Morta answered.

"The spring here," Vanth suddenly said. "Are the stories true?"

Morta grinned, an unsettling sight. "I suppose you'll have to find out."

27

Ryvin

Ara was struggling to walk even with me, carrying most of her weight as she leaned on me. She was trying to hide it, but her breathing gave her away. The ragged sound was a warning. A sound that indicated it was time for any family to say their goodbyes.

That wasn't going to happen.

I scooped her into my arms and she leaned her head against my chest, not even protesting the help. That told me everything I needed to know. I was dangerously close to losing her. I kissed her forehead. "Stay with me, Asteri."

Each step deeper into the earth felt more perilous. The spring under the oasis was supposed to have extraordinary healing abilities. It was the reason so many came to this island, only to seal their fate as a meal for the cyclops. I now suspected its waters were what created the garden above me. It was a good sign if it could create that much thriving life on such an otherwise barren island.

The steps weren't actual steps. More like indents on a decline. I slipped on the green moss and held tight to Ara, bracing her against my chest so I didn't drop her. My hip slammed into the ground and hissed out a curse. Ara didn't even react.

My pulse raced and I brushed her dark hair away from her face. Her eyes were closed and she was so pale. Sweat covered her forehead in a sheen, but when I touched her she was as cold as ice. "Asteri?" I pressed my fingers to the side of her neck and held my breath while I waited for her pulse. It was so faint I wasn't sure if I was imagining it. Leaning down, I lowered my cheek so it was right next to her mouth and nose. The rattling was gone, but her breathing was so shallow and rapid I wasn't even sure how she was getting the air she needed.

Determined to make it to the spring, I stood, readjusting her so I was holding her with one arm. I used my other hand to help me balance against the moss-covered wall. It was just as slick and damp as the steps.

There was nothing ahead of me but darkness. Morta hadn't given any indication as to how far down the spring was. I wondered if I was traveling into the Underworld itself.

I sent two fae lights ahead, then clenched my jaw with frustration when I only saw more stairs and more darkness. There was no giving up, though. There was only one option, and it was saving my mate.

"I never told you what I wanted to do after I eliminated

my father." I looked down at her, foolish hope making me think that maybe she'd open her eyes. They remained closed. I paused my progress and removed my hand from the wall so I could feel for her breath. When I found it, I started walking again.

"I had plans, you know," I continued. "But you came along and changed all that." I chuckled to myself. "I suppose I did the same for you. Sometimes I wonder if it would have been better for you if I never met you. If your life would be easier. Happier. Without me."

I paused again, then kissed her cold forehead. "But I'm too selfish to let you find that out. Now that I have you, I'm never letting you go."

I waved the fae lights forward, urging them deeper as I continued the decline. "But you've made it clear you're the same. That stupid move you made by saving me instead of saving yourself. I might never forgive you for that. You know that, right?"

The sound of water dripping echoed around me and my heart swelled. I looked ahead, willing the spring to appear in the darkness. It was still nothing but slippery steps. "I hear something. Hang on, please, hang on."

After a few more steps, I checked her breathing again. "Asteri, can you hear me? I need you to wake up. I have so much I never told you. Did you know I never planned to be king of Konos?

"I never admitted that to anyone. I wanted Nyx to claim the throne. She'd have more children. It's what the gods do. By the time she tired of ruling, I figured her other children could fight it out amongst themselves. I'd be long gone. I always thought maybe I'd find out what was on the other continents. I aways thought it would be worth battling the monsters in the sea to find out. Maybe you'd go with me. Maybe you'd tame the monsters along the way."

I paused again, leaning down to feel breath.

I waited.

And waited.

Panic surged, and I pressed my fingers to her neck.

Nothing.

No pulse.

No breath.

My shadows billowed around me, angry surging tendrils that blotted out the fae lights, but I was blinded by my rage. I was not going to lose her.

I fell forward, letting the shadows catch me, then I ran. The shadows propelled me along, letting me bypass the steps. I was moving into darkness as fast as I could. After a few breaths, my mind cleared enough that I thought to throw out fae lights as I raced down the tunnel.

They blurred as I passed them, throwing more and more as I flew toward the bottomless pit. If this was a dead end, I was going to kill all the fates. And then I was going to find and kill my mother.

My shadows reared up, forming a barrier that I crashed into. I let out a frustrated scream and they scattered. Leaving me standing at the bottom of the chasm.

I'd made it.

And there, just as promised, was a pool of clear water. I didn't wait before jumping in with Ara in my arms.

28

THE COLD WATER stole my breath, but I pulled us both under completely, holding Ara with me for several heartbeats before emerging. I moved to the side and leaned Ara's unresponsive body against the rocks. "Come on, wake up."

I pushed the hair from her face and leaned closer, feeling for breath while I pressed my fingers to her neck. I felt the faintest flicker of a pulse. "Asteri, wake up."

Warm breath ghosted my cheek and I pulled her to me, a burst of elation surging. I hadn't lost her yet. I was certain she was doing better, but until she opened her eyes, it meant nothing. "Please, please wake up."

I pressed my cheek against hers, feeling her skin against mine. I whispered in her ear, telling her everything

I thought she'd want to hear. "We're going to have a long, happy life together. We'll see your sisters all the time. We'll stay in Athos if you want. We'll travel far away if you want. Anything. Anything you need if you just stay with me. Please, Asteri, please wake up."

I pulled her close to me, holding her tight. I could feel her warm breath against my neck, feel her heartbeat against my chest. Then I heard the smallest sound. It was a little squeak or moan. Something I couldn't quite place, but I knew it was Ara.

I adjusted, letting her fall against my arm and giving space between us so I could see her better. Her eyelids were fluttering, her brow furrowed adorably.

My heart felt like it was going to explode. "I'm here, Asteri, I'm here. I've got you."

She grunted and made more squeaking noises that made my heart soar. I kissed her cheek and smoothed back her wet hair again. "Please wake up."

"Ryvin?" Her eyes were open in little slits, but she was looking up at me.

"I'm here." Joy surged through me, and I had to hold myself back from squeezing her in my arms. "I'm here. You're going to be alright. You're going to be fine."

Her eyelids fluttered again, and she opened them, glancing around the darkened cave. The few fae lights flickered around us, but it was largely shadowed. I sent a few more fae lights into the air, creating a dazzling display like little stars above us.

Her lips parted. "It's beautiful." Her voice was gravelly, but she was speaking. "Where are we?"

"Do you remember what happened?" I asked gently.

Her eyes widened. "Am I dead? You didn't kill yourself, did you?"

"No, no." I smoothed her hair again, trying to reassure her. "We're in a healing spring hidden under the oasis where Nona lives."

She looked around again. "The poison?"

"You nearly died," I confirmed.

"The spring cures it?" she asked.

I nodded, my throat suddenly too thick to speak. I couldn't let myself think about what would have happened if I'd been too late. If the spring hadn't worked.

She laughed, the sound musical. It made me join in and I pulled her into my embrace. She threw her arms around me, still laughing. "I'm alive. I can't believe it. Thank you."

"I can't do this without you," I confessed. "I thought I was going to lose you."

"You saved me." She leaned back and stared at me, her gaze penetrating and searching. "I came here to save you, and you ended up saving me."

"I told you long ago, I'll never let anything bad happen to you," I reminded her. It was a promise I'd made her that I'd had to abandon too many times. I couldn't keep it when she went off on her own, but she was strong and capable and I trusted her. She needed a lot less saving that she did when we first met. Every time she gained power and confidence, my love for her deepened.

She wasn't the same woman I'd met in Athos. She was stronger, fiercer, braver. And I couldn't wait to see how much more she'd become as she truly welcomed and developed the magic she'd been cut off from for so long. "But maybe you should be making that promise to me instead."

"How about we agree no more monsters for a while?" she teased.

"I like that agreement." I cupped her cheek, studying her. "I'd rather take you somewhere far away where I know you'll be safe."

"You know we can't do that," she replied.

"I know. But gods, Asteri, watching the life leave your body..." I blew out a long breath.

"I know how you felt," she replied. "If my mother hadn't had that antidote..."

"No more poison, then," I said, trying to lighten the mood.

Tears fell down her cheeks and she chuckled. "Agree. No more of that, either."

I wiped her tears with my thumb, then kissed her cheekbones, hoping to send the tears away. She captured my face in her hands, then pulled, her lips meeting mine in a hungry kiss. I picked her up and she threw her legs around my waist, making me tumble forward slightly. She was pressed against the rocks on the edge of the spring, and I leaned into her, devouring her mouth with mine.

Our tongues clashed, and I felt her fingers reaching for my tunic. The sopping wet fabric was stuck to my body, making it more difficult to remove. I pulled away from the kiss, gasping for air and hurrying to strip my clothes. I tossed the sopping wet tunic outside the spring before removing my trousers.

Ara was working the fabric of her clothing and I stepped in, helping remove the clothes and throwing them with mine outside the spring. She was back on me the moment I released her soaking clothing from my hands.

I kissed her back with urgency, unable to shake how I'd almost lost her. I held her tight, unwilling to let her go. "Please, don't ever choose me over yourself again." I whispered against her ear. "I can't lose you."

"I can't make that promise," she said, her brow furrowed as she stared at me. "I would save you every time. You know that, don't you?"

I did know that, because it was the same way I felt. I answered by claiming her mouth. She returned my passion with her own sense of urgency. The kiss demonstrated all our relief that the other was alive. I couldn't get enough of her. I needed her.

She wrapped her legs around me again and a shiver ran down my spine as she brushed against my cock. Holding her tightly, I entered her, a groan passing through my lips as I did. She moaned into my mouth, then kissed me even more fervently.

The water splashed around us, cool against my hot skin. I leaned her against the smooth rocks and she lay back, her chest rising and falling as she sucked in rapid breaths. Her hands trailed against my chest and I grabbed her hips, thrusting deeper into her. Her eyes closed and she moaned as her hands moved to my arms. She gripped me hard, her fingernails digging into my biceps. The bite of pain sent a rush of pleasure through me as I continued to thrust.

Leaning down, I kissed her again, desperate to maintain closeness to her. She threw her arms around me, holding me down close to her. I continued to thrust, breathing in the scent of her hair mixed with the sulfur of the water. I kissed her neck and collarbone before returning to her lips.

She was tensing under me, her breaths hitching, occasionally halting as little shivers of pleasure overcame her. I could tell she was holding back, resisting climax. I was close but I wanted her to give in. "Let go, Asteri. Don't hold back."

She whimpered, then gasped before a series of tiny cries escaped her lips in rhythm with her exhales. Her back arched and she closed her eyes, the sounds growing louder with each thrust. I leaned down and nipped at her nipple, then moved to the other, alternating between gentle kisses and using my teeth.

Her whole body tensed and she screamed, her hips bucking as she finally gave in to her release. It sent me over the edge, and I groaned as I joined her in climax, finishing as she began to tremble, her body responding to the pleasure.

I lifted her from the rocks again, pulling her close to me so I could change positions, putting myself against the rocks. She relaxed into me, her body melting against mine. I kissed her brow, then her cheek. "I'm the luckiest man alive."

She gave me a sleepy smile. "We're both lucky."

As she closed her eyes and took steady breaths, I said a silent prayer to the gods. They'd never responded to me, but if honoring them was something I could do to keep her alive, I'd do whatever it took.

"We should get back to the Oasis," I said after we'd both caught our breath.

"It's tempting to stay there, isn't it?" she asked.

"I could do it, even if it meant dealing with Nona, but I don't think you could," I replied.

She was quiet for a moment, then looked up at me. I could see the sparkle of life in her eyes again. I wasn't sure the last time I'd seen that look from her. "You're right. I guess we better go defeat the king so we can go anywhere we want."

I helped her out of the spring and we managed to get our sopping clothing back on. The walk out wasn't nearly as long or tedious. I could walk behind this woman for the rest of my life and never get tired of watching her.

We were two steps out of the entry to the cave when Ara was tackled by Vanth. She laughed as he lifted her and swung her around in a circle. For the first time, I didn't feel any jealousy. I saw friendship and love that I was grateful for. I knew if something ever happened to me, I could count on Vanth to support Ara.

I'm not sure what was in that water, but I was grateful.

Vanth released Ara. "I'm so glad you're alive."

"I'm happy to be alive," Ara said. "What did we miss?"

Vanth glanced over at me, then looked back at Ara.

"The fates left. Something about being needed for cutting a lot of threads."

The joy hanging in the air around us faded, and I watched as Vanth and Ara tensed, their expressions hardening into those of warriors.

"Let's go help them determine which threads they should cut, then, shall we?" Ara asked.

29

ARA

THERE WERE a dozen ships in the harbor as Athos came into view. "Those aren't fae ships."

"No, those aren't," Rvyin agreed.

The captain approached us, his face pale. "We have to turn around. Our ship isn't prepared for battle."

"They aren't here to fight us," Vanth told him.

"It's Thebes, isn't it?" I said, recalling Aspasia's promise. Ryvin nodded.

"Vampires? Here in Athos?" The captain was sweating now. "I thought we were expecting the fae. We can't fight off both."

"They're here to help," I said. "We've made an agreement with them." It was a bit of a lie. Athos had never negotiated with the vampires as far as I knew. We were taking all this based on Aspasia's word.

"She'll honor what she said," Rvyin whispered.

I gave him a look, hoping he could interpret it. It was both annoying and reassuring when he guessed what I was thinking. He took hold of my hand and gave it a squeeze.

"There's nobody in the ships," someone called.

The captain walked toward the bow, squinting into the distance. "I don't see anyone either."

"They must be in the city," I suggested.

"Maintain course," the captain called.

The sailors were quiet as we pulled into the harbor. I could see the empty ships sitting there. Though they were similar to the ships used by Athos and Konos, they were just different enough in their shape that they stood out. "They're going to tip off the fae that we have help by leaving those there."

"I'm sure there's a plan," Rvyin said. "I hope."

"We won't be here when this all goes down," the captain said suddenly. "We're restocking supplies, then we'll travel to Telos to wait this out."

Ryvin removed something from his pocket and handed it to the Captain. "If anyone questions you, show this."

The Captain inclined his head. "It's been an honor sailing with you, Your highness." He turned to me. "Princess."

He left us and began to shout orders to prepare for docking. I looked over at Ryvin. "What did you give him?"

"Fae coin with my father's royal seal. They're very rare and only used by the inner circle. It should help him survive if we aren't successful."

I turned and stared at the city, trying not to dwell on

his statement. It was the first time I'd heard him mention the possibility that we'd fail.

The city was nearly abandoned when we walked through. I longed for the days when my biggest fear in town was the stares I'd get from the citizens who knew who I was. As we neared the road out of town toward the palace, we saw a few groups carrying bags and bundles.

"Looks like your sister opened the gates," Vanth said.

"That's good. Hopefully, we'll be able to keep them safe," I replied.

None of the people walking seemed to notice us as we passed them. They were too focused on carrying their goods and keeping their children moving to worry about anything else.

Athos had been through too much in such a short time. They needed us to defeat the Fae King so we could finally find safety. Maybe we could open our doors, expand trade and travel. I found a giddy sense of hope as I considered our potential alliance with Thebes and our newfound alliance with Drakous. I glanced over at Ryvin. "Are you planning to take over Konos when this is done?"

He stiffened. "I never planned to rule Konos."

"Will Laera take over, then?" I asked.

"Please no," Vanth cut in. "Besides, she'll be heir to the Court of Vipers."

"Let's defeat the current ruler before we worry about who takes his place," Ryvin replied.

It was interesting to see how he reacted. Growing up, it was always expected that Lagina would rule. I was next in line, but planned to pass it to Cora if anything happened. I wondered what Ryvin's plan had been since he was the eldest. Was it never discussed since the Fae King was immortal?

We were nearly to the palace and could see the wide open gates. Beyond them, there were people everywhere. I noticed blue uniforms dotted throughout the masses. The guards looked like they were directing people while others were handing things out.

Ryvin stopped and lifted his arm into the air. "Do you feel that?"

I stilled next to him and glanced over at Vanth. The shifter was also reaching his hand into the air.

"It's like the one on the island," Vanth said.

"Not as strong, though," Rvyin replied.

"It's easy to breach," Vanth said, extending his hand.

Brows furrowed, I followed their motions and touched something cold and strange in the air. I couldn't see anything, but there was a definite change. "What is that?"

"Shield. They must have gotten an old one up and running," Ryvin said as he stepped forward. He frowned. "They'll need to fortify it better. It didn't keep me out and I'm half fae. It won't be of much use if fae can walk right through."

Vanth crossed the invisible line next, shrugging when he was beside Ryvin. "Didn't stop a shifter, either."

Nervously, I took a few steps. Cold sliced through me, making me gasp. But it was gone so quickly, I wondered if I'd imagined it. "So that's a magical shield?"

"Yes, but it's weak," Ryvin said.

"We were hoping you'd return before we finished setting it up," Laera called.

I grinned when I saw her.

"Welcome back. It's nice to see all of you still breathing," she said. "Come on, I'll walk you in and catch you up on what you missed along the way."

We found Lagina in the study, pouring over maps and plans with Argus and two generals who'd worked under my father.

They all stopped when we entered, and Lagina abandoned her maps to race toward me. She pulled me into an embrace. "Thank the gods you've returned." Holding me out at arm's distance, she studied me. "You're alright?"

"I'm fine," I assured her.

"And you did it? Bested Nyx?" she asked.

"I survived her challenges," I replied. "I wouldn't say I bested her. She got her licks in."

"I'm sorry. I want to hear all about it, but Laera says her father is on his way," Lagina said. "And we're having some concerns with our new allies."

"She wants us to work with vampires," one of the generals said, not hiding his disdain.

"You're looking for sympathy in the wrong place," I retorted. "I'm half god." I pointed to Ryvin, Vanth, and Laera. "And you've got a half-god, half fae, a shifter, and a full fae. And those vampires are offering to help us."

"We lost half our men because of him," the general snarled, turning his glare on Ryvin.

"And I killed your king," Ryvin replied.

"Not helpful," I said.

"Enough. Mortagan, you've served Athos longer than I've been alive. You served my father well. If you are no longer capable of doing what's best for us, you will receive full honors in your retirement," Lagina said.

General Mortagan's eyes widened. "You'd do that?"

"I would. We have one chance at this. If you want to help us, you're welcome to stay. If you're going to be a complication, I need you to leave." She stared at him with all the power I'd seen used by her mother and the authority of our father.

I pressed my lips together to keep from smiling. She was stepping into the queen thing better than I could have ever imagined.

"Fine. But if they betray us—" Mortagan began.

"—the fae will kill us all anyway," I finished for him. "We take our chances working together or we surrender. There's no other option."

He grumbled, but nodded once. "I will meet with the general from Thebes."

"I'll go with him," Vanth offered. "You worked with me once before. I fought with your men. You know I'm honorable."

"I have no problem with you. It's them I don't trust," he threw a sideways glance at Ryvin and Laera.

Laera made a show of checking her nails, as if this was the most boring conversation she'd ever had to withstand.

"We should invite their leader to our meeting," the other general, who'd been silent until now, said as he moved away from the table. "They should be part of the plan. We need to know their strengths and how to best position them against the fae."

"I agree," Lagina said.

"We'll return soon," Mortagan bowed to Lagina. "Your highness."

Vanth patted Ryvin on the shoulder before following the general out of the study. The other general joined them, leaving me with my sister as the only other Athonian in the room.

Her shoulders drooped and she let out a slow breath, as if she was releasing all the tension she'd been holding for weeks.

I crossed to her and took her hand. "How are you doing?"

She let out a sound that was almost like a laugh. "This is not what I expected my time as queen would be."

"When was the last time you rested?" I asked.

"I did get some sleep last night after we got the shields up," she said. "Don't worry about me, I'll be fine. You're the one who just returned from trials I can't even imagine."

"You're doing amazing," I assured her.

"It's not over yet," she said.

"And there's the wedding," Laera added.

My brow furrowed, and I looked over at the Fae Princess. "What wedding?"

"Tonight. The Dragon King came all the way back to Athos just for Cora," Laera explained.

"Really? He's making her do that now?" Anger made my face feel hot.

"Ara, you're hurting my hand," Lagina said.

I released her quickly. "Sorry."

"It was Cora's idea," Lagina said.

I shook my head. "I don't understand."

"Maybe the bond got to her," Laera suggested.

"She wanted to ensure the alliance," Lagina said. "I tried to talk her out of it, but you know Cora. Once she's made up her mind on something, it's happening."

"Tonight?" I asked.

"Sunset," Lagina said.

"Is this really the best use of our time?" I asked.

"You should invite the people," Ryvin said. "Do it somewhere they can see it and be part of it. Give everyone something to celebrate. A moment of distraction."

"That's a good idea," Lagina said. "You really do think like a king, you know that?"

Ryvin looked a little pale.

Someone knocked on the door, and Argus crossed the room to open it. Sophia's whole face lit up when she saw us. I didn't even get to say hello before I was wrapped in her arms.

"I'm glad you're back. I could use some help," she said as she released me from her embrace.

"Whatever you need," I offered.

"Great. You find the flowers for Cora's bouquet," she said cheerfully.

30

THE DAY WAS a blur of flowers and silk and mountains of pastries. The kitchens made as much food as they did for the Choosing, only this time, it was for a celebration.

Sophia took over, just as Ophelia would have, making sure that everything was going to be beautiful. Even Ryvin and Vanth joined in, helping to build a platform for the bride and groom to stand on during their ceremony.

The only thing missing was Cora. I hadn't seen her since arriving and every time I tried to make my way to her rooms, I was given another task to complete. She'd been completing as much of the pre-wedding traditions as she could, but I hated that she was doing them alone. She'd traveled with Argus to make offerings at the temples, and I knew Lagina had sent some of the special oils their mother had used for her to bathe and prepare for the ceremony.

When we were nearing sunset, I finally made my way to her room to check on her.

"Come in," she called in response to my knock.

I entered the room and found her sitting in her undergarments, staring at a pile of gorgeous saffron colored silk. I brushed my fingers over it. "This is beautiful. Did your mother set it aside for you?"

"It was a gift from Bahar. Apparently, he had it brought when he first arrived, but asked Lagina to store it for me so he wouldn't scare me away." She looked up at me and fixed a diplomatic smile on her lips. "How are you? I haven't seen you enough lately."

"Don't do that, Cora," I said. "Don't entertain me. I'm here to check on you, not ask you to play hostess."

She hummed, then returned her attention to the dress. "I know she wasn't the best mother, but I miss her. I wish she was here."

I moved closer so I could put my arm around her. She leaned into me, resting her head on my upper chest. "I'm sorry she's not here. I'm sorry for everything you've had to endure the last few weeks. You shouldn't be doing this so quickly."

She sat up and turned her stunning blue eyes on me. "I think I feel the mating bond."

I lifted my brows, surprised by the change of topic. "Oh?"

"He wasn't going to marry me. I might have used some of my... special skills to change his mind," she confessed.

"He was going to marry you eventually," I replied. "That was why he came here in the first place."

"I know. But when he returned and said he'd wait, it was like it changed something in me. I don't know how to explain the sensation. I know he cares about me. Which makes no sense. We don't even know each other," she said.

"Mating bonds are..." I struggled to come up with the correct word, "different."

She chuckled. "That's one way to put it."

"I think he's a good man," I added. "He has demonstrated that he cares for his people, and he's been helping Athos to show he cares for you."

"I thought I understood men. I thought I knew what they wanted. I thought I was there to look pretty and fill their beds. I don't know how to be a queen," she said.

"You'll learn," I said.

"Will you? You never wanted to be queen, and now your mate is next in line for Konos while we actively try to kill their current king," she pointed out.

My mouth felt dry. "That's complicated."

"Tell me about it," she answered with a heavy sigh.

We both sat in silence for a long moment. I wished I could say something comforting, but I wasn't sure which of her concerns I should address.

Suddenly, she stood. "You'll help me dress."

I rose. "Of course."

She picked up the shimmery saffron fabric, then passed it to me. I took it from her and noticed that it was embroidered with small orange flames along the hem. A fiery dress for a future Queen of the Dragons.

I helped her into the chiton, draping and pinning it as I

went. When I was finished, I stepped back, taking her in. "It's stunning. A perfect color for you."

She smiled, but it was a tight, tense smile.

"Would you like me to help you with your hair?" I offered.

"Please." She sat down on the small stool at her vanity.

The servants were either helping with the influx of people we had on our grounds, or they'd left to be with their families. A pang of sadness made my chest ache as I recalled all the times Mila had helped me with my hair. What I wouldn't give to have her back with me, just so I could tell her how much she meant to me. We'd had so much loss and I knew there would be more before this was over. I wondered if the ache in my chest would ever fully cease.

I did my best to twist and pin her hair. I added pearls and gold beads to add some sparkle. Carefully, I applied shimmery pink and gold powder to her eyes and cheeks, then lined her eyes with kohl before helping her paint her lips a deep red.

When she stood, I took a step back to take her in. My lips parted. With her gold hair, icy blue eyes, and perfect curves, she was always the most beautiful of the four of us. With the stunning chiton dress, shimmery makeup and sparkling hair, she was ethereal. She was the embodiment of what royalty was supposed to look like. "You look like the Queen of Drakous."

She gave me a skeptical look before peering at herself in the mirror.

"Are you ready for this?" I asked carefully.

When she turned to look at me, she seemed taller. "You did your part, Ara. Now, this is how I do mine."

A gentle knock sounded on the door. "I'll get it," I said as I crossed the room. I opened it just a crack, unsure if Cora was ready for anyone else to see her dressed for the ceremony.

"The Dragon King sent me with this gift for his bride," a dragon soldier who'd come with the king held out a wooden box. "He would be honored if she'd wear it for the ceremony."

I accepted the box. "Thank you. I'll make sure Cora receives it."

The soldier bowed, then left. I closed the door, then returned to Cora.

Her brow furrowed as she accepted the box from me. She took a seat, then wordlessly opened it. We both gasped as we stared at an intricate crown. Gold flames were carefully crafted and connected in a circle, making the whole crown look like it was burning. Along the base of the flames were red garnets, orange amber, and yellow citrine. The shining stones helped give the illusion that the flames were burning, made even more pronounced by the excellent craftsmanship of the varying sizes and shapes of the overlapping flames.

"This is too beautiful," Cora said. "I can't." She held it away from her as if it might actually burn her.

I took the crown from her, surprised that it was much lighter than I thought it would be. "You can." I lifted it, moving slowly, in case she objected. Instead, she closed her eyes and tilted her chin.

I set the crown atop her head. It fit her as if it was designed for her. I didn't know where it had come from, or how he'd had it made, but it was like it had always meant to be on Cora's head.

"It's perfect," I said.

She grabbed my wrist. "I'm afraid, Ara. What if I don't ever love him? What if it's all just lust that fades?"

I knelt down so I was in front of her. "Close your eyes."

She did.

"Think about Bahar. What do you feel when you imagine him standing in front of you?" I could have reminded her about her duty to Athos. That would have been enough. But I took a chance, certain she was already at the point of no return with the bond.

She took a deep breath, then released it slowly. "I think of how annoyingly self-assured he is." Her jaw tensed and her lips pressed together into a line.

I worried I'd made things worse.

"I think about his strong arms, and his stupidly handsome face," she added.

A smile tugged at the corners of my mouth.

"I think of how he looks at me like he might devour me whole, but also like he's never seen anything as fragile as me. How he cares about his people. How he went from demanding I give him heirs to refusing to marry me…"

She opened her eyes. "Why do I feel so warm? It's different than how I felt about Tomas. I always thought I loved him, but what I feel for Bahar is not what I felt for Tomas. Is that what it's like for you with Ryvin? Was it different than how you felt for David?"

My throat tightened as I tried to compare my feelings for Ryvin to David. He was the closest thing I had to someone I loved before Ryvin. The guilt of what I did to him would never leave me, but her words made me realize what I felt for him wasn't love. It never had been.

"The closest thing I have to what I feel for Rvyin, is what I feel for you and Sophia and Lagina. There was never a true connection with David. Not like I have with Ryvin. It's like he's part of me, and I'm part of him. It's hard to explain."

She nodded. "I think I understand."

"I know it's strange," I said.

"Sometimes, I'm angry that the fates took the choice from me," she confided. "Tell me it's worth it."

"It's worth it," I said, without hesitation.

"Alright. But when I have babies that can turn into dragons, you're coming to stay with me," she teased.

"I wouldn't miss it," I said.

Another knock sounded, and I returned to the door to find Lagina and Sophia. They were both dressed for a wedding. Lagina in a reserved deep blue peplos, and Sophia in an airy turquoise chiton.

"You're not dressed," Lagina chided.

"It's time, Cora," Sophia added.

"She can wear one of my dresses," Cora said, hurrying to the wardrobe. She pulled out a pale blue silk chiton. "How about this?"

Lagina walked over to the wardrobe and selected a deeper blue dress. "This. There should be no doubt that she's representing Athos."

"Perfect," Cora said as she returned the other dress.

My sisters quickly helped me dress, then fussed over my hair and makeup. When they were finished, I was more elaborately dressed than I usually allowed. My hair dotted with pearls, my face shimmered with gold, and my lips were painted crimson.

"If only mother could see us all now," Cora said.

Sophia winced and Lagina and Cora sandwiched her between them before Cora dragged me into the hug.

"Don't do that, Sophia," Lagina said. "Mother would be proud of you, and you know it."

"Nobody cry, it'll ruin our makeup," Cora said with a laugh that was half sob.

Another knock forced us apart, and I had a momentary pang of sadness as we separated. When the fight was over, Cora would leave to Drakous, Lagina would continue to rule Athos, and I had no idea where I would be. But I knew, despite my blue dress and the love I felt for my people, I didn't belong in Athos anymore.

This time, it was Ryvin and Vanth, along with Argus. Ryvin's eyes widened when he saw me. He opened and closed his mouth a few times, as if struggling to find words. "Wow."

"I'll take that as a compliment," Cora said from next to me.

My cheeks heated. "I'm not covered in blood and dirt for a change."

"You're gorgeous when you're covered in blood and dirt, as long as it's not your blood, but I never even imagined what you'd look like as a queen."

That took away my ability to speak.

"We're here to escort you to the ceremony," Vanth cut in.

"It's time?" Cora asked, glancing to the window.

"We'll be right there," Lagina said before shutting the door on the men outside. She turned to Cora. "It's time for your veil."

Cora was tense when she nodded, then followed Lagina. I hadn't even noticed that Lagina had brought a veil into the room when she arrived. It was sitting on the little table next to all the makeup.

Cora sat, then Lagina carefully pinned the veil over her crown. Covering her face and her hair with the sheer, white fabric. When she was finished, Cora stood and it was as if she'd transformed. The veil making her into a bride. My eyes stung, but I held in the tears, knowing Cora wouldn't want me to cry.

"I'm ready," Cora said.

"Who would you like to escort you?" Lagina asked, her voice a little choked sounding.

Traditionally, our father would escort her. If not him, the next male family member would step in. We didn't have anyone for that role. I imagine she'd have asked her mother, but that option had also been stripped from her.

Cora stepped up to Lagina and looped her arm through our eldest sister's.

Lagina nodded, and I could see the shimmering, unshed tears in her eyes. I knew she couldn't speak or she'd lose control, so I went to the door and opened it. "We're ready."

The men moved aside, letting Lagina and Cora walk first. We followed them. It was an unusual procession. Cora should have had friends in beautiful matching dresses. She should have spent all day yesterday being pampered and making offerings to the gods. She'd had most of the traditional preparation taken from her, but she never once complained. She wasn't the same person I'd left behind when I traveled to Konos the first time. But I supposed I wasn't, either. None of us were the same.

We walked to the kitchen so we could use the back door to the gardens. The ceremony would take place in the orchard and everyone who'd sheltered within the shield of the palace grounds was invited. It was just like the Choosing, only this time, we were celebrating life.

31

ARA

THE GATHERED Athonians erupted in cheers as we walked down a flower petal strewn path toward the waiting platform. Strips of blue and gold silk were draped across the top, creating a shimmering canopy. Behind the platform, we could see the sun dipping low into the horizon as it made its descent to night.

Bahar stood patiently, a look of pure devotion in his shining eyes. He wasn't aware of anything around him. His attention was completely focused on Cora. Warmth spread in my chest and I felt hopeful for them. Next to him, a priestess in a white peplos waited silently for the bride's arrival.

I noticed the few dozen dragons who'd traveled with Bahar. He left most of his men and his brother behind to try and retake Drakous while the king was occupied here.

We'd be fighting a difficult battle on both fronts against the fae.

Music began and I forced myself to the present moment. This might not be the wedding Cora imagined, but I was determined to make it special for her. Fixing a smile on my face, I looked around at the faces of these gathered. The vampires from Thebes were standing to one side, the Athonians keeping their distance from the group. Soldiers in uniforms and citizens were intermingled, everyone striving for a view of the bride. A perfume of jasmine and tuberose filled my nose, their scents thick in the warm evening air.

Aunt Katerina was standing about halfway down the path in a formal teal peplos. Cora paused, releasing Lagina so she could give the older woman a hug.

"You're going to be a wonderful queen." Aunt Katerina said, her voice thick with emotion. She held her in her arms for a few heartbeats, and when she stepped back, she wiped tears from her cheek. "You make all of Athos proud."

Cora kissed our aunt on the cheek, then whispered something I couldn't hear, before looping her arm through Lagina's again. We continued along the flower petal strewn path.

We reached the platform and Lagina held Cora's hand as the bride climbed the steps. A breeze made Cora's skirt ruffle and flow as she stepped onto the platform. Lagina released her hand, then moved to the side next to me and Sophia. Ryvin, Vanth, and Argus joined the crowd nearby.

As Cora faced Bahar, he looked like he'd just had every

wish he'd ever made come true all at once. Cora's expression was similar. It made my heart swell to see the joy in their expressions. I knew she'd dreaded this, but I was so grateful that she wasn't anymore.

The priestess lifted her hands, indicating that the ceremony would begin. She began by dedicating the ceremony to Hera, the goddess of marriage, then she guided the couple through making offerings of oil and wine. A jeweled knife was used to cut a lock of Cora's hair, another offering to the goddess.

"This union will not only unite two great kingdoms, Athos and Drakous," the priestess said, "but it unites two people who will become one. As a symbol of your connection, please join hands."

Cora and Bahar took hold of each other's hands and I noticed a pink flush on my sister's face.

"Under the protection of Hera, we ask that you bless this marriage with harmony and prosperity," the priestess said. "King Bahar, you may unveil your bride."

Bahar didn't move. He and Cora were staring at each other so intently, I thought they might have forgotten there was anyone else present. The priestess cleared her throat and Bahar caught himself, looking over at the priestess.

"You may unveil your bride," she repeated.

Sophia and Lagina took hold of my hands and squeezed. We were all leaning forward in anticipation.

Bahar gently lifted the veil, folding it back so it uncovered Cora's face. His whole expression softened. "My wife."

"My husband," Cora whispered.

"Under the watchful eyes of the gods, I declare you husband and wife," the priestess called.

Bahar closed the distance between them and pulled Cora into his arms. She leaned up expectantly as he leaned down. They met in the most careful, gentle kiss I'd ever seen. It was sweet and cautious. It was nothing like Cora, so I knew that was Bahar trying to be a gentleman.

Cora threw her arms around his neck, then pulled him tighter and the kiss intensified. Everyone cheered and people threw flower petals into the air. I joined in the celebration, clapping and cheering along with everyone else.

When the newlyweds came up for air, they were both beaming. They lifted their arms into the air, huge smiles on their faces.

Suddenly, dark shadows swirled around them, blocking them from view. The cheers turned to screams, and I frantically looked for Ryvin while feeling for my magic. Had I done that? Had my emotions brought shadows? More shadows descended from the sky, creating an ominous cloud over the whole orchard.

People were shoving and screaming, everyone fleeing from the orchard back to their tents or away from the smothering darkness. Ryvin found me and wrapped his arms around me. "That's not you, is it?"

I shook my head. "It's not you, either, right?"

"No." His jaw tensed, then he released me. "Where are you, Mother?"

The shadows swirled around us, forming a vortex right in front of the platform. I ran around it, trying to reach Cora. She was huddled in Bahar's arms, but thankfully, the swirling shadows weren't touching them. I stopped in front of them, my arms outstretched protectively, ready to fight if needed.

The spiral of shadows narrowed, swirling and twisting until it finally shrunk away, revealing Nyx standing where they'd once been.

"I didn't realize I'd arrived on such an auspicious occasion." Nyx inclined her head. "My congratulations to the bride and groom."

"Why are you here?" I demanded. "I completed your tasks."

People were still screaming and running, but some of them had stopped to watch. It wasn't everyday a goddess dropped in. Until I traveled to Konos, I'd never seen a god or goddess. Now, I couldn't seem to get away from them.

"You proved your point," Ryvin said, moving closer to his mother. "You nearly killed Ara."

"I knew she'd go after you, truthfully, but I didn't expect that you would find a way to keep her alive," Nyx replied. "I'm impressed."

Ryvin tensed, his hands balled into fists.

"Don't," I warned. "She has to keep her word."

"Oh, I'll keep my word," Nyx said, glancing at me before returning her attention to her son. "And I am here to give you my blessing."

"I'm not sure I want your blessing after what you did," Ryvin gritted out.

"Forgive me if I didn't truly believe that any human could be worthy," she said. "But your mate proved me wrong. More than once."

"Powerful Nyx, how honored we are that you've graced us with your presence." Lagina had approached the platform and was in a low curtsy in front of the goddess.

Nyx cocked her head to the side like a cat investigating something unusual. "And you are?"

Lagina maintained her low curtsey, keeping her head down. "I am Lagina, Queen of Athos."

"I keep forgetting that old monster is dead," Nyx said. "How unfortunate that you had to have him as a father."

"I am not my father," Lagina said, a note of defiance in her tone.

Nyx arched a brow. "Rise, Queen of Athos."

Lagina stood. "If you'd give me the honor of your time, I'd like to show you the temple we are erecting in your honor." Lagina clasped her hands in front of her and waited patiently.

"You actually are building a temple? I thought it was just an idea when it showed up in Ara's dream," Nyx looked from Lagina, to me, then to Ryvin. He nodded.

"So the humans learned their lesson from the darkness I bestowed on them," she said.

"It was an excellent reminder of your power and your abilities. It made me realize how wrong it was that my father never honored you properly. You are just as worthy of a grand temple as Athena," Lagina said.

Nyx straightened, her chin rising even more. "Finally, someone with sense ruling the humans. Please, take me to this temple."

They started to walk, then Nyx turned back, returning to me. She stretched out her hand, then opened her fingers to reveal two items in her palm. "I believe I owe you these."

Gratitude overcame me. I never thought I'd see my mother's gifts again. I took them from Nyx, then quickly affixed them around my neck. "Thank you."

Nyx gave me a half smile. "Do come by and visit Obsidian sometime. He took a liking to you." Then she glanced at Bahar and Cora. "You two make a lovely couple."

She stepped closer to them, and Bahar tightened his grip around Cora. My sister was shaking. Nyx waved her hand and a spiral of shadows appeared, then she reached into the shadows and pulled out a knife. Bahar quickly pushed Cora behind him, and Ryvin unsheathed the sword at his side.

"Everyone calm down." Nyx turned the weapon so she was holding the blade, presenting the hilt toward Bahar. "Now, remove yourself sir. This is a gift for the bride."

Bahar hesitated, but eventually moved enough that Cora could reach for the hilt. She took it awkwardly.

"This weapon will instantly kill your mate no matter where you strike him with it. Even if it's just a graze on his flesh." Nyx was smiling.

Cora held the weapon out away from her as if it were poisonous. She looked up at Nyx, wide-eyed.

"You don't have his powers. This will even the play-field." Nyx winked. She turned her gaze to Bahar. "If you take it from her or have it destroyed, I will know, and I will come for Drakous."

"What a lovely gift," Lagina said loudly.

"Yes, lovely," Bahar grunted.

"Thank you," Cora managed.

"It won't harm her, if you're wondering," Nyx said to Bahar. "So she can sleep with it under her pillow every night if needed."

"I hope she won't feel the need, but if it makes her feel safer, it's welcome in our bed," Bahar said.

Nyx gave him an appreciative nod, then turned to Lagina. "Shall we?"

It wasn't until Lagina and Nyx were out of sight that the music began again and the party truly started. Platters of food were brought out and people ate and danced and laughed. Torches were lit so the party could continue long after the sunset. I couldn't remember the last time I'd seen this much joy.

Ryvin offered his hand. "Care for a dance?"

I grinned, accepting it. We both knew this happiness was fleeting, but we took it, spending the next few hours spinning and dancing until we were breathless.

By the time the celebration slowed, I was so exhausted I had to lean on Ryvin on the walk back to my room. It had been so long since I'd been tired for a good reason.

That night, I fell asleep with Ryvin's arms around me, and my mother's returned gifts. For the first time in a long time, I felt hope.

32

ARA

"I CHECKED the wards again and they've gotten stronger. They should keep out anyone with fae blood, but I don't think there's anything we can do to prevent a god from getting in," Laera said as she entered the breakfast room.

"That should work. I don't think any of the gods have an interest in being in Athos when the fae arrive." I was the only one in there, attempting to eat something before returning to more training with Ryvin.

The morning had been a flurry of activity already, everyone doing what they could to prepare. The breakfast room had been set with snacks that could be grabbed by anyone who needed something, though most of it was untouched.

"I'm sure they're enjoying the show." Laera took a seat next to me and reached for a honey cake.

"How much time do you think we have?" I asked.

"They can already see the ships." She took a bite, then chewed slowly.

I stood. "What?"

"Sit down." Laera grabbed my arm and pulled. "They're coming either way. You getting panicked about it now does nothing but wear you out before it's even time to fight."

Her eyes dropped and she pressed her lips together. "See what I mean?"

I followed her gaze and saw shadows twisting around my middle. "I didn't do that on purpose."

"I know." She set down her cake, giving it a look like it personally offended her. "The food here is terrible."

I couldn't help but smile at that. "It's not that bad."

She waved her hand dismissively. "It doesn't matter right now. What does matter is that you're still letting your emotions get the better of you when it comes to your magic."

I opened my mouth, and she held up her hand. "Let me finish."

I closed my mouth and crossed my arms over my chest. I felt like a child being scolded.

"Listen to me. If you were raised fae, you'd have had decades to hone your skills. We're not expected to learn it quickly. We make mistakes. We break things. Some of us accidentally kill people. In Ryvin's case, a lot of people. But we learn. Slowly. You don't get that luxury. And yes, I know it's not fair. It just means you have to be better than all of us. Especially since you have dual powers to tap into."

I lowered my arms to my side. "I know."

"But you don't. You're not trusting yourself. You don't have time to learn anymore. You have to be a master of your magic and Ryvin's. Now. Today. Not five years from now."

"You realize that's impossible, right?" I countered.

"You're not even supposed to be alive, Ara. Don't forget that the gods were so afraid of you that they wanted you dead. I think it's time for you to show them just how terrifying you can be." She reached for an olive and popped it into her mouth.

I took a breath, letting her words sink in. I wasn't used to seeing myself as someone powerful, but I was. I was an asset in this fight and it was time I started acting like it.

Grabbing a honey cake of my own, I made myself eat. It was going to be a very long day.

Vanth walked into the breakfast room, his whole body tense and ready for a fight.

"We already know," Laera said. "They still have to set up their blockade. You should eat, shifter."

Vanth glanced over at me.

"She's right. They're not going to breech our walls this second." I was trying to follow Laera's lead, to keep my emotions under control.

Vanth narrowed his eyes. "I'm not sure I like you two spending time together."

Laera laughed. "If you eat something, we'll go with you to the war room."

He growled.

"If Laera is trying to take care of you, you must be in bad shape," I said.

"You're in my head," he accused.

"I don't have to go into your head. You're projecting all of your emotions so clearly I could feel them on the opposite side of the palace," she replied. "And you're hungry. Eat."

He stomped to the table and grabbed a honey cake.

"Oh, not that," Laera said quickly.

Vanth sniffed it, then wrinkled his nose before setting it down.

"It's not that bad," I said, taking the last bite of the one I'd been working on.

He reached for some dried fish, then ate a few olives and some fruit. I'd never seen anyone eat so quickly. "Happy now?"

Laera stood. "Very. Shall we?"

I tried to imitate her calm as we left the room, even as anxiety was starting to build in my chest. As we entered the hallway, I paused to look through the colonnade at the sea beyond.

There they were. Hundreds of ships. Red sails were joined by white, gray, and green. All the fae together to attack one single human city.

I balled my hands into fists. They were here to annihilate us. The king was here for our blood.

"The shields should hold," Laera said.

"But for how long?" I asked.

"Longer than your people have without access to the sea," Vanth said.

While we feared those waters, we were dependent on them for fish and trade. We could grow much of our own food, but without access to all of Athos, we were limited to only what could be produced on the grounds that were protected by the shield. We couldn't bring the livestock with the people when they evacuated here. We couldn't afford to have this war drag out.

"Let's go." I started walking again, heading for the study, which had become our war room.

Argus, General Mortagan, Bahar, Lagina, Cora, Sophia, Ryvin, and Erebus, the leader of Thebes, were staring out the window at the incoming ships. They turned when they heard us approach.

"Come to join the fun?" Bahar asked.

Ryvin crossed the room to me. "Looks like our training is on hold."

"I'm ready," I assured him.

His jaw tightened and he nodded, attempting to be reassuring, but failing. I could feel his tension. I took his hand and gave it a quick squeeze, then released it and walked toward the others. "What did we miss?"

"They're establishing a blockade," Mortagan explained, pointing to the ships that were moving into position. "The others are getting closer to shore so they can release their soldiers."

"There must be five-thousand already," Argus said.

"They'll send more," Mortagan commented. "This can't be their whole fleet."

"They might have left some behind in Drakous," Bahar said.

"Laera, can you find out?" Ryvin asked.

She nodded. "I'll do my best."

"Kabir is at the winter camp near Drakous, if you need a familiar mind," Bahar said.

Laera frowned. I knew she didn't like when people guessed at her abilities, but she didn't argue.

"I must prepare our archers," Mortagan said suddenly. "They're fae. They move faster than us. We might not have the day to prepare."

"We should anticipate at least one attack before nightfall," Erebus said. "They will camp tonight. They never fight at night. They need that time to let their magic replenish."

"Let us know what you need," Lagina said.

Mortagan inclined his head. "We'll fight to the end, Your highness."

Erebus also bowed to Lagina, then joined Mortagan, the two of them heading out to prepare the soldiers. We weren't certain how well the shield would hold to a mass attack, so our archers and foot soldiers needed to be ready to go.

"He left five-thousand men behind to hold Drakous," Laera said.

"Five thousand?" Bahar asked.

She nodded. "I get the sense he feels that's the more important target. And he doesn't see Athos as a threat."

"I really hope Nona removed that extra magic," I said quietly.

"We'll find out soon," Vanth replied.

"The good news is that he's here," Laera said. "My father came to Athos."

Despite the rising tension, the information made me smile. That meant we had a chance. If we could get to him, his alliances would unravel. We'd be able to end this war.

I HATED WAITING. I hated standing there watching out the window, doing nothing. Our people were huddled in tents, sharing the provisions we could provide, waiting. Our soldiers had taken over every spare corner of the palace, finding anywhere they could to rest while they waited. Bahar's men and Erebus's men did the same, camping in the training grounds or taking over spare rooms. We were overflowing with people who could do nothing but wait.

I almost wanted the battle to begin. At least then I could do something.

I watched as the ships sailed toward land. I watched as thousands of fae flooded our shores. Once they entered the city, I couldn't see them anymore, but I knew they were in the streets, destroying anything they crossed, pillaging and attacking anyone who'd stayed behind. It made my stomach churn.

They'd be at our gates soon.

By late afternoon, thousands of fae marched toward the palace. They stopped just beyond the gates, where the shield began.

"They know it's there, don't they?" I asked Ryvin. "They can sense the barrier."

"I'm sure they can," he said.

"Is it going to hold?" Lagina asked.

"We're about to find out," Laera replied.

None of the fae attempted to cross the barrier, but they were clearly preparing to fight. Archers stepped forward and began to fire arrows into the shield. They fired until they emptied their quivers, then they retrieved their arrows and started again.

Every time the arrows hit, the shield glittered and sizzled. Every time, it made me tense with anxiety. It was holding, for now. Meanwhile, I could see the tents dotting our sandy shores as soldiers settled in for the long haul. They could wait for our shields to fall. Using it as target practice was nothing more than an intimidation tactic. They knew they couldn't penetrate it, but it was unnerving to listen to the pings of their arrows as they ricocheted off the barrier.

The sun was setting, sinking into the sea. I knew we'd have a reprieve tonight. But that only meant that tomorrow would be the real thing. The fae would attack with everything they had.

33

The sunrise brought dragons.

Huge creatures with massive wingspans flew over Athos, breathing fire along down on the barrier. Dozens of them circled, lighting up our shield with orange flames.

Our soldiers were stationed at the edge of the barrier, waiting in case the fae broke through. Laera, Selena, and Aspasia stood in the rear, ready to reinforce the shield with whatever they could. I stood nearby, my hands already trembling as I resisted the urge to call forth the shadows too soon.

Ryvin was near the front, standing next to Vanth. Bahar's men were hidden among the fae, staring skyward, probably anxious to join the aerial fight. We didn't want to risk the king knowing we had dragons. Not until necessary. All we could do was wait until the shield fell.

Thousands of fae soldiers marched for us, surrounding the palace grounds. Their armor gleamed in the early morning light. I watched in horror as they prepared the battering rams.

Our soldiers readied their catapults.

Teams of fae raced forward, battering rams slamming into the barrier, making the ground shake.

Catapults released, launching heavy stones skyward, before they crashed into the fae army. Only the first two hit before the fae began to use magic to catch the stones and throw them back toward us. They bounced off the shield, but every time they hit, I winced at the sound.

Flames roared as they lit bundles inside the catapults, launching them at the fae beyond. The fire was extinguished before it hit any of our enemies.

Battering rams slammed into our shields again, making the ground shake once more. The barrier buzzed and flickered, but it was holding.

Twice more they charged the shield, but the battering rams didn't get through. Dragons continued their onslaught from above, but their flames were ineffective.

I started to feel like maybe we could do this. Maybe they'd realize they couldn't win. But even that was a false victory. We couldn't stay barricaded in the palace grounds forever.

The fae soldiers parted, making a path. A group walked toward us, led by the king himself.

Ryvin moved closer to the shield and Vanth held his arm out in front of the prince, preventing him from taking another step. I left my position, pushing my way through our lines to reach the front.

When Vanth saw me, he lowered his arm, and I made sure I was standing slightly in front of Ryvin. He wouldn't risk accidentally pushing me beyond the shield.

The Fae King stopped only a few foot spans from us. His lips were upturned in a thin, unsettling smile that promised chaos. "Son, how good to see you again. I see you did let this Athos whore win you over."

Ryvin's fists clenched and he took a step forward. I grabbed his arm. "Don't. He's trying to bait you."

The king turned his attention to me. "I found out something about you recently. About your parentage. You could be quite valuable once you're trained up a bit and you learn to bite your tongue."

"I have enough training to send you to the Underworld," I sneered. Until he mentioned it, I hadn't even thought about the fact that I might be able to use my magic against him. Now, ideas flooded my mind. If Bahar and his dragons failed, I was another option.

The king held up his wrist, showing several gold bracelets that reminded me of the one Ryvin wore. "I've been collecting these over the years. They prevent your mother from using her magic against me. I'm guessing they'll work exceptionally well on you since you're only half goddess."

"Coward," I hissed.

"No, not a coward. I'm prepared. I strategize. Which is how I know I'll win, and you'll lose." The king's eyes left mine, as if noticing something, then he returned his gaze to me. "It seems I'll be in the market for a new queen once I execute my old one for treason. If you're seeking more power, I can make you an offer."

"Stay calm, Princess," Laera whispered as she walked past me.

I felt a strange cooling sensation crawl through my body. I knew I was fuming, but everything inside me was suddenly so light I might float away. I realized Laera was using her magic on me. I should be furious, but she probably prevented me from doing something stupid.

"Father," Laera said flatly.

He clicked his tongue. "I expected eventual betrayal from Ryvin, but I thought you were loyal."

"You always underestimated the women in your life," she replied.

"That I did. I won't make that mistake again," he said.

"No, you won't. Because you'll be dead," she said.

He laughed, letting it linger as he rested his hand on his stomach and threw his head back. The people who had accompanied him and were waiting right behind him looked at each other uncomfortably. I could tell they weren't sure if they should join in. He stopped abruptly, and they looked relieved that he was finished.

"You won't even leave the safety of your shield, how exactly are you going to kill me?" The king asked.

She glared at him.

"We are prepared to spend months camped outside your shield. We have provisions to last us through winter. But I have the feeling we won't need to stay that long.

There are other ways to solve this, you know," the king said.

"We are not going to surrender our city to you," I said.

"You are not the queen," he hissed.

"But I am," Lagina called as the soldiers parted for her to join us. She stood tall and proud, staring down the king as if he was nothing more than a slug. "And Athos is done bowing to the fae."

"Then Athos will cease to exist," the king said.

"You can try," Lagina snapped. "But humans are stronger than you realize."

"We'll see about that," the king said. He turned to his men. "Begin the attack." He turned and walked away.

The soldiers with the battering rams fell back and a new group pushed forward. These men were not clad in armor. Instead, they wore loose fitting tunics and trousers in expensive materials. They were polished and clean, none of them had the appearance of a soldier.

My brow furrowed as I took them in. Were they here to try diplomacy? They had to be nobles. They were far too nicely dressed to be anything else.

Just as I was about to ask Ryvin, the men raised their hands and the shield began to vibrate.

"Throw everything you've got at it!" Laera yelled as she raced back to where her mother and Selena were standing. The fae women lifted their arms to the sky, offering their magic to the shield.

I looked back at the line of fae. They were attacking our shield with magic. Wide-eyed, I turned to Ryvin. "Can they do that? Is that going to work?"

Ryvin's jaw clenched, and I didn't need him to respond. We were on borrowed time.

Dark tendrils began to swirl around me, shadows billowing up, responding to my stress. "Can you take them out? The fae? Can you use your magic?"

He shook his head. "It won't penetrate the shield. Only physical things can get through. I'll have to leave."

"Not yet," Vanth replied. "Get back there, Ara. We've got archers and catapults and we might as well use them."

Rvyin fell back with me. Our job would begin once the shields were down. For now, all we could do was watch.

Archers stepped forward and struck quickly, knocking down several of the fae at the barrier. The fae soldiers moved forward, creating a wall with their shields in front of the magic users. Our archers fired back, occasionally getting something through before the fae changed tactics, sending some of their magic wielders to protect the others rather than focus on the shield. At least that would slow them down.

We launched catapults, but the payload never hit anyone. The fae stopped it before it reached the ground. So our archers took to shooting at random intervals and in irregular directions to try to catch the fae off guard.

The shield cracked. The sound like a whip, followed by a rumbling. It was weakening. I glanced over at Ryvin.

It was late afternoon when our archers ran out of arrows. We had craftsmen making more, but they couldn't keep up. Our soldiers fell back, retreating from the barrier.

Half of them were sent to rest, while the others were

given rations and waited, just in case. There wasn't anything else we could do.

Suddenly, the attack ceased. The magic on the shield stopped. The fae troops began to leave. Our soldiers whispered and shuffled their feet, some of them moving closer to the shield to get a better look.

"What are they doing?" I asked.

Ryvin looked to the sky. "I guess he's calling it early tonight. They must be close."

I saw Laera walking toward us. Her face shone with sweat and she had dark circles under her eyes. "There isn't much left. He could break it before nightfall if he wanted, but I think he'd rather they save some of their magic."

"He plans to break it and then attack immediately," Ryvin said.

"That's my guess." Laera rubbed her eyes, then shook out her hands. "I'm nearly spent. I need to sleep or I won't be able to help tomorrow."

"Go on," Ryvin said. "We'll need everyone at their best in the morning."

"If he waits until morning," she replied.

"He'll want them rested," Ryvin said.

"What's happening?" Mortagan asked as he approached Ryvin. "Where are they going? We can't have won."

"No, we didn't win." Ryvin explained his theory and Mortagan looked grim. "I'll inform my men."

"What happens in the morning?" I asked.

"We fight," Rvyin said.

I looked out at the retreating soldiers. We had a

depleted Athonian army, a few hundred vampires, a handful of dragons, and Ryvin. His magic was enough to take down many of our opposition, but I didn't think it would be enough.

"I can tell where you're going in your head." Ryvin put his arms around me and pulled me closer. I looked up into his silver eyes. He seemed relaxed, but I had a feeling that was for my benefit.

"Stop trying to think about everything," he said. "That's what you're doing, isn't it?"

"How is it that you're always so quick to know what it's in my head?" I narrowed my eyes. "Do you have some of that power that your father and Laera share?"

He kissed my forehead. "No, you're just very easy for me to read."

I frowned, hoping that wasn't the case for everyone. "It's hard not to think of how many soldiers your father brought."

"You have to remember, they're loyal to him out of fear. And we have dragons, which they aren't expecting." His smile was genuine and there was a confident spark in his eyes. "He's nothing against dragon fire. We only have to take him down to end this whole thing. With him gone, the fight is over."

He pulled me into an embrace and I leaned against him, trying to release my tension, but it wouldn't ease. We'd failed so many times to take down the king, but every time that happened, it had been us taking the risk. This time, it was my sisters and my whole city. If we failed, everyone went down with us.

34

GENERAL MORTAGAN WAS ARGUING with Erebus, each one insisting their men should take the front in the morning. I didn't realize exactly how desperate they all were to die in the glory of battle.

It made me feel nauseous.

Aunt Katerina walked in and I turned to watch her enter the room. Both men stopped arguing when they saw her. She greeted them with a nod, then continued over to where I was sitting with Lagina, Cora, and Sophia.

"How are you girls doing?" she asked as she took a seat on the couch next to Lagina.

"We were safely tucked away in the palace," Cora replied, indicating her and Sophia. "How are you?"

"The men are restless," she answered. "They want their

chance at the fae. Today just made them more anxious for death."

"That's grim," Cora said.

"It's true. They're all dreaming of being a hero, which makes people sloppy," she explained.

General Mortagan walked over to us and greeted Aunt Katerina with a stiff nod. "Lady Katerina, we could use your guidance on this topic."

I lifted a brow and mouthed the word, *lady* to Cora. She covered her mouth to stifle a giggle. Aunt Katerina threw us all a silencing look before she rose, then joined the general and the leader from Thebes.

Restless was a good way to describe the feeling of waiting for the inevitable. But even though I knew I would fight, I wasn't in a rush to die. I rose, giving my sisters a small smile, before moving to the other corner of the room where Ryvin and Vanth were deep in conversation with Bahar. They looked up as I approached.

"Shouldn't you be talking with Mortagan and Erebus?" I asked.

"They know what they're doing with ground forces," Bahar replied.

"So we're not going in with magic first?" I asked.

"We can't afford to show our full strength until we wear them down a little," Ryvin said. "And we need to know what we're fighting against."

"We're going to lose a lot of lives," I replied.

"We'll lose more if we show our cards too soon," Bahar said.

"You're staying back until the king comes out to gloat, aren't you?" I asked.

"We have to get him out in the open," Vanth said. "We won't get another chance. If he thinks he's at risk, he'll flee."

"Coward," I bit out.

"He doesn't have Ryvin to do his dirty work for him anymore," Vanth said.

"I have to say, I appreciate knowing I'll never have to go up against you on a battlefield," Bahar said.

"You wouldn't be in your human form anyway," Ryvin replied.

"True, but I've seen you take down dragons," he answered.

I blinked a few times. "Dragons?"

"I've done a lot of things I'm not proud of," Ryvin said.

"But that ends now," Vanth said. "We're going to defeat him and then you write your own stars."

"Our own stars," I said, looking at my friends. "All of us."

"I like the sound of that. Now, if you don't mind, I'm going to go spend some time alone with my wife." Bahar was already walking away from us, single-mindedly focused on Cora, who was staring at him with a seductive grin on her lips.

It felt intrusive to watch as he scooped her up and murmured something to Lagina and Sophia before carrying a giggling Cora from the room.

"Well, I suppose our meeting is over," Vanth said.

Mortagan and Erebus walked over to us, both men

wearing satisfied expressions. "We've decided," Mortagan said.

"I'm still not convinced it's for the best, but we know the casualties will be high either way," Erebus added.

"There's nothing else we can do?" I asked.

"We can't risk them keeping the king hidden. We have to lure him out, but we'll do it as quickly as we can," Ryvin said.

"Our men know what they signed up for," Mortagan said.

I heard laughter and turned to see Aunt Katerina, Lagina, and Sophia throwing their heads back as they tried to contain their joy. I couldn't help but smile. I was glad they were getting at least a moment of happiness amidst all this chaos.

"That aunt of yours is something special," Mortagan said. "If not for her bargaining with the dragons, I don't think any of us would even have a chance."

"She is great," I said. "They all are."

"I'm not going to pretend I know what it was like for you growing up under your father," Mortagan said. "I worked for him as long as I can remember. I thought I'd die under his rule. I'm honored that my death will be under your sister's."

It was an odd statement, but I managed a smile and a nod. He inclined his head. "Have a good evening, Your highness."

"We'll see you at dawn, Your highness," Erebus said, taking the cue to leave from Mortagan.

I watched as the men left the room, then walked over

to my sisters. "I'm going to get some rest. I'll see you all in the morning."

"Sleep well, Ara," Lagina said.

Sophia stood, then stretched her arms skyward. "I think I'm going to turn in."

Aunt Katerina rose. "Our night guards will do their jobs. They'll alert us if anything happens. We should all rest."

I hugged my family, then walked toward the door where Ryvin was waiting for me. He took my hand, and we walked silently down the hallway toward my room.

Absentmindedly, I played with the charm on my necklace. Running it back and forth along the chain as we walked. I brushed against the other cord. I had forgotten about my mother's gift again. Lowering my hand, I felt for the small pouch through the fabric of my tunic and thought back to my mother's words.

What was inside the pouch? She'd told me not to open it until it was absolutely necessary.

If I didn't use it now, there might not be another time. How would I know when it was the right time?

Her voice seemed to float up from my memories in that confident tone of hers, *You just will.*

My heart pounded and I dropped my hand as the idea took root. It was insane. Reckless. Likely, it was suicide. But it was possible I might be able to save everyone I loved. I was certain this was why she'd given me the gift. I had no clue what it was or how I was supposed to use it, but I knew I had to use it tonight. If this gift was as powerful as I thought it was, I could kill the king.

Ryvin would never agree. I'd have to sneak out once he was asleep and hope he'd understand when he found out.

"You alright?" Ryvin asked as we stopped at my room.

I opened the door and leaned against it, waiting for him to enter. "I've got a lot on my mind."

"It'll be better after we get through tomorrow," he said.

"I don't want to think about tomorrow. I only want to think about right now." I closed the door, then pulled off my tunic. If this was my last night with him, I was going to make it count.

Ryvin smirked as he began to remove his clothes. "I like the way you think."

As soon as his trousers hit the ground, I dropped to my knees in front of him, giving him a seductive grin before I swiped my tongue from the base of his cock to the tip.

He sucked in a shuddering breath, then let it out in a low moan. I grabbed his hips, then repeated the action, working my tongue up and down his shaft until it stood at attention.

I lowered my mouth, closing my lips around him, then began to move up and down. My tongue flicked and swirled as I moved and Ryvin's breathing changed, little gasps escaping his lips. His fingers wove into my hair and when I looked up at him, his eyes were closed, his lips parted. He was completely lost in the sensations I was creating.

I continued, working up and down, changing pace and motions with my tongue, sometimes grazing my teeth along the sensitive skin. Suddenly, Ryvin reached for me, setting his fingers under my chin so he could tilt my head. I looked up at him, his cock still in my mouth.

He shook his head, but had a delicious smile on his lips. "You're going to make me finish too soon, Asteri."

I swirled my tongue in response.

He groaned, his eyelids flickering for a moment before he came back to his senses. "My turn." He gently pushed my chin down, then he stepped away before offering his hand.

I took it and he helped me to my feet. As soon as I was standing, he scooped me up and tossed me onto the bed. I squealed as I sunk into the softness of the mattress.

He didn't waste any time before removing my clothes and settling between my thighs. His tongue swiped over my clit and he teased me with quick flicks before one of his fingers entered me.

I moaned, my hips rising. He added another finger, turning them in a way that allowed him to reach that perfect spot inside. That spot that made me grip the sheets and buck my hips uncontrollably. His tongue added to the intensity, making me come apart at the seams. I was crying out, over and over, my breath stolen by the gasps. Eyes closed, I existed only in the moment. There was nothing other than pleasure coursing through me. Anything could be happening around me and I wouldn't care as long as he kept going.

His fingers pumped in and out, his tongue swirled, and I failed to catch a single breath as I gasped and moaned and screamed. Tension built, tighter and tighter until I was wound like a spring ready to explode. Teeth grazed my clit, and I lost all control, the climax roaring through me like waves crashing against the shore, followed by smaller waves, rolling in again and again.

I was shaking when he stopped. My forehead damp with sweat, my whole body tingling. I finally opened my eyes and looked up to find Ryvin's face above mine. He looked incredibly smug, but he earned that look.

I reached for his face and set my palm against his cheek, then caressed him with my thumb. I was still too breathless for words. He grabbed hold of my hand, then pressed a tender kiss to my palm. Then he lowered his face until his lips found mine. He kissed me softly at first, the intensity escalating as I kissed him back with more passion.

Breaking the kiss, I gave him a playful smile before I wrapped my arms and legs around him, then rolled. He helped, but I managed to get him on his back. Straddling him with my hands on his chest, I leaned closer to him. "My turn again."

He lifted a brow and moved his hands to my hips, caressing my ass and lower back. "I can't wait."

I rose, then lowered my hips onto him, not taking my eyes from his face as he groaned, his eyes closing when I slammed completely down. His hands began to guide me, working with me as I lifted and lowered. His hips rolled and rose. I leaned forward, claiming his mouth with mine. Then I straightened, focusing on making him lose control the way he'd done for me.

I guided one of his hands to my breast and as soon as he cupped it, he groaned again. I rocked and undulated, watching him as I tested out new movements of my hips. His breath caught and I smiled, knowing I'd found the right motion. I continued, repeating the movement as I watched his eyes roll into the back of his head.

He dropped his hands to my hips, holding me as his breathing grew more rapid. I continued on, my own breaths growing quicker as the position sent little shockwaves of pleasure through me. I started to moan, closing my own eyes as the sensations became more consuming. The thrill of pleasure escalated, and I let out little gasps to keep myself from losing control.

Ryvin's fingers dug into my skin and I could feel him tensing under me. He was so close. I leaned down and ran my fingers along his chest, then up his neck and into his hair, before stealing a kiss.

His hands moved to my back, pulling me in tight. It was enough to push me over the edge. The sensations peaked, sending a shock through my body that had me crying out into his mouth. Ryvin groaned, his body shaking under me. He deepened our kiss as we both breathed through our fading climaxes.

When I climbed off of him, he quickly pulled me into his arms and I rested my head on his chest. I listened to his heart beating fast and strong. He casually played with my hair, running his fingers through it over and over in a soothing way.

"What if we just stay like this forever?" he asked sleepily.

I looked up at him, noting that his eyes were already closed. I kissed his jaw. "One day, we will."

35

RYVIN TOSSED and turned every time I took a step and I held my breath as I pulled a tunic over my head. I couldn't risk staying too long or making too much noise. I stared at my desk, wishing I'd thought to leave the supplies out to write him a letter. If I opened the drawers, he'd be certain to wake. Instead, I left the necklace my mother gave me on my desk, hoping Ryvin understood it as my way of saying goodbye.

With my trousers and sandals in hand, I carefully opened my door and closed it as quietly as I could. Thankfully, there were no guards in my hall. I hurried to pull on my trousers and stepped into my sandals. My heart raced, certain I was going to be caught at any moment.

When I crossed into the main hall, I paused, glancing around at all the milling soldiers. Some of them glanced my way, but they either knew who I was or didn't see me as a threat.

I could feel their eyes on me as I walked, but I continued along with my chin high, acting as if walking through the palace in the middle of the night was something I typically did.

Hoping that Laera was staying in the same room she'd been in last time, I walked with purpose, knowing it was possible Ryvin could wake at any time. I needed to be beyond the shield before that happened.

There were no guards stationed in the halls. Probably because they needed everyone to rest tonight for tomorrow's potential slaughter. My jaw tightened and I walked faster, hurrying to Laera's room.

I didn't bother knocking and was surprised to see the princess was sitting in a chair staring into a crackling fire in her fireplace.

"I wondered how long I'd have to wait before you came," she said without turning to look at me.

"It's not polite to be in other people's heads," I replied.

"I didn't have to be in your head to know you'd do something to make yourself into the sacrificial hero." She stood and turned to me. "It's your story, Ara. Why the fates wanted you dead. I can't recall another who fought for those they love rather than glory or selfish reasons. Even I have a hard time believing your motives and I can read it all. I know it's real."

"So you know what I'm going to ask," I said.

She sighed. "I knew as soon as I mentioned that the shield wouldn't keep a god out."

"So?"

"In theory, you can leave the shield without any trouble. Getting back in could be tricky, but I don't see that as relevant since it won't matter by morning, anyway."

"Because the shield will be gone, or because I will?" I asked before I could stop myself.

"Even I don't know that," she said.

"You're not going to try to stop me." It wasn't a question. I knew she wouldn't and it made me respect her even more.

"I'll make sure his dreams are pleasant for the next hour to give you a head start," she said.

My brows lifted. "You can keep people asleep?"

She shrugged.

"Thank you."

"Go. There's not a lot of time before sunrise," she said.

I walked to the door, then turned to give her a nod of gratitude before I closed the door behind me.

EXITING through the front would draw too much attention, so I headed toward the kitchens. I didn't expect to find Cora sitting on a counter, kicking her feet while she ate grapes from a bowl.

Her eyes widened when she saw me. She set down the fruit and hopped off the counter. She scanned my clothing, her mouth twisting to the side as she took in my all black outfit. "Where are you off to?"

"Please don't tell anyone," I said.

She frowned. "You're sneaking out."

I nodded.

"To do something really, really stupid."

I didn't argue with her.

She sighed, her whole body looking as if she'd just surrendered. "I'll give you until sunrise. But if you're not back, what do you want me to tell them?"

"If I'm not back by sunrise, and the Fae King still attacks, tell them I'm sorry I failed," I said.

"Fuck, Ara. You know you don't always have to be the one who does everything for everyone else." She stepped closer to me. "Do you need help? Want me to come along?"

I almost laughed. She looked genuine, but there was a bit of fear I caught in her eyes. As if she was concerned I might take her up on her offer. "I need to do this, alright?"

She moved closer, then gave me a hug. I wrapped my arms around her. "I will try to come back."

"I know." She stepped back. "Good luck."

I smiled, then walked to the back door, not letting myself look back. As soon as I was through, I blew out a long breath. I trusted that she'd keep quiet about seeing me, but it was possible that Ryvin could wake any minute. I needed to get as far from here as I could before that happened.

Quickly, I checked that the pouch was still attached to the cord around my neck. I could feel the object inside it. It was a small, round ball, but I still had no idea what it was or how it could help me.

The gardens and grounds were full of people. Some were in tents, others were sharing blankets spread on the earth. A few guards mingled, and I even saw a couple of citizens walking around. Nobody seemed to care that I was walking toward the shield. I suppose after watching it keep the fae out today, there wasn't much risk in anyone going in or out. It would be suicide to leave if the shield was guarded by any fae.

I stopped right at the point where I could feel the magic, and after a quick backward glance at the palace, I called Ryvin's shadows. Breathing steadily, I summoned them around me like a cloak of darkness. Shielding me from view the way we'd done when we arrived in Drakous. I could have used this to get out of the palace, but I'd never tried it before and wasn't sure how long I could hold the shadows.

Before I could talk myself out of it, I stepped through the invisible barrier, sucking in a breath from the icy cold, before emerging on the other side.

My pulse raced as I walked down the road toward town. I expected to encounter fae soldiers at every step, but the roads were silent.

Once I reached the city, I scanned for any signs of movement. Buildings were destroyed everywhere I turned. Doors torn from hinges, roofs caved in, the contents of shops and homes tossed into the streets. My chest tightened as I took in the destruction. We'd have a lot to rebuild once the fae left our shores.

I could feel my hold on the shadows fading, so I released them and kept to the natural shadows as I crept through the city. I'd need them again to get into the camp and didn't want to waste them all now.

Laughter sounded and I darted through a doorway,

moving quickly to the side so I was hidden from view. I peered around the edge of the doorframe, catching sight of a small patrol of six fae. They were talking and laughing as they walked up the street. One of them was throwing something into the air and catching it repeatedly as they walked. Another was smoking something, blowing out perfectly formed rings.

They had to be the most unbothered, casual patrol I'd ever seen. They were either off duty and exploring the ruins of Athos, or they were certain they had nothing to watch for. A smile tugged on my lips. That would work to my advantage. If all the fae were this relaxed, there was no way I'd be caught sneaking into their camp.

As soon as I couldn't hear their voices anymore I continued along, meeting no other guards or soldiers as I crept through the silent city. The last few times I had walked through here I had felt the desolation and sadness. I didn't think it could get any worse, but I was going through a defeated city. A place that no longer resembled the home I remembered. My people deserved better. They deserved happiness and peace and a chance to truly thrive.

I tried to keep those thoughts at the forefront of my mind as I stared down at the beach. My chest tightened and I could feel the blood draining from my face as I stared at a thousand tents squashed together, spread across the sand. They had taken over, claiming the space as theirs.

I could hear the crash of the waves and I wondered if I could call to them and have them rise up and pull the entire camp back into the sea. Something told me that wouldn't be enough. There were thousands more fae in Drakous and I knew that to end this, we had to eliminate the king.

It took several tries to find that dark spot inside where my magic resided. I had to shut down the fear and that part of me that was warning me to turn back. Finally, I regained a sense of calm, shutting everything else out the way as I had done in the past. I had to turn it all off. All the fear, all the love. I settled into numb indifference and the shadows came. They swirled around me like an old friend, familiar and comforting. Almost as if Ryvin were here with me, guiding me through what I needed to do.

I kept my mind clear as my feet touched the sand, abandoning my sandals after only a few steps. I buried them, hoping that no one would find them before I revealed myself.

The camp was alive. Soldiers sat around bonfires laughing and drinking fae wine. Others were going in and out of tents or stumbling around, clearly already several glasses of wine into their revelry. The camp had an air of celebration, even though they would return to battle in the morning. It was as if they were already counting their victory. That drew a flicker of anger that made my shadows tremble. I shoved it away, working to keep my emotions at bay so that I could maintain absolute control.

I knew the king would likely be protected by guards and that he'd be in the largest and grandest tent. The camp was massive, but I had a feeling he wouldn't risk being too close to the sea. I walked toward what felt like the middle of the mass of tents and began to look for signs that might point me toward the Fae King's tent.

From here, it was difficult to tell any differences or direction at all. All the tents looked the same, but there was less activity here than there had been on the outskirts of the encampment. It was quieter, and I took that as a good sign.

Instead of walking toward the sounds of guards playing games of chance, or telling lewd tales around campfires, I walked toward the silence.

As I continued along, there were fewer guards walking around and no signs of amusement or activities. My heart pounded so loudly I was worried someone else might hear it. Every hair was on edge and a trickle of cold ran down my spine. My instincts were telling me to turn and run. I had to be close.

I continued forward until I caught sight of a large group of guards making a perimeter around a tent that looked the same as all the rest. Narrowing my eyes, I studied them, watching their movements. It could be a prisoner. Moving a little closer, I caught a strong floral scent. That wasn't likely to come from a prisoner's tent. It had to be the king.

There was only one additional row of tents between the king's tent and the sea. My fingers itched, feeling that connection to the water, begging to be used. I thought about it again, about trying to send him to a watery grave, but it wasn't enough. If I could guarantee a monster tearing him apart limb by limb, maybe I would use the magic my mother gave me.

I felt for the pouch, pressing my finger and thumb against the small circular object inside. I was going to use the magic my mother gave me, anyway. Part of me wondered if this was what she always intended it for. I had thought it was something that might save me if I were in mortal peril, but I knew deep in my gut that the object she gave me was not something that gave life, but rather something that would take life away. I knew it was a weapon, even if I couldn't explain how I knew that.

I stood behind the tent next to the king's tent wondering how I could get past his guards without alerting them. The shadows were a good cover, but once the tent flap moved, they'd know.

I glanced again toward the sea, feeling an urge to connect to it the way that I had before. Then I realized it wasn't the water that was calling to me, but something within the water. Someone who was starting to feel like an old friend.

I smiled, then worked to keep hold of the shadows around me while I reached for my other magic. The magic that had been stripped from me just as I was learning how to wield it. After my deal with Nyx, I no longer had to fear using it.

It came easier than it ever had before. As if it were relieved to come back to me, back to where it belonged. The sensations like reconnecting with an old friend. I felt strong and ready as I called to everything I had. I pulled on the water, bringing it toward me, willing it to come all the way up to that first row of tents.

The waves roared to life and crashed into the shore,

causing the sea to swell and surge as the tide rose. Water surged over rocks, spreading beyond its normal reach. It continued to rise, the tide creeping farther until it began to kiss the bottoms of the first row of tents.

Screams and movement surrounded me as soldiers emerged from their tents and started to hastily pack them up, preparing to get out of the way of the water.

The guards around the king's tent were curious, watching with furrowed brows, but maintained their positions. As I continued to bring the water higher and higher and closer and closer, the guards around the king's tent began to get a little restless.

I pulled back just enough that they would think they were safe to stay where they were and the guards who'd started to disassemble stopped and waited. Dozens of men stood near their tents, staring out into the sea as if they could command it to retreat.

I asked the water to grow a little calmer to lull them into a false sense of security. A couple of the soldiers re-entered their tents, apparently satisfied that the water would go no higher. Others stood and watched, cautious about the will of the sea. They were the smarter ones, but they were about to regret that they were standing so close to the edge without any weapons.

I caught the faintest glint of scales under the moonlight a moment before the sea serpent's head rose from the water and attacked, grabbing one of those waiting soldiers and pulling him into the ocean.

His scream was short lived as he was dragged below, but it got the attention of the other soldiers who quickly ran away or returned to their tents and emerged with weapons. The sea serpent swam farther down the shore, grabbing more of the men even as they aimed their swords or attempted to blindly shoot arrows into the dark water.

I let the water rise, giving the serpent more depth so it was easier for her to hunt. She attacked again and again, dragging screaming fae into the depths before returning to take more victims.

I looked over at the king's tent and noticed the guards getting increasingly agitated. They were talking to each other in hushed tones and finally half of them drew their swords and raced to the aid of their companions. Still under the cover of shadows, I moved closer to the king's tent, and while the guards were busy staring at the massacre happening at the shore, I slipped inside.

36

Ara

The interior of the tent was lit by one small fae light flickering in a jar on a table near the bed. I could see the king's sleeping form bundled under the blankets. It was a small soldier's bed, in a simple room. I expected him to travel with opulence after seeing how he lived in his court. Quietly, I reached for the bag around my neck and began to loosen the draw strings.

The screams outside were fading, but there was still enough noise to mask my footsteps. I crept closer to the bed; afraid my heartbeat was too loud. I could see the gentle rise and fall of the king's breathing. I was incredibly lucky that he was a sound sleeper.

I took another step closer, then paused, trying to figure out the best way to move forward. What was I supposed to do with the item in the bag? Did I just release it or throw it at him? Was there a trick to using it?

"I'm disappointed by how easy you were to fool. I thought for sure you'd realize it was an illusion," a deep male voice said.

I spun, reaching for the pouch and tearing it from the cord. The king moved with preternatural speed. He had me on the ground, his knee on my chest, my wrists pinned. I closed my fingers around the pouch, hoping he didn't notice I was holding something.

"I wondered if you'd come to take me up on my offer," he said, his voice gravelly and low.

I shuddered, turning away from his warm breath on my face. Then I made myself look at him with defiance. I would not allow him to see how he got to me. "You know why I'm here."

"Your reputation as a martyr is well known at this point, Princess," the king said, leaning down so his face was directly over mine. "I wonder, could I get my son back if I have you in chains? What do you think he'd do if I hold your life in my hands?"

"He knows better than to fall for that. He'd rather see me dead than work for you again," I said.

The king grinned, showing straight white, slightly pointed teeth. "I doubt that very much. I know what he did for you in Athos. Imagine what he'll do this time."

I moved under his weight, struggling to free myself. It only seemed to make him smile wider. Holding me here was effortless for him.

"You don't know him as well as I do."

He laughed. "You think you know him better? I created him. Everyone always thought the minotaur was my monster, but my greatest monster was my son."

I glared at him, letting all the hate I felt for him seep into me, filling me like a dark creature, hungry for blood. Gritting my teeth, I worked to hold the shadows back, to let them build without the king knowing what I was doing. I wished I could make him explode the way I'd done with the vampire back in Konos but I couldn't even sense the faintest thread of my own magic.

"Lochlan," the king bellowed.

A soldier rushed into the tent, his head bowed so low I wasn't sure if he even saw that the king had a woman pinned to the ground.

I started to slowly move my fingers, working at the little pouch to access the contents.

"Send a messenger to the palace. Tell them that if Ryvin wants his mate back, he'll surrender to me before the sun rises."

The round object was cool to the touch as I fished it from the bag. I tightened my fingers around it, careful not to let it roll away.

"Yes, Your highness," Lochlan called with another bow. He quickly retreated.

The king turned his attention back to me. "I should be thanking you right now. You're going to get me everything I ever wanted."

"I am nobody's pawn," I hissed. Fury swirled, making my vision narrow to the man in front of me. I was done being used by the men around me while they strove for power they didn't deserve. It was time to do things on my terms.

With a scream, I let the shadows explode, sending all the anger and frustration and hate and fury toward the Fae King.

He was thrown from me, letting out a surprised scream as the shadows sent him across the tent. I reached out, ordering the shadows to catch him, preventing him from knocking the tent over.

Guards burst through the door and I shoved them away with more shadows, letting the darkness wrap them in cocoons of death.

The king was stammering, struggling to get words out. "H-How?" His eyes were wide as he took me in. And this time, he wasn't looking at me like a prize. Like someone below him. Now he was looking at me with fear in his expression.

I approached slowly, then turned to launch more shadows at two more soldiers. They were smothered by the power I wielded, their bodies vanishing in the embrace of darkness.

"It's impossible. Ryvin would never give up his power," the king said.

"He didn't have to." I hardly recognized the snarl in my voice. "He's not you. He's not the monster you think he is."

"You're wrong. You can't change him." The king's nostrils flared. "You can't kill me with his magic. It won't work. He tried once when he was young. Did he tell you that? He tried to kill his own father. Succeeded in killing yours. That's the man you defend?"

I stopped in front of the king, staring at the man who'd taken so much from my people and still wasn't satisfied. I pinched the little ball between my forefinger and thumb. Without hesitation, I shoved it into his mouth, then sealed his lips with shadows.

I wasn't sure what the object was or why I knew I was supposed to shove it into his mouth, but it was instantly clear I'd made the right choice.

I stepped back, my eyes widening, unable to hide my disbelief as gray streaks spread from the king's mouth, expanding like spiderwebs across his cheeks and down his neck.

Startled, I lost control of the shadows and the king fell to the ground. He landed on his knees and clutched at his throat. Gasping and choking, he struggled for breath even though the shadows no longer bound him.

His eyes widened in terror and he dropped his arms, his fingers digging into the dirt as he clawed toward me. The streaks were spreading down his arms and across his hands. He stilled, one arm outstretched, reaching forward as if trying to grab something. He looked up, his eyes locking on mine showing nothing but fear. His whole body stiffened and the streaks of gray seemed to continue to grow, expanding until his whole body was the color of stone.

No, not the color of stone. He was stone.

It was impossible.

The king stared at me with solid gray unseeing eyes. His lips were parted in a frozen attempt at a last breath. His one hand was still on the ground, fingers curled into the dirt, as if reacting to pain we couldn't see. His other arm was outstretched, forever frozen in a last attempt to reach his killer.

My hands were trembling as I moved closer to him to investigate. Slowly, I touched his elevated hand, then drew back in surprise. I gasped.

It was solid stone.

I knew what had been in that bag. I knew why my mother insisted I not open it until I needed it.

My mother had given me a medusa stone. I thought they were a myth. The stories said they were given by a gorgon and could only be used by women who were in danger. Only the bearer would be unharmed by the stone. If I'd opened this around anyone else, it would have been catastrophic.

And now the Fae King was dead.

I stared at the statue that used to be the Fae King, feeling numb. I wasn't sure where to go from here. I hoped I could take the king down with me. I didn't plan on being able to escape with my life.

The ground shook and the sound of screams filled the night, sending me into action. I ran for the door, peering out to find there were no longer any guards outside the king's tent. My stomach twisted in guilt when I realized I'd killed them all.

Flames shot across the sky and soldiers screamed. Men raced past me, still tugging on their armor as they charged. I looked up just as four dragons flew across the sky, unleashing flames on the tents below.

I paused, taking in the flying beasts, trying to figure out how they were there when the king was gone.

Then I recognized the midnight blue sheen of a familiar dragon's scales. That had to be Bahar. If that was him and his men, it meant Ryvin and my friends were out there somewhere. They were attacking the fae. My stomach twisted in a mixture of anxiety and excitement. After all this time, we were finally initiating the battle we'd been waiting for.

I ducked back into the king's tent then ran over to where the statue knelt in the same place I'd left it. Pressing my foot against his side, I shoved until the whole statue toppled over. It cracked when it landed, his arm shattering in the fall.

Somehow, that made me feel more confident that he was actually gone. I glanced around for a weapon and saw a massive ornate sword propped against the small table. I grabbed it and lifted it, quickly realizing it wouldn't do me any good. It was far too heavy. Then I remembered the training sessions with Rvyin. The only time I won was when I used magic, not traditional fighting skills.

I shook out my hands and made my way to the exit, ready to join the fray.

Smoke filled the air, and the night sky was illuminated by burning tents and streaks of fire coming from the circling dragons above. Fae soldiers ran past me, none of them stopping to notice a woman walking through their camp.

I hurried to follow them and ran right into battle. Steel clashed and fighters brawled. Fae were attacking Athonian soldiers and vampires from Thebes. Dragons attacked those who were trying to flee to the ships.

A fae soldier noticed me, then charged, a sword over his head. I lifted my hand, calling the shadows. They came to me with ease. The man didn't stand a chance as the darkness swallowed him.

Another soldier standing nearby turned and ran after watching me, but an Athonian soldier shoved his sword through his gut before he could retreat.

I continued through the masses, using my shadows to help where I could while I hunted for my friends. The deeper I got into the battle, the more my anxiety peaked. I kept reminding myself that they were strong fighters, that they were likely in less danger than I was.

A sword swung in my direction and I jumped, just barely saving myself from being sliced open. I glared at my attacker, a fae male with antlers who glared at me in disgust. I gave him a glare of my own as I sent shadows to swallow him whole.

He made a gurgling sound as the shadows did their work, smothering him until nothing was left.

I focused more on my surroundings after that, knowing that my friends were likely looking for me as well. I continued to fight, picking up a knife someone else had dropped. I made quick use of it, stabbing a fae who was toying with a fallen Athonian guard.

"Thank you," the guard called, accepting my hand as I helped him off the ground.

I didn't get a chance to say anything back before a knife

was plunged into his neck. Gritting my teeth, I stared at the killer.

"What do we have here?" A tall fae in the red uniform of Konos said. He held the bloody knife in one hand and a large, also bloody sword in the other. "They really shouldn't let humans come play in their battles."

"I'm no human," I warned.

"Half-breeds don't count," he snarled as he charged me.

I called to my shadows, but he was so fast I had to dodge, which sent the black wisps I'd managed away. He charged me again, swinging with the sword, then swiping with the knife.

His movements were brutal, and it was taking all my concentration just to avoid him. I couldn't focus enough to call the shadows. I couldn't use my magic.

"I can't wait to show Ryvin your corpse," the man spat. "I'll show him that his magic wasn't enough."

The thought of Ryvin seeing me dead sent a surge of rage through me and I stopped thinking. My vision narrowed until all I could see was the gloating expression on the man sizing me up for a kill. The sound of the battle ceased, the air seemed to still.

Darkness billowed around me and I welcomed them as I charged forward, leaping into the air with the aid of the shadows under my feet, my knife ready. The soldier's eyes widened as I came down on him, jabbing my knife into his throat.

The shadows caught me before I hit the ground and I moved away before his toppling body could land on me.

Taking heaving breaths, I stared down at the man who'd found so much joy in the thought of seeing me dead. I was glad he was gone. Glad he wouldn't have a chance to carry that bloodlust any longer.

Suddenly, a cacophony of screaming filled the air, and I spun to see dozens of fae soldiers falling to their knees, clawing at their throats. The screams died as they began to gurgle, blood pouring from their mouths. As they quieted, they fell, unmoving.

In the center of the bodies, covered in blood, was Ryvin.

"Ryvin!" I started running, weaving around fighters without concern.

My mate saw me and the hard expression on his face melted instantly to one of relief. He sent out a wall of shadows on either side of him, knocking everyone in their wake to the ground, then he ran for me.

We met in an embrace that felt like coming up for air after being under water. I kissed him quickly, then pulled away. "I'm sorry. I'm sorry. Please forgive me."

He kissed me hard, his lips almost punishing, then they softened, and he breathed out a sigh before breaking the kiss. "Just stay alive."

I nodded, then turned, the two of us fighting the men who were charging toward us, all of them coming to take down the Prince of Darkness.

I called to the shadows again, finding them returning with ease. I wondered if it was because he was right next to me. It didn't matter the reason, I was just grateful I could call on the magic. We moved in a circle, sending shadows after anyone who charged us. Bodies piled up, but I knew we'd killed even more than were showing because sometimes, we sent them straight to the Underworld without a trace.

Finally, soldiers began to come closer, then flinch before charging. Then, they stopped coming at all. They knew coming for Ryvin was a death sentence.

A horn sounded, loud and low, bellowing with a forlorn call. I stiffened, then turned to my mate. "What is that?"

"Retreat," he said.

I laughed, still gripping the knife in my hands. Nervously, I looked around, not sure I believed it was all over. But all I saw were Athonian soldiers and vampires from Thebes letting their shoulders slump as they took their first deep breath since the battle started.

Fae were running to their boats, but the dragons circled, taking them out as they made their escape. Flaming men ran toward the sea, only to die screaming as the creatures of the deep made them into a meal.

I whispered a thank you to the monsters, and to my mother, knowing that somehow, they knew I was grateful.

Footsteps sounded, and I turned to see Vanth and Laera walking toward us. Vanth was wincing as he limped. Laera was covered in blood, but walking with such dignity I was certain none of it was hers.

"Well done, Ara," she said as she approached.

Ryvin growled. "You knew."

"Of course, I knew," Laera said. "But she's fine, isn't she? And she succeeded where all of us failed."

"He's really dead, then?" Vanth asked.

I nodded.

"How?" Vanth asked.

"The gift from my mother," I replied. "It was a medusa stone."

Laera smirked. "Clever woman. I knew I liked Ceto."

"You did not," Ryvin said, a hint of their old sibling rivalry showing in his tone.

"Well, I do now," Laera said.

"Where are my sisters?" I asked. "Did anyone make it through the shield? Are the people safe?"

"We turned off the shield as soon as Laera told us my father was dead," Ryvin explained. "They didn't expect us."

"I don't think anyone got past the beach," Vanth said. "And we did leave a few soldiers, including your Aunt Katerina and Argus, and two dragons behind."

"Thank you." I knew I wouldn't feel better until I saw them myself, but it sounded good. It sounded like we won. My brow furrowed.

"What is it?" Ryvin asked.

"Did we actually do it? Did we actually win?" I looked at my friends in disbelief. It didn't seem possible that it was over.

Laera chuckled. "Imagine that. I think we actually did."

Ryvin pulled me into his arms. "No more running off to save everyone, alright? Can we leave that to someone else from now on?"

I turned my head, and he lowered his face closer to mine. "I think I'm retiring from battle." I rose up on my toes and gave him a kiss.

"Queens don't typically fight in wars," Laera said.

I tensed, then turned to her.

She had an amused look on her face. "What, you think I want the Konos crown?" She shook her head. "Sorry, but that's his, and I'm pretty sure where he goes, you go."

"I never wanted to be king," Ryvin said.

Vanth dropped to one knee, lowering his head. My mouth parted in surprise. I was certain Vanth had never bowed to anyone.

"Your highness, I would be honored to serve under you, King of Konos." Vanth kept his head down, but I could see his shoulders shaking slightly.

Ryvin released me, then shoved his friend. Vanth fell to the ground, bursting into laughter.

"I'll work on it, I swear. By your coronation, I'll be able to do it with a straight face," Vanth said.

"Come on, I want to see the look on my mother's face when she finds out my father is actually dead," Laera said.

37

ARA

WE ARRIVED BACK at the palace gates to cheers and shouts of joy. Soldiers were swept up in the arms of loved ones and the people of Athos broke into victory songs I'd almost forgotten. Casks of wine were brought from the palace stores and a massive bonfire was erected where the platform for Cora's wedding had been. I suspected they'd used the platform to start the fire.

I saw my sisters standing on the balcony, waving and smiling while the people below shouted praise for their new queen. It was such a contrast to the last time she'd stood there, a grieving daughter, watching as too many of her own people were sent to the Underworld.

I managed to slip into the palace with Ryvin and Laera, seeking the more subdued venue after everything we'd endured. It was still night, and I knew that once the sun rose, we'd have to face the realities of the aftermath. Athos was in shambles. It would take time and resources to rebuild. There were also the casualties that would start to become reality as people failed to find their loved ones. I knew my actions saved some lives, but I wished I could have prevented all the loss.

We left a trail of bloody footprints on the marble tile as we walked in. Mine were barefoot, as they often were. It felt like a hundred years ago since I left muddy footprints on the gleaming floor after training sessions with David. It hadn't been all that long, but I wasn't the same person I'd been that day Konos arrived. That Ara had died, and a stronger, more confident version had taken her place.

"Ara, thank the gods," Argus called as he ran down the long hall. "Your sisters are asking for you."

I looked over at Ryvin and Laera. Laera smiled and Ryvin nodded. "Go. We'll catch up with you later."

I followed Argus through the halls, past guards who hollered and cheered when they saw us. The entire palace was alive with celebration. I found myself forcing a smile and cheering with them, but my emotions hadn't caught up to reality yet. There was a numbness in my body, a sense of doubt. It was hard to believe we'd succeeded.

Guards were stationed outside the room, and it felt so familiar. They'd gone back to their places, protecting the royal family. I nodded to them as they parted to let me through, Argus following me.

My sisters were still waving and smiling at the crowd below when I joined them on the balcony. Cora was the first to notice my arrival. She spun to face me, her shoulders sagging in relief, her eyes filling with tears. "I thought I'd never see you again."

Lagina and Sophia turned, both of their expressions changing from their diplomatic smiles to true joy. They moved toward me, embracing me in a sandwich between the two of them. Cora joined them, the four of us holding each other while we alternated between laughing and crying.

It felt real then, with my sisters' arms around me. I let it out. Let myself feel the weight of what I'd done, both the good and the bad. I let the tears flow and let myself feel the exhaustion of the last few weeks. So much had happened, but there was hope.

When we parted, I heard a fresh eruption of cheering. We'd caused a scene, with many of the citizens standing below us, their fists in the air as they chanted. It took me a moment to understand their words, but when I figured it out, I couldn't help but chant along with them. As I shoved Lagina forward, I joined in, "Long live the Queen. Long Live Athos!"

Tonight, we needed to celebrate. Tomorrow, when the sun rose, we'd start the process of honoring our dead, rebuilding, and strengthening Athos into the city it was always meant to be.

Something nudged inside me, a feeling I was getting more familiar with. I turned and saw Ryvin standing in the room, out of view of the people below. He was watching us with pure pride in his eyes.

I left my sisters, joining him in the background. "You don't look like you're too angry at me."

"I understand why you did it," he said with a sigh. "There's a part of me that wishes you hadn't, but I'm just too grateful that you're alive to care about anything else."

"I'd kiss you right now, but I'm pretty sure my entire face is covered in blood and I'd really like to wash it off," I said.

He laughed. "Don't worry, after the dust settles, I'm taking you somewhere private where we can spend a few weeks alone without leaving the bedroom."

"I like the sound of that," I replied.

The door opened and Bahar burst through, clothed in only his trousers. His eyes were wild, his hair a windblown mess.

My heart thundered. "What's wrong?"

A wide smile spread across his face. He ran over to where I was standing, holding a small scroll of paper in his hands. "We've retaken Drakous! My brother Zyan was hiding in the palace. He poisoned the wine in our stores and those stupid fae drank themselves to death. He signaled Kabir and our forces liberated the city before the Fae King even arrived here."

The dragon shifter wrapped his arms around me, lifting me off the ground, then spun me in a circle. "Drakous is safe! My kingdom is safe!"

He set me down and I laughed as I watched him race toward the balcony where he captured Cora in his arms.

Ryvin took my hand and led me back to the balcony. I was surprised to see that the cheering and celebration continued, even with the Dragon King and the Prince of

Konos by our sides. No, not prince, King, if Laera was to be believed.

"Will you take the throne?" I asked.

He looked over at me. "What do you want? I know neither of us wanted to rule."

"You'd be a great king," I said.

"You'd be a great queen," he replied, then he leaned closer, so his lips brushed against my ear. "Either way, I want you as my wife."

My brows lifted and I turned toward him. "Are you asking me to marry you?"

"If you'll have me," he said.

The smile on my lips was so wide it made my cheeks hurt. "Dion is going to be so disappointed."

He laughed, then pulled me into his arms. "We'll break it to him gently."

THANK YOU!

Thank you for taking this journey with Ara and Ryvin and all their friends and family. I hope you enjoyed the Blood and Salt Series!

Need a little more? Get a free epilogue when you sign up for my newsletter. https://tinyurl.com/5n7x3cte

Sign up here or scan the QR code below:

ALSO BY ALEXIS CALDER

Rejected Fate Series

Darkest Mate

Forbidden Sin

Feral Queen

Royal Mates Series

Shifter Claimed

Shifter Fated

Shifter Rising

Academy of Elites Series

Academy of Elites: Untamed Magic

Academy of Elites: Broken Magic

Academy of Elites: Fated Magic

Academy of Elites: Unbound Magic

Brimstone Academy Series

Brimstone Academy: Semester One

Brimstone Academy: Semester Two

Romcom books published under Lexi Calder:

In Hate With My Boss

Love to Hate You

ABOUT THE AUTHOR

Alexis Calder writes sassy heroines and sexy heroes with a sprinkle of sarcasm. She lives in the Rockies and drinks far too much coffee and just the right amount of wine.

facebook.com/AuthorAlexisCalder

instagram.com/author_alexiscalder

tiktok.com/@authoralexiscalder

amazon.com/stores/Alexis-Calder/author/B07TP5VCGZ

Hope might not be enough this time.

The fae king continues to claim victories and Nyx is awake. As if that wasn't bad enough, the gods are after us and we're running out of time.

The Fae King has power he shouldn't from a sorceress who holds the key. To defeat him, we have to go through her. But the gods are hunting us, and Nyx asked for me personally.

I'll have to face her alone while my friends work to save everyone I love.

I'm afraid we aren't going to make it out alive this time but I will do whatever it takes to give Athos a chance.

The problem is, I'm not sure we ever had a chance to begin with.

It all ends now. One way or another.

9 781965 182093